CRIME WITHOUT CONSCIENCE

THE SETTLERS
BOOK FIVE

REG QUIST

Crime Without Conscience
Paperback Edition
Copyright © 2023 Reg Quist

CKN Christian Publishing
An Imprint of Wolfpack Publishing
9850 S. Maryland Parkway, Suite A-5 #323
Las Vegas, Nevada 89183

cknchristianpublishing.com

Paperback ISBN 978-1-63977-459-3
eBook ISBN 978-1-63977-458-6
LCCN 2023941237

ALSO BY REG QUIST

Novels

The Church at Third and Main

Hamilton Robb

Noah Gates

Terry of the Double C

Just John

Just John: The Complete Journey

Just John

Northward to Home

Reluctant Redemption

Reluctant Redemption: The Complete Series

Reluctant Redemption (Book 1)

A Winding Trail to Justice (Book 2)

Rough Road to Redemption (Book 3)

Mac's Way

Mac's Way: The Complete Series

Mac's Way

Mac's Land

Mac's Law

Danny

Danny: The Complete Trilogy

The Truth of The Matter (Book 1)

CRIME WITHOUT CONSCIENCE

FOR THE PAST SEVERAL MONTHS, THERE HAD BEEN constant rumors about the telegraph coming to Stevensville and the Fort. In other parts of the West, centers much smaller than the two towns Sheriff Rory Jamison patrolled, had been blessed with the modern, fast communications. But the towns in question still relied on stagecoach-handled mail or a fast rider making the trek to Cheyenne or, even further away, to Denver to reach a wire.

The sheriff was riding towards his newly built home. He was expecting to join his wife of only a couple of weeks for lunch. As had become her habit in the short few days since the marriage, she stood at the edge of the covered porch, waiting, shading her eyes to protect them from the sun's glare. Grinning in happiness, Rory knew that under the shading hand, her lips were holding a welcoming smile.

A rider, pushing a sweating and heaving grey gelding almost to exhaustion, was heard hollering, "Sheriff! Sheriff!"

Rory pulled his JJ Ranch-bred, blood-red bay horse to a stop. He half turned in the saddle to see who it was that was flagging him down. Waving his hat in the air while kicking the last of the gelding's strength out of the animal, Trey Preveau, the young man Tippet often hired to help in his livery, hollered for the sheriff to 'wait up.'

Trey was so out of breath a listener could be forgiven for thinking the kid had been the one doing the running. He started to speak, stopped to catch his breath, started again, and, while the gelding heaved and trembled in exhaustion, managed to say, "Fire. Livery. Marshal's Office. Bank. Couple a others. Bank robbed. Horses burned up. Banker shot."

Rory said, "Alright, Trey. I get the idea. Now you step off that animal before he drops from under you. Walk him back to the livery. Slowly! Get Kegs to help you. He knows more about horses than anyone around. He might be able to save the animal. You stay and care for the horse. There's nothing you can do down in Stevensville that others can't do. I'll ride down."

Rory turned back to his house and the woman waiting on the porch. A few seconds of riding brought him to the tie rail. As he walked up to the house, he was about to speak when Julia said, "I heard. I've got lunch ready. You sit and eat. I'll grab a change of clothes for you to take along."

Before the wedding, the young lovers had discussed the demands of the sheriff's job in a large county. That they both had hoped the call to action would take a break while they settled into married life, hadn't held off whatever was happening twenty miles to the south. Nor was there any guarantee on how long the sheriff would be gone. This would be the first test of their new marriage.

One-half-hour later, Rory turned the red horse back to town and the road south. Julia kissed him goodbye.

"I'll pray for your safe return."

~

THE SHERIFF, knowing his new bride would be worried in spite of all her brave talk, was worried himself. A young woman alone a half mile from town could be a temptation to a wandering man. His concerns for her safety were mostly put to rest by the fact that she would soon be spending the days at her job at Mr. Sales' saddle shop. She had stayed home for a couple of weeks after the wedding to arrange the new furniture and settle in to married life. But that time was about up.

Scout, the big shepherd dog that had adopted Rory and doted on him, had also adopted Rory's new bride. The faithful animal was protective, almost to the extreme. His place of rest during the night had become a folded blanket inside the cabin door. Although his blanket was pushed to the side every morning, every night—when all were settled down—he pulled his thin mattress in front of the door so no one could come in or go out without him moving.

In addition to the dog, Rory had purchased a double barrel twelve-gauge shotgun, a .32-pocket pistol, a .44 Colt to match his own, and a .44-40 carbine. Julia was proficient with all of them. She wouldn't be without protection. And if more was needed, Deputy Sheriff Cap Graham had decided to live long-term in the older cabin on the property. Still, Rory wished he was home.

~

Tippet's barn was sure to be a smoking wreckage by the time Rory kissed his wife goodbye. And if the banker was indeed shot, he would have received medical attention hours ago. As to the marshal's office and jail, it was probably time for a new one anyway. He had no idea what Trey meant by 'couple 'a others.

Holding to a steady trot, just short of three hours after leaving home, the sheriff was riding into Stevensville. The streets were busy with horse and wagon traffic, much of it stopped or tied off at the various railings. There was just a whiff of smoke rising above the blackened remains of the marshal's office.

Andy Speth, the soot-blackened bank clerk, with the remnants of his shredded and burned shirt hanging loosely from his shoulders, his bare arms and chest exposed to the sunlight, stood guard over the remains of the bank. The shotgun in his hands held the message that he was serious about holding to his responsibilities.

The livery was a mass of half-burned timbers, laying every which way across the bed of smoldering hay and straw. Tippet and several other men were hauling buckets of water from the pump that stood like a sentinel to things passed, outside what had been the front of the livery building. Surprising, but pleasing nonetheless, Rory noticed a begrimed Boon Wardle among the workers.

Other men and women stood a distance away, clogging the street. Many held handkerchiefs over their noses, a questionable defense against the stench of burned horse flesh. Idly, Rory wondered why, if the stench was so disagreeable, they didn't turn away from the ugly sight and smell and go home or back to their businesses.

As he sat the gelding, wondering where Ivan was and

what anyone could possibly do to relieve the situation, a shout of warning cleared the street. A farmer who lived on the edge of town was riding his stone boat and directing a team of Belgians toward the livery. The job he was about to undertake would be the most miserable of this miserable day.

When the fire started, Tippet had run to the corrals at the back of the barn and turned the horses out. Most got out and ran freely on the street until a couple of riders gathered them up and drove them to the north end of town. A rope corral was quickly put together. Now, those same two riders lowered a section of rope and eased Tippet's team into the street. Tippet's harness had all been lost in the fire, but the resourceful men dropped their catch ropes over the animals' necks and led them to the fire site. Backing the unharnessed team into the mess as far as they dared, without injuring the horses, they threw the ends of their ropes toward the burned horses. Tippet rushed to pick up the ends with the intent of roping the downed animals, but another man stepped up and took the ropes. "Let me do this, Tippet. You go over to Ma's and have a coffee.

Tippet took a final look at the animals he loved and passed over the ropes.

With much pulling by the team and directing by the men, the first carcass was slid onto the stone boat. The second was more difficult, given that the stone boat really wasn't large enough for the job, but they got it done. It was a horrible task, with chunks of burned flesh being ripped off as the heavy carcasses slid across the blackened timers and onto the big sled. Something no one would wish to repeat. Two or three of the workers turned and threw up whatever they had eaten that day. And perhaps the day before.

With the two dead animals roped together and tied to the stone boat, the farmer, walking beside his team, led his Belgians south, and out of town. Idly, Rory wondered where his destination was, knowing that the worse odors were yet to come as the spring sun did its work on the hundreds of pounds of flesh.

Exhaling a deep breath and wishing he had meaningful words for Tippet, he turned to where Andy Speth was standing over the remains of the bank.

"Howdy, Andy. Not a good day. What can you tell me? I'm told that Jessie was shot. Is he over at Doc's?"

"I guess he is. That's where they took him."

"How bad is it, Andy?"

"Bad enough. He's dead."

2

THAT STATEMENT KNOCKED THE WIND OUT OF RORY. Even knowing his banker friend had been shot, he never once suspected that.

While he was trying to figure out where to take the talk to, Andy, desperate to control his emotions, swung his arm behind him and looked pleading at the sheriff.

"Now I don't know what to do with this mess."

"I'm just terribly sorry and upset to hear about Jessie, Andy, but that mess your standing in doesn't appear to hold much promise. It all looks to be burned through. What are you hoping to still find in there?"

"Nothing, if I'm ready to be honest about it. I'm not quite ready to be that honest yet, though."

"I see the safe door standing open, Andy. Where's the money? Did it burn up before you could close the safe door?"

"Thieves took it. The same ones that shot Mr. Ambrewster."

"That's the first I've heard about thieves. Tell me about it, Andy."

"Four men. Walking. Not riders. First thing, they lit the livery hay on fire. Not the loft. The outside stack. What Tippet kept for the corralled horses. I'm thinking anyway. Nothing else makes any sense.

"Barn burned like all the fires of hell were after it. Seems every man in town was there within a minute or two. Everyone shouting. Tippet loosening horses from their stalls. Loose animals so stupid that they got outside, then turned and ran right back in. Knocked Tippet over twice.

"Boon Wardle, him who's been sore all over for weeks after you shot him off his horse, he worked harder than anyone to save the horses. Then, when he thought Tippet had control of the last couple, he set in to dragging saddles out. By then, the loft was afire, and everyone had to get out.

"Tippet and Wardle...they helped each other, arms around each other's shoulders, coughing and staggering at the last second, before the whole thing almost exploded...as the loft hay fell onto the flames. Two horses couldn't be saved. Wardle had to drag Tippet away from the stalls. Firebrands were flying everywhere.

"Men were running, hauling water from the two town wells, and Tippet's own, when the heat didn't dive them off, sloshing half of it on their own pants and the boardwalk, while women pumped. They were wetting down the roofs across the street, hoping to save the rest of the town. Bank. It was on fire before I even knew it. Jessie. He was busy grabbing up bank records and stuffing them into his leather satchel. He was just reaching for the vault cash holdings when a voice said, 'I'll take that.' I heard and saw him.

"There were four men. Never seen any of them before. No masks. I'm thinking they wanted to blend in with the crowd. Jessie, he reached for that little pocket gun he always carried, but before he could get it, he was shot. Shot right in the chest. He wasn't more than five or six feet away. He was probably dead before he hit the floor, but the men, they hauled him over to Doc's anyway.

"Robbers, they left the leather satchel, grabbed the cash box and what little was in the day drawer, and ran. The shooter, he turned the gun toward me, but the one with the box of money, he grabbed him by the arm and shouted, 'Let's get out of here.'"

"Do you know where they went?"

"That's the strange thing. I ran after them, hoping to see and maybe do something, but they ran right into the woods behind here. I saw no horses. The only thing I could hear above all the noise of the fire was a crashing of bush and shouts of 'hurry.' I have no idea where they were heading for in that bush."

"I do. Now, Andy, I'm pretty sure you can leave this mess. There's just nothing at all there to guard. Except that satchel of bank records. You guard those with your life."

Rory meant it as an emphasis on his statement, not a life sentence. But Andy said, "Seems my life is what this bank might require of me."

"Go home, Andy. Get some rest."

"I know you're right. I'll leave. Pretty soon."

The sheriff still sat his gelding. As he turned to leave what used to be the bank, Key Wardle, the town marshal, hailed him from across the street. Rory wound his way through the traffic, much of it sitting idle, and tied off in front of the mercantile at the only empty spot he could see. He stepped down and walked back to where Key stood waiting. Key welcomed him with, "I have a table in Ma's dining room. Come join me for coffee."

When the two men were seated, Rory said, "Andy filled me in on the bank robbery. Did he have it right? Is Jessie dead?"

"I'm afraid that's true. Shot right off, as if that was the plan the whole time. Can't figure that. A fella robs a bank, and he may one day be able to walk out of prison and hold his head high again. But if he kills someone, all those options are off. Came near enough to losing Jessie's body too, the little building burned so fast. Lost the office and jail too, but of course, you've noticed that already.

"Just seems like there's no limits to crime when a man turns his life to that direction."

Ignoring that statement, Rory asked, "What are your first moves going to be?"

"First moves are already made and done. The southbound stage had to swing onto the back street to get through town, but I managed to catch him. Held him up while I wrote out a wire. Tate was driving today. He promised to get to the Denver telegraph office with my note. If they get that out wide enough, there should be a whole lot of folks knowing about the killing, the fire, and the theft. And, of course, the four fugitives.

"Next, I rode up to Ambrewster's house. Nice place. Bigger than some, but not so grand that the townsfolk will think he's living high on their money. He never locked it, but I found a key hanging on a hook in the kitchen. I'll keep it locked up during the day. I'm thinking I might stay there tonight. I lost my sleeping space and my bedroll in the fire. I think the fugitives are on the run, but I can't be sure.

"There's no doubt they were willing to do anything to

get their hands on the bank money. The fire was to distract us all from the holdup. If they should circle back through the bush, they might decide to see what they can find in the banker's house. It wouldn't hurt to have it guarded for a few nights."

Rory thought about that for a moment before saying, "Clear that with the town council first. Just so there's no misunderstanding."

3

Rory didn't figure his time around the remains of the fire to be wasted time. He needed to re-assure a few that had been hurt, and he wanted to know as much as he could about the thieves. The last valuable bit of information Key passed along was when he said, "Ivan mounted up almost immediately after he heard about the murderers' running into the bush. It was as if he knew where they were going."

"He did know. And so do I. Now, to be clear, Key. The fire, theft, and murder are town business. Catching the escaping thieves is county business. You've got your hands full here. Stick to what you have to do. Don't get involved in any hunt for the four men. Leave that to Ivan and me. I'm riding out now. I'll either be back or somehow get word to you as soon as possible."

Knowing Ivan would have taken the trail to the I-5 Ranch, Rory followed. He was hours behind. The I-5 was

Ivan's family's cattle spread. His parents and older brother ran the outfit. Across the well-grassed, high mountain hanging valley was the bush-shrouded trail to Kiril's cabin. Abandoned after Kiril's death, most figured the land and the cunningly built log cabin and barn belonged to Ivan, Kiril's one friend.

Rory had discovered the carefully disguised trail from the back of Kiril's barn through the bush and down the hill to the back of Tippet's barn, a distance of several miles. It would appear as if the thieves had reversed the trail, choosing to raid the town on foot and escape up the hill. They were attempting quite a climb, but with the aid of the rope Kiril had left hanging from a stout tree, the worst of the hills could be conquered. But the climb and run through the forest would be slow. A man on a horse, taking the longer, but easier route, might reach the cabin before the climbers.

There was every possibility that Ivan was facing four desperate men, and Rory was nowhere near being able to help his friend. Ivan had stood beside Rory on several manhunts. Now it was time for Rory to do the same for Ivan.

He took the familiar hill at a faster pace than was good for any horse, but he would switch his saddle to an I-5 animal when he got to the ranch. Cresting the hill and trotting into the I-5 ranch yard, he was greeted by Pavel, Ivan's older brother.

"Yo, Pavel. I need a horse."

"That's exactly what Ivan hollered when he rode in here a couple of hours ago. He didn't even stop to explain. We saw smoke from down the hill. What burned?"

Rory had swung off his saddle and loosened the cinch. He lifted it into the cradle of his arm and started walking to where Pavel had pointed to a gelding already tied to the outside of the corral. With no discussion, Rory began fitting his saddle to the unknown animal.

"Livery burned. Bank and jailhouse too. Couple of small, unused sheds. Banker Ambrewster shot and killed. Bank robbed. Four men. They took to the forest where Kiril's hillside path reaches town. Ivan will be on their trail. Thanks for the horse."

"Knew you'd be here and wanting. That's a good animal. He'll give you what you need."

"Take care of that bay for me, please."

"Without even asking, my friend."

Rory only heard half of Pavel's last statement. He had the gelding running full out before he was even firmly seated.

THE LAST HALF-MILE of trail to Kiril's cabin was familiar to the sheriff. He could have taken it at a run but chose instead to be cautious. And quiet. The men would have had time to climb the hill, and Ivan certainly had time to fort up, either in the barn, the cabin, or in the surrounding forest. That situation had to lead to a confrontation.

Ivan would have checked the barn for horses. It was certain the men would not attempt to climb further than the cabin. In any case, it would make no sense. The hill above the cabin, leading to the uphill gold country, was a steep one. Climbing on foot would be slow and tedious and would certainly look out of place, gathering attention from any observers.

Rory had all these thoughts circulating in his mind when he heard a shot. Only one, and that seemed strange. If Ivan had spotted the prey and opened the ball, the fugitives would surely have replied in kind. Still, he held to the quiet walk. Not too far ahead, if it had not completely overgrown, was a narrow side trail that would take a rider around the cabin, holding to the trees all the way. There would be an extra half-mile of riding, but if it kept the fugitives from spotting him, it would be worth it. He came to the turnoff and grimaced. The brush had been pushed down by the heavy winter snows and had mostly held to that position. Only a bit of it had sprung back up. Still, it was a trail.

Explaining the situation quietly to the horse, and perhaps reassuring his own mind, he turned in. He lifted his hat off, knowing he wouldn't get far without losing it. He snugged the hat between his own lap and the pommel and horn. If it got crushed, he could always try to re-block it.

The horse balked a bit but kept moving. Once, he was behind a low hill that rose to screen his view of the cabin, and the brush was standing almost completely upright. There must have been a difference in the snow load or the wind. In any case, he was able to move at a trot. The trail put him a bare hundred yards above the cabin when it joined the main uphill path. Rory stepped to the ground and tied the animal carefully. He lifted down both the carbine and the Sharps Big 50 he was in the habit of carrying. Hunched over. He hurried across the path and into the light forest behind the cabin.

He eased down the slope until he was within easy talking distance of the cabin. There was one window in the back wall. Rory fished around until he had picked up a small handful of pebbles. He found a space behind a couple of large boulders and slid in, resting on one knee with his other foot providing balance. Cautiously peering around the rock toward the single window, he threw one pebble, hoping it would tap against the glass. He missed by an embarrassing distance. The tap on the log was virtually unnoticeable. The second pebble came closer, and the third struck the glass. There had been no noticeable sound before, but now, the silence seemed to become profound. Rory hunched back and waited.

Listening carefully, he thought he might have heard a boot heel settling on the floor. The sound was slight, but it was there. No doubt about it. He flicked another pebble that struck the glass again. There was no returned sound, but there was a distinct shadow moving across the glass. A hatless head appeared briefly, just enough to allow a quick look, and then moved away. Rory threw another pebble. This time the look from inside was longer, as if the searcher was scanning the hillside. Rory moved into view and waited. He was rewarded by the sound of a window sliding open and then a smiling Ivan whispering, "Where did you come from?"

The pointless question didn't really deserve an answer.

As Rory was moving toward the cabin, he asked, "What was that shot I heard?"

"Our gang of four fools is in the barn. One of them seems to be shoot-crazy. Hollered a threat and took one random shot toward the cabin."

"How did they know you were in the cabin?"

"Just a guess, I'm thinking. But logical, even to a simple mind."

"You're holding back on me, Ivan. How did they know anyone was anywhere around?"

Ivan could no longer hold back his grin. He pointed at the floor behind him. Rory stood on his tiptoes to see over the sill and squinted against the sun's glare.

"Is that what I think it is?"

"Well, if you think it's four bridles, off'n four horses, horses that bunch was depending on riding, you'd be right. Of course, they may be wondering where their saddles are too. And then, they may also be busy figuring out how to catch their loosed horses without getting shot."

It was only then that Rory, peering through the cabin and out the front window, noticed a horse grazing beside the unused chicken coop. He had to assume the others were somewhere in the yard as well. Breaking through his serious sheriff's demeanor, he couldn't hold back a laugh.

"My friend, I think you've about wrapped this hunt up. All we need now is for those boys to realize it's over. Have you talked to them?"

"No. I'm just letting them stew for a bit. Soften up some is what I mean to say. They've been in there now for an hour or more. I'm thinking it's nearing the do-or-die moment in their planning. Maybe come out with their hands up without me wasting a lot of breath hollering at them."

While Rory was trying to sort that possibility out in his mind, another shot was fired. This one hit the front door of the cabin but didn't penetrate. The shot was accompanied by a shout of frustration. Rory listened to the sound of the shot and the dying echo of the shout fade to nothing before he said, "It don't appear as if they plan on doing this the easy way."

"You're usually right, my sheriff friend. What do you suggest? This window is nowhere big enough for you to crawl through, and there's nothing to be done from behind this cabin, so I'm thinking you have another idea."

Saying nothing, Rory passed his Sharps through the window, butt first, and then held out a handful of shells for the monster gun. Knowing that Ivan would understand what to do with the Big .50, Rory slid to the uphill side of the cabin and into the bush.

Ivan walked to the front window and slid it open. He was hoping to finish this matter with no broken glass. Compared to life or death, the glass seemed like a minor issue, but it represented a ride to town for replacement glass and a ride back up to do the job. He'd rather avoid that if possible. Of course, on the other hand, it might be that Tempest would be prepared to join him on another ride up the hill. She seemed to have enjoyed their first visit to the cabin. But for the moment, there were more pressing matters.

Rory had to crawl uphill, further into the forest, to be covered enough by brush to be invisible from the barn. He knew Ivan would be watching for any sign of his movements while also keeping his eye on the barn for threats.

Crawling, whether through forest or cactus-laden grass, always seemed to take longer than it really did. In fact, he was behind the bole of a big mountain pine within a matter of minutes. He couldn't get a clear view of the cabin windows, but he could see the front of the barn alright...if he squinted around the edge of the tree. He had seen no sign of aggression from the barn, so he had probably not drawn the thieves' attention.

Shouting, without exposing himself, the sheriff hollered, "You men in the barn. There's no getting away. We have you covered from two directions. Your horses are in our control. We know every trail through the forest behind you. If you run, we'll catch you. You can't escape. Throw down your weapons and come out."

As if his voice had been the trigger to his violence, one man—screaming in rage—stepped halfway out of the barn door, raised his rifle, and levered off three shots in the direction the voice had come from. In answer, Ivan shot just once. The distance would have been comfortable for his own carbine, but he had the Big 50 resting in the crook of his arm and ready, so why not? While the shooter's attention was totally on the sheriff, Ivan rose from a crouch and laid the Sharps on the windowsill. The time for a slow, careful aim, which, in reality, took only a bare second, was all he needed. The screaming shooter's head and shoulders were visible above the corral's top rail. He squeezed the trigger. As always, he was rattled by the roar of the mini cannon, as well as the recoil. But the weapon shot true. There was a splattering of flesh and blood, and the body of the shooter flew sideways a bit before falling out of sight. The man's hat floated for a short moment and then tumbled to the ground. He would certainly do no more shooting.

Rory allowed the situation to settle for a half minute before he hollered, "How about it, men? Had enough?"

In response, a hand appeared, waving a colored piece of shirt. It wasn't a white flag but close enough. Along with the flag, a voice hollered, "Don't shoot. We're coming out."

Rory hollered back, "This is County Sheriff Rory Jamison and Deputy Ivan Ivanov. You're under arrest. Come out now. Slowly. If I see any sign of a weapon, I will shoot. I hope you understand that."

"We understand. We're coming out."

Rory moved to the side of the tree, with his carbine in the ready position, watching carefully as the men appeared. Two of them glanced downward at their dead partner and took a step away from him with startled looks on their faces. The third man avoided looking altogether.

"Walk to the center of the corral and turn to face the barn."

When the men complied, Rory stepped fully into view and began walking down the slope. He knew Ivan would have the men in his sights.

At his first close look, Rory thought, *'Amateurs. Cowboys thinking they're on a lark. An adventure. Fools.'*

He walked up to the three and searched them for weapons. Except for a couple of camp knives, they were clean. He waved for Ivan to join him. With only two sets of handcuffs between them, the two lawmen simply linked the three bank robbers together, wrist to wrist, with one of them on the outside of the corral and the other two inside. Without tearing down that section of the corral, they weren't about to go anywhere.

Rory gathered the weapons from the barn floor while Ivan caught up his own mount and drove the prisoners' horses into the corral. He closed the corral gate to hold the animals, and climbed into the loft. He opened the big front door, built there to aid in the loading of hay, and dropped the saddles onto the ground. Rory lifted the rifles from the saddle scabbards, unloaded them, and then searched the saddlebags for weapons.

After climbing back down from the loft, Ivan walked to the cabin and retrieved the bridles.

One by one, Rory released the men, saying, "Saddle your own animal and stand by."

With all the horses saddled and ready, Rory said, "Now, lift your dead partner into the saddle and tie him firmly."

It was an unpleasant job, given the damage the Big 50

had done, but the men did as they were told. While that was being taken care of, Ivan remounted his own horse and rode to the bush behind the cabin to retrieve Rory's gelding.

Rory unloaded all the other weapons before tying them on the saddle behind the dead man.

Within minutes they were ready to ride. Rory held them up long enough to enter the barn and close the back door, the one that led onto the bush trail. Ivan had closed the loft door, and now Rory closed the bottom door, sealing the small building against weather, roaming animals, and hopefully, snakes.

Ivan led out with the thieves following. Rory brought up the rear. The man riding in front of Rory, a fellow no more than nineteen or twenty years old, frightened and wanting to explain, started to talk.

Rory said, "I simply don't want to hear it. So, hold it. You burned out a friend of mine, and you murdered another friend, a man who had done you no wrong. So don't say one word."

The young man hunched his shoulders and fell silent.

4

THE RIDE BACK TO TOWN, ALONG THE BUSH TRAIL TO THE I-5 Ranch, the swap of horses, and the long trail to town, riding much more slowly than they did on the ride up the hill hours earlier, took till nearly dark.

They rode into a town in mourning, with anger growing, feeding their other feelings. The first man to spot the riders let out a shout. Soon the boardwalk and the road were teeming with people. There were a couple of shouts of 'hang them,' 'leave the rest to us, Sheriff,' and a few other insincere suggestions for retribution. Rory and Ivan ignored them all.

Before the body was unloaded into the shed behind the doctor's office, Andy Speth was called. Someone ran to the banker's house and brought Key Wardle down as well. Rory called Andy close and asked, "Andy, which one of these men shot Jessie?"

Andy looked carefully at the three mounted men, all of whom had their chins pushed down into the jackets and their hats lowered over their eyes, hiding a part of their faces. Still, the bank clerk was able to say, "None of these."

The Big 50 hadn't left much of the fourth man's face to use for identification, but Andy, after reluctantly taking the short walk around the horses, bravely bent down, then craned his neck upward to look at what was left. He glanced and then glanced again before standing up. "I'd know from the shirt if nothing else. But I could see enough of him to say for sure. This is the man."

The captured thieves had been led to the shed. Rory didn't want them out of his sight. When Andy identified the dead man as the shooter, one of the other thieves blurted out, "Arch was always shoot-crazy. Don't know exactly why we ever rode with him."

"Shut up," hollered one of the others.

The dead man was laid out inside the shed while the others sat their saddled, waiting.

Browning, the owner of the mercantile and leader of the town council, helpfully said, "The jail's burned and gone, Rory. What do you propose to do with these men?"

Someone hollered, "Shoot them."

Everyone ignored the shouter.

Rory, tired beyond explanation and knowing Ivan was the same, determined to remain civil. Browning had been a friend and helpful in times past. He would say nothing to damage that relationship.

"I think what we'll do, Mr. Browning, is handcuff these fellas to a log. Somewhere they can spend the night looking at—and smelling—the results of their actions. We'll stand a guard over them and size the situation up in the morning."

That moved two men to walk toward the now cooling fire. Ignoring the filth they were grinding into their clothing, they dragged out a half-burned beam.

They dropped it on the ground close to the back of the burned-out livery. The smell of burned horse flesh and timbers, turning slowly to charcoal as the flames were reduced to a smoldering, smoky mess, was an evil concoction sure to scar the nose and throat of any man subjected to its presence for any length of time.

"This do for you, Sheriff?"

Ivan took the initiative, saying, "That'll do just fine."

Marshal Key Wardle had a set of handcuffs on his belt. He walked to one of the mounted men and said, "Get down." When the man was on the ground, he clipped one cuff on the man's wrist and took him by the elbow, leading him toward the chosen timber. The thief took a breath, pulled back against Key's hand, and said, "I can't. You can't mean to leave me here. It ain't human."

"You lit the fire; you burned out the livery and the horses with it. You killed a man. And you stole the bank funds. That's not very human either. Now sit down."

Key was choking and gagging as he cuffed the man, but he never backed out of the job. Before long, all three were chained there.

A series of men had offered to stand guard. Key named them off in pairs for two-hour stints, telling them to hold back, as far from the stink as possible, but to stay alert.

When Ma Gamble, owner of the hotel dining room, offered to feed the prisoners, a howl of protest began to rise up among the gathering, but Browning himself quieted it down with a hand gesture and a, "Let's not sink to their level, folks. Of course, we'll let Ma feed them.

"And now it would be best if most of you went home. The excitement is all over."

THE HOTEL STAFF had been kept on the run that afternoon, filling and draining the bathtub as soot-blackened men scrubbed off the remnants of the fight. Browning gave discounts on the many new sets of clothing he had sold to those that had decided their own was beyond fixing. Now Rory and Ivan took turns getting themselves put back to rights.

THE NEXT MORNING the men were again fed. Their saddled mounts were led up to them. They were to be taken to a nearby farm where the farmer had cleaned out a small building for their temporary jail. Key would again organize a rotation of guards. Rory had felt it was only right that the trial take place in Stevensville. He would ride for the judge and be back in a couple of days.

Browning again called for attention from the crowd.

"I'd like if the town fathers and Ma Gamble, who also sits on council, would join me in the dining room. We'll want the sheriff and deputy, as well as Andrew Speth, to join us. It would be good if a half dozen known citizens would come along as witnesses. Key, will you take charge of the prisoners?" The question was really an order. Taking it that way, Key didn't bother to answer.

Those named, as well as a few witnesses, were soon gathered, squeezing into the small dining room, wondering what it was all about. Browning wasted no time getting down to business.

"Folks, several townsmen have left private and confidential documents with me for safekeeping over the years. You will recall that I had a metal safe in the store before the banker came to town. My friend, Jessie Ambrewster, was one of those, even though he had his own safe in the bank. Sadly, as you all know, Jessie was murdered yesterday. That, of course, brings up many questions, but those questions will have to wait. Right now, what should be dealt with is the will Jessie made out and lodged with me."

He held out a sealed envelope and said, "Sheriff Jamison, I think it would be appropriate for you to open this and read it before the people."

Rory quickly replied that Browning himself should read it, but the merchant refused, still holding the envelope toward Rory. Reluctantly he took the packet, lifted a camp knife from his belt, and slit the folded flap open. First, looking around the crowded room as if asking for final approval, he slid the paper out, opened it, and began reading.

Last Will and Testament of Jessie Ambrewster, Stevensville, Colorado.

This being the only will I have ever written; no other documents will supersede it.

My possessions are simple. They consist of my home, furnishings, private possessions, and the Stevensville Bank, along with a small personal deposit in that bank.

I have no living relatives near or dear to me.

Therefore, in the event of my death, I leave my house, all its possessions, and the personal bank deposit to my dear friend Ma Gamble, a fine and worthy lady.

Secondly, I leave the Stevensville Bank, with one stipulation, to my clerk, Mr. Andrew Speth. The stipulation is that he will find and employ an experienced and trustworthy banker to complete his training and supervise the banking actions for a period of one year. I am directing that Sheriff

*Rory Jamison be asked to oversee and assist in the location of
a trustworthy assistant.*

God bless you all.

Signed----------------

Beyond a couple of collective gasps from the crowd,
there was nothing said. Rory glanced first at Ma Gamble
and then at Andy. Both were looking as if they had been
struck by lightening.

5

As Rory was preparing to head north to the Fort, the Stevensville leaders were huddled over coffee in Ma Gamble's dining room. The question wasn't whether a new marshal's office and jail building should be built or where it should be sited. The question was how large the building should be and what building materials should be used. Wood had proven the day before to be vulnerable to fire, which was no surprise to any in the gathering. That alone pushed the discussion toward adobe or brick, with each choice having supporters on the town council.

Costs and the choosing of a builder consumed enough time that Browning finally said, "Look, folks, I have a business to run. I vote for brick and the builder up at the Fort. Both choices have proven their merit. And I vote for three iron-barred cells. Now, I'm going to re-open my store. You can move forward without me from here on."

Hip Dawson, mayor and town baker, also stood. "I'll

vote along with Browning in all the choices. I have a business to run too, and I best get at it."

With the decisions seemingly made and the meeting winding toward a visiting time, one man hollered after the baker, "Go make some donuts, Hip. Ma is about to run low."

Hip Dawson walked out the door with a roar of laughter encouraging him along his way.

ENTERING THE FORT, Rory went first to the marshal's office. He dismounted and walked in, looking initially at Marshal Wiley and then glancing at the cell, where it appeared, by the odor and the rattling of the man's snoring, that Wiley had housed a drunk.

His greeting to the marshal was, "Can you let that drunk out, Wiley, or have you placed more serious charges on him?"

"He can go. I'd love to see the last of him."

With that, he rose from the desk, picked the cell key off the wooden peg it hung from, and opened the cell door. He rattled the key ring across the bars, back and forth twice, before nudging the man's boot with the toe of his own boot. "C'mon, tough man, on your feet."

His voice was received with a groan and then more snoring. Wiley lifted the man's hat off the chair it was lying on and lightly whapped the drunk across the face with it. That got some attention beyond the groan the kick on the boot had pulled out of the fellow. When one eye finally opened, Wiley said, "Get up and get out of here. If you figure to tear the saloon apart again, I'll stand you before the judge. Take that as a warning and get gone."

It took a half minute, but the feet finally hit the floor, and with a sigh of pain, and a one-handed push against the thin mattress, the man rose to a sitting position. Wiley was patient for a few seconds before he again picked up the hat and threatened to use it as he had already done. Ducking his head and hunching his shoulders, the drunk reached for the hat and struggled to his feet. Wiley pointed to the door like a schoolteacher might do to a recalcitrant first-grade boy who would rather stay outside playing. The man, whom Rory had never seen before, wobbled and staggered, but he made it out the door and onto the street.

Wiley slipped on a pair of well-worn leather gloves and carried the slop bucket to the back door. He set it outside to be dealt with later. He slipped the gloves off and washed his hands.

By that time, Rory was coming back in the front door with a large canvas pannier resting across his shoulder. He laid it on the desk and opened one side. From the large pocket, he drew the bank record books Andy had gathered up and saved. From the other pocket, he pulled out the metal box from the bank safe and a smaller canvas sack holding coins and loose bills. He carried the items into the cell, laid them on the bunk, walked back out, and said, "Lock 'er up. Don't open it for anyone."

Rory walked to the saddle shop where his new wife was working and tried to open the door. The wooden door opened a bare two inches before a light growl was heard from inside, then a shrill laugh from Julia. That was followed by the order, "Scout, move away."

Rory finally got the door open, walking in to receive an excited and aggressive greeting from the dog and a happy smile from his wife. The scowl on Mr. Sales' face might have been signaling a different response. Rory stayed only a few moments, just long enough to show that he was home safe and sound and to very briefly mention the burned buildings, and more seriously, the shooting of Jessie Ambrewster. That news even had Mr. Sales laying down his tools and listening carefully. Although the saddle maker offered no response, his concern was obviously genuine. Rory ended the talk with, "I'll see you at home this evening."

6

RORY'S NEXT CALL WAS TO THE JUDGE.

"Sir. If you can spare a few minutes, we need to talk."

"Come in, Mr. Jamison. A rider yesterday afternoon brought some news from the south, but we have no details. I'm assuming you are going to close that information gap."

"Sadly. Yes. The livery, two horses, the bank, the marshal's office and jail, and a couple of small, unused buildings were all burned to the ground. The good news in that, I suppose, is that the town was saved. Saved by the hard work of the women pumping water from the two town wells and the men carrying it up ladders to wet down the close-by roofs.

"The very unhappy news is that the banker, a friend of mine and a friend to the town, was shot and killed. Deputy Ivan outsmarted the thieves and trapped them in an unused barn. When I showed up on the scene, the men were being forced to either shoot their way out or surrender. It turned out to be a bit of each. One man placed his faith in his gun. He will be buried today in

Stevensville. The other three surrendered. They are under arrest and guarded in a building on a close-by farm since the jail is gone.

"Now, as you are well aware, we don't have the facilities for long, drawn-out proceedings. Nor do we have easy access to lawyers. I'm thinking the folks down at Stevensville will demand that we move quickly, if for no other reason, to put the thing behind them.

"So, here's the question. I would like you to take the stage to Stevensville and hold a trial just as soon as possible. However, if you thought justice would be better served with lawyers and all, I could transfer the three men to Denver and let the larger court preside."

Rory then sat silently while the judge filtered that information through his active mind. When a full minute had gone past, he said, "It would appear that your case is cut and dried. Here's what I think is best. I'll travel down tomorrow. We'll hold a hearing, not a full trial. Not at first, in any case. If your prisoners find it to their advantage to plead guilty, we can decide their case. Bear in mind that you have not told me who did the shooting or who the dead man is. It is best that I not know at this point.

"If the men choose to ask for lawyers, we can transfer the case to the city."

Rory stood to his feet, saying, "That sounds like a fair enough position, Sir. I'll not join you on the stage. There seems to always be a need for me to ride somewhere else, so I'll leave early and ride down. I'll hope to have arrangements complete when you arrive."

~

It WAS early afternoon when the judge called the informal hearing to order. The chairs in the hotel lobby had been re-arranged, and a desk for the judge was moved into place. Rory called the prisoners to identify themselves as he called out: Keith Crain. Vic Stanley. Muir Adams.

The men stood to identify themselves as the judge sat silently, noting the appearance and features of each man. When the last man sat back down, Sheriff Jamison said, "The fourth man, Arch Majeska, was shot and killed resisting arrest."

As a first order of business, the judge explained to the three men that they had three options. The first was to simply plead guilty to theft, destruction of property, and accessory to murder. The second was to go to trial in Stevensville and plead their case, claiming innocence, without lawyers. The third was to transfer the case to Denver, where the men could hire lawyers.

In the silence that followed this explanation, the accused looked from one to another, with guilt and sorrow, or perhaps it was shame, showing in their faces. Finally, one man spoke up.

"Sir. I was asked earlier to speak for the three of us. If we are accused of theft only, we will plead guilty. If you intend to include the murder of the banker, which was done by Arch alone, who is now dead, we will ask for a lawyer."

Judge Anders P. Yokam leaned back in his chair and looked over at Sheriff Jamison. Knowing the judge didn't like it, but that he would accept the informal process, as was often the case in small settlements, Rory said, "Sir. The bank clerk, Mr. Andrew Speth, has testified to me and to others that it was the man named Arch who did the shooting. As was noted earlier, that same man was shot and killed in the capture of the thieves. Andy was an eyewitness to the killing of the banker. Whether or not the shooting was a planned action between the four men, we only have the survivor's word that it was not.

"However, I will testify that, during the ride down the hill from the place of capture, one of the men claimed that Arch was shoot-crazy and that they should never have followed him. Again, we have only the man's word.

"As to these men before you, I have seen no signs of remorse other than the remorse over being captured. If the destruction and death that resulted from their actions has them facing those actions with regret, I have yet to see it. In fact, if any of them have a troubled conscience at all, there's been no visible sign of it."

Judge Yokam again turned to the three prisoners.

"Men, the law would allow the sheriff to charge you with being an accessory to murder, and a trial in a larger center may, in fact, find you guilty of that charge. But it is my understanding now that you will plead guilty to theft and destruction of property if the other charge is removed. Is that the case?"

Again, the spokesman took the lead. Very quietly, he said, "Yes, Sir."

"That being the case, we will move from a hearing to a trial. You have already been sworn in."

Speaking to each man separately, the judge said, "You, young man, are charged with theft and bank robbery, as well as destruction of property. How do you plead?"

The quietly spoken word came quickly, "Guilty, Sir."

With all pleading guilty, Judge Yokam said, "On the evidence and on your plea of guilty, I sentence you each to ten years in the State prison. And it is my hope that you will come out, when your time is fulfilled, as better men than you went in. Court is dismissed."

7

KNOWING THERE WOULD BE THE NEED TO TRANSPORT THE prisoners, either for trial or to prison, before he had left the Fort, Rory ordered a special stage that would run all day and night, with regular changes of horses and drivers. That stage was waiting outside the hotel when the judge wrapped the table with his little wooden hammer. But because of the time of day, it was decided to have Ma Gamble feed the prisoners, the stage whip Rory, and Cap —who had agreed to accompany the sheriff on the trip.

With the meal completed and the horses fed and watered, the whip had the stage rolling out of town at a smart trot. As soon as he reached the town limit, he had the animals running at their normal, mile-eating gait. Two days later, with its weary passengers, the unit halted in front of the state office. Leaving Cap to watch over the prisoners, Rory walked inside. He had no treat for Bertha, as had become his custom, but he greeted her pleasantly and walked directly to Oscar Cator's office.

Without sitting down and with no preamble other than a quick 'hello,' he said, "I'm here with prisoners for the State facility. I'll detail it out for you later, but right now, we need to get these men housed."

Oscar stood and called over the office partition that stopped two feet from the high ceiling, "Tubs. Come in here."

Tubs Cardinal, a tall thin man, defying the imagery of his name, was soon at the door.

"Tubs, this is Sheriff Rory Jamison. You've heard of him, but I'm not sure you've ever met."

Not bothering to pursue that statement, Oscar said, "Stage outside. Three prisoners on it. One weary sheriff's deputy. Gather up a couple of men and take over. Get the prisoners down to the lockup. The paperwork will follow, probably tomorrow."

When Tubs hesitated, as if there was to be more talk, Oscar said, "So go already."

Rory said, "Cap and I need to hit the pillows. I'll come by tomorrow and we'll sort out the judgment and whatever other paperwork you need."

With no more said, he turned and followed Tubs. But he stopped at the door and said, "Bertha, I'm remembering your shock at the work I and others do. I'm sure whatever it is you're doing will hold for a minute. Come with me."

With a questioning look on her face, the state office secretary and keeper of the door stood and followed after first glancing back at Oscar Cator, who was her boss. Rory gently pushed Tubs aside and opened the stagecoach door himself. He asked Cap to step out and then asked Bertha to come closer.

"Have a good look at those three men in the back, Bertha. At first glance, you could think they were your neighbors' sons or nephews you haven't seen for awhile. Give them a shave and a new shirt, and they could be choir boys or the kid from a close-by ranch that's come to court your daughter. But what they are is bank robbers. Burned the livery and the jailhouse to cover their crime. Two horses were burned in the fire. Their accomplice shot and killed the banker. That thief and murderer lost his life when he challenged Ivan, you will remember Ivan in the arrest. Don't these boys look innocent?

"Looking at these men, you can see, I'm sure, that a lawman never knows who he's dealing with. There are no signs on these men that announce that they're thieves and building burners or that they rode with a murderer, but that's exactly what they are."

Bertha held her gaze on the men for only a few seconds before she backed away. Slowly she lifted her eyes, first to Rory and then to Cap. She then, uncharacteristically, patted Rory on the chest. She did the same to Cap before silently turning back to the office door.

Cap watched the woman walk away and then turned to Rory with an unasked question on his face. Rory said, "Later," and closed the stage door after Tubs was seated.

BY NOON THE NEXT DAY, Cap and Rory had visited the state office, laying the court papers on Oscar Cator's desk. Questions were asked and answered. The current gossip and rumors around the territory were exchanged. But finally, with no more to talk about and with Oscar needing to attend to other business, the men shook hands and were ready to take their leave. But as Rory's hand fell on the doorknob in Oscar's office, the state man said, "Don't skip town without going over to the federal office. I'm sure Block would like to see you, but the more important thing is that there's another Washington man in town. He has everyone over there walking on their tiptoes, afraid to speak or move. The message to me was that he especially wanted to see you."

"I'm getting really sick of this Oscar."

"I know you are my friend, but it's going to continue until either a full solution to the stolen bank boxes is found or half the marshal's service is fired and replaced with more trustworthy men. And you're wrapped up in it whether you like it or not."

Rory shook his head and turned the knob.

Outside, Cap asked, "What do you figure to do about the marshals?"

"Nothing I can do. It isn't much, but I can delay for a few hours. Come, we have a bank to visit."

Both men wore their weapons but had left their carbines in the hotel room. With their coats, which were really not necessary on a warm day, tied with the leather straps and allowed to hang naturally, the gun belts were not easily visible. Anyone taking a careful study might notice a bulging at the waist, but neither man was concerned about it.

At the bank, Rory asked to see Mr. Tremblay. Hebert Tremblay's wife was rescued from an unfortunate incident during one of Rory's visits to the city. He and the banker hadn't become personal friends, but still, there was a two-way respect building between them. It didn't hurt that Rory had two significant deposits held by the bank, one personal, the other for his county.

They had to wait a short while as Tremblay finished his work with another customer, but before long, they were seated across from the banker. Rory introduced Cap and then explained the purpose of their visit. When

Tremblay heard about the murder of Jessie Ambrewster, his face fell in shock.

"I only met the man once. Fine fellow. We hold a large portion of the long-term deposits for the Stevensville Bank. Did Jessie leave instructions in case of something like this?"

"He did, and that's why we're here."

It only took a few minutes to explain the situation fully. When that was done, Rory asked, "Do you have a man in your branch that you could spare from time to time to fulfill the will's instructions."

Tremblay stood to his feet and left the office. He was back almost immediately, followed by a young, dapper-looking man.

"Sheriff Rory Jamison, Deputy Cap Graham, I'd like you to say hello to Phil Canning. Don't be fooled by the clothes or the big city demeanor he has successfully taken on. Phil is a rancher's son. He won't be intimidated by anything you tell him.

"Phil, Sheriff Jamison has a short story to tell you. And an offer."

Again, the story was abbreviated to just the pertinent facts. The offer was brief and to the point; "Banker Jessie Ambrewster left a stipulation in his will that before Andy Speth could take ownership of the bank, he was to have a senior assistant to guide him along and help him get re-established. Finding that man was left to me. I immediately thought of this bank and Mr. Tremblay. He, in turn, thought of you. If you took this on, I don't know what kind of a schedule you would have to develop. After the first short while, I can't imagine that you would be needed more than a few days per month. But then, I'm not a banker, and I don't know what at all goes into the business. You and Andy and, perhaps, with Mr. Tremblay's guidance, could figure that out.

"You would, of course, be paid. What arrangement you would make for your current job is between you and Mr. Tremblay. But Jessie did not see Andy needing an assistant at all after some more training."

When Canning sat silently, Tremblay said, "How does that sound to you, Phil? It would get you out of the office and into the country from time to time. And you'd be helping a young man put together what was broken."

~

RORY AND CAP were walking along the Denver Street that led to the federal marshal's offices. Cap had been silent the entire time at the bank. Now he said, "You seem to know that banker pretty well. Never had much to do with bankers my own self."

"I'll tell you all about it sometime Cap. But right now, I plan to face up to whatever these federals have in mind. You can come along or go back to the hotel, whatever you wish."

"I'll come along."

Rory used just one knuckle to rap on the crinkled glass with the lettering 'U.S. Marshal's Office' on it and turned the knob. He and Cap walked into a room where every eye was on them. On previous visits, Rory had wondered if it wouldn't be better to keep the door locked, given the nature of the work undertaken by this group. There was no telling when someone bent on revenge might burst into the room with guns blazing, seeking revenge.

"Afternoon, men."

He said no more, figuring someone there, probably

the branch manager, Donavan Gaines, would have something to say. He did. What he said was, "Sheriff Jamison, get yourself into my office."

Rory grinned at Gaines as he said to Cap, "Make yourself known, Cap. A couple of these are good men. See if you can figure out which ones they are."

That brought a series of catcalls and groans from the group. Block Handley stood from his chair in a small side office and greeted Cap.

"You're keeping questionable company, Cap, but everyone makes mistakes. I'm Block Handley."

Cap introduced himself. No one else shook hands, but that didn't surprise or bother Cap. It was common for lawmen to stand loose when first meeting someone.

In his private office, Donavan Gaines pointed to a seated man, a man showing some stature and the self-confidence of position.

"Sheriff Jamison, this is Deputy Marshal Col. Oliver Staveley. Oliver just arrived from Washington a couple of days ago. Your visit is timely. Oliver very much wanted to meet you. I believe he has some questions for you."

There was no offer of a handshake from the Colonel. Neither was there any respect shown by standing to meet the visitor. Rory's father would have written the man off immediately as untaught and arrogant. Rory held back final judgment, although he agreed with his father's assessment of this easterner.

Rory managed to tip his hat a bit and say, "Colonel."

To break the ice, Donavan said, "I'm happy to see you, Sheriff. But what brings you to the city this time?"

"Bank robbery and murder. Up at Stevensville. Messy business. Four men. Robbed the bank. Murdered the banker, a friend of mine. Burned the stable and some other buildings to create an escape. It didn't work. One man is in his grave, and three were brought down to the state penitentiary. The judge gave them ten years each for robbery. The murderer was killed resisting arrest."

For the first time, the Colonel spoke. His words almost sounded like a sneer.

"Shot resisting arrest. Handy."

Rory glanced at the man and then turned to Donavan.

"Oscar Cator said you wanted to see me. I hadn't figured on a long stay in town. What can I do for you."

At this, Col. Oliver Staveley appeared to find his opening.

"You'll tell me the entire story of the trip to Texas and the arrest of Webster Cunningham. After that, you will tell me why you struck and then insisted on arresting one of our senior deputies, Glover Harrison, and what right you had to treat deputies Carlton and Byway as you did.

"And you might just as well know…I'm holding great suspicions on you. And as for you being in a hurry to return to your village, or whatever it is, you will stay in Denver as long as I wish. And that may be a while. I have serious matters to dig through."

Rory almost smiled before asking, "Do you intend to arrest me, Sir?"

"No one said anything about arrest."

"Fine, then I'll be taking my leave."

Rory turned his head away and spoke to Donavan. "Have you given this man my written report?"

"I have. And Deputy Handley has supported both your written report and your verbal report to me."

"Alright. I have nothing at all to add."

When Rory turned to the door, the Colonel finally rose from his chair.

"If you open that door or attempt to leave, I will arrest you."

"No, you won't. You'd look a fool. You have no charge to arrest me for. And make up your mind. I am leaving."

~

TWO MINUTES LATER, Rory and Cap were back on the sidewalk. He wondered what was being said back in Donavan's office, but he would probably never know. They walked a few blocks, then crossed the street and turned down a short side alley. A half block along was the livery that Rory was in the habit of using.

"Hi'ya there, Sheriff. What brings ya ta the big city this time?"

"Hello, Kris. I came just to see you. If I'm away too long, I get to where I'm feeling sad. Yearning for your bubbly personality. I thought you would have known that. If I don't see your smiling face for a while, I can't sleep at night.

"Kris, say hello to Deputy Cap Graham. Cap and I, we're going to be needing a couple of horses in the morning. Buy, not rent. You got any good ones around?"

"Too bad you weren't here a few days ago. Those you left with me for sale were good animals. Sold the last two not long ago. Got the money for them right there in the office. I planned to take that and the money from the other sales to that bank you told me about the first chance I got."

"You find us two good horses, well shod, saddles, and gear. We'll be here in the morning to do business."

With that, the two men walked back to the hotel.

They would eat and then go shopping for bedrolls and some camp supplies.

~

THAT EVENING, as Rory and Cap were settling back in their chairs to enjoy a last cup of coffee—after feasting on the dining room's standard beef and mashed potatoes —Col. Oliver Staveley wound his way through the crowd, stopping beside the two lawmen. With no other greeting, the federal deputy marshal asked, "May I join you, Sheriff?"

Rory's head snapped around. He hadn't seen the man approaching, although Cap certainly had. Rory had noticed Cap studying on something, but with all the movement, the crowds, the ladies in fancy dress, and the prosperous ranchers and businessmen to take note of, there was no shortage of people to look at, admire, and wonder about.

Not sure what to expect, Rory indicated an empty chair. "As you wish, Colonel."

The man took the seat and said, "First off, let's get rid of that ridiculous Colonel title. I was an officer in a supply depot during a time when they were throwing officer titles around like kid's penny candies. I did nothing at all to earn such a title. In fact, I have tried everything I know to leave it behind me. But somehow, the marshals feel that those of us who wore a uniform, no matter what color it was, should carry our titles with us. I disagree, but that hasn't changed anything. My name is Oliver. Or, if a person wished to be more formal, Deputy Marshal Oliver Staveley. But I am fine with Oliver."

Neither sheriff responded to the change in attitude

from their previous meeting, although the deputy may have seen just the lightest tilt of Rory's head in acknowledgment. Oliver Staveley cleared his throat. He fidgeted with his hands a bit, as if he wasn't quite sure where to start. He was relieved of that decision when a young lady in a dining room uniform approached with a cup in one hand and the coffee pot in the other.

"Coffee, sir?"

With that matter dealt with, the marshal said, "I suppose I have to confess to you men that my subordinate officers have, this afternoon, taken me to the woodshed, as my father would have said back on our Tennessee farm. I'm sure you will understand that is not a common occurrence in the marshal's service."

There was a slight pause as Oliver Staveley gathered the words he wished to speak. When he did speak, he ignored Cap while directing his words at Rory.

"Sheriff, you have created quite a fuss in Washington. I'm not sure you understand that. I'm also not sure how much information you have been trusted with. It's quite possible that you landed in the middle of something outside of your normal work or even your intelligence. By intelligence, of course, I mean the private information held by a limited number of people. The word bears no weight on your personal intelligence, which I am assured by those same subordinates, is quite likely equal to, or perhaps even superior to, the majority of the population.

"I refer, of course, to the theft and subsequent disappearance of two federal government strong boxes containing newly printed currency, as well as freshly struck gold coins.

"Now, lest we be overheard in this crowded room, if you have completed your meals, I suggest we move into the lobby where we can pull some chairs together in a quiet corner."

Neither Cap nor Rory had spoken yet. As if on signal, the three men rose. Rory led the way. The other two men followed. At the door, Cap said, "Perhaps I should leave you two alone."

"I'd like you to stay if Oliver has no objection."

"Stay deputy. I have nothing to hide at this point. Well, to be honest, I have quite a bit that must stay hidden, but none of it applies to our conversation this evening."

Rory was starting to feel as if the Colonel was a man who enjoyed talking. Or, perhaps, more accurately, enjoyed being listened to.

Taking the lead, Rory selected an overstuffed wing-back chair and pushed it into a corner. The other men followed suit. They formed a triangle that would have them isolated from the crowd. Rory spotted a small, round table that would sit about knee-high. He lifted it over the back of one chair and set it in the center of the triangle.

If they leaned forward as they spoke, their heads would almost touch. For privacy, it was the best they could do without moving into a separate room. When they were seated, Oliver Staveley started again.

"As you are well aware, Sheriff, and you will come to understand, Deputy, if you stay on the matter, the theft was a great embarrassment to a government at war. The theft showed organization, cunning, incredible bravery, and awareness of knowledge that was meant to remain private. It, unfortunately, also demonstrated something close to treason.

"A small group of riders managed to surprise the transport troupe. With no shots fired. No deaths. And no identifications of the masked men, the transport troupe was overcome, dismounted, tied, gagged, and left on the side of the road. The thieves were gone in a matter of minutes.

"Since no one was supposed to know about the movement of the boxes, or even of their existence, for that matter, the suspicions in Washington rose to fever pitch. I have no way of knowing how tuned-in either of you are on the political world. But by explanation, I will say that when I say fever pitch in Washington, I am talking about the bureaucracy, and those men who hold the real reigns of power. The average citizen likes to think that our elected representatives are in control, and that is true, but only to an extent. The true control of the nation rests with those unnamed and unknown men who sit in quiet offices and pull the strings of government. But among those quiet workers, or among the senate, there is always much ambition. In the case before us, the matter fell at the feet of one who has great political ambitions indeed. It is because this matter could well spell an end to those ambitions that it has, as I already said, reached fever pitch.

"There has been no cooling off at this point, although it was thought the matter had been brought to a close when the boxes were located a couple of years ago. Although, as you already know, Sheriff, the identity of the original thieves has never been discovered."

As if he had lost the trend of the story, Cap said, "Located?"

"I apologize, Deputy. The sheriff is aware that the boxes disappeared without a sign. They remained lost for some years. None of the fresh bills nor the gold coins were ever seen in circulation. Washington was beyond reason or comfort, and by Washington, I really mean one man. One very powerful man who was in charge of the entire matter—from forming the original idea to the last printing in a New Orleans mint that was in danger of being lost to the Confederate forces, to the loading and transfer of the two boxes, and to the route to follow to arrive in federal territory.

"It was a great embarrassment to that man and a threat to his personal political hopes. Before either of you ask, know that he shall remain nameless. But that he still holds to those same political ambitions is well known to the inner circle.

"How or where the boxes were lost, or secreted, has never been discovered. If they had been lost forever, like the British crown jewels, everyone involved would have been just as happy, and it may have all gone to sleep by this time. But, Deputy, when your sheriff here came into the possession of a tarnished gold coin and started asking questions, the whole nasty matter had fresh light shone on it."

Cap, showing his merit as a lawman, said, "And Washington suspects that Rory is somehow more involved than he has admitted to."

The marshal leaned back in his chair and studied Cap. After a moment, he said, "Alright, men, here's where I eat crow, as the saying is."

But instead of simply proceeding, he asked, "Do you suppose we would be allowed to have a pot of coffee brought out here?"

Rory stood, slid between two of the closely packed chairs, and disappeared into the dining room. In a few minutes, a waiter—pushing a small trolly holding a silver tray of mugs, some kind of small pastries, and a steaming pot—followed Rory back to their private corner of the lobby. The waiter poured while the men sat silently.

It was clear that the marshal would prefer to be doing almost anything else, but he did finally take up the narrative again.

"Sheriff, like the men who have come west before me to deal with this matter, I was of the suspicion that you might be in this thing up to your eyebrows. You might be willing to admit that you keep popping into the story at all critical moments. You are far too young to have played a part in the original theft, but that matter will stay closed. We are satisfied that the identities of the masked riders are forever lost. We are also not pursuing the question of how the boxes got lost or where they have been all those years. But how they were located and by whom is of great interest. That's where you fit in, Sheriff."

Not wanting to disrupt the flow of information and still waiting to hear the man explain about eating crow, Rory and Cap both remained silent.

"You have friends, Sheriff. As it turns out, you have a lot of friends. Friends who like and trust you. And some of those friends are, in turn, men I know and trust. It was two of those men, to name them, Deputy Block Handley and Deputy Donavan Gaines, both trusted men, that took me to the woodpile after this afternoon's unhappy meeting. They explained your history to me and advised that your time and whereabouts could be easily accounted for. They also advised that I consult with Oscar Cator, which I have, in fact, done. There appears to be no evidence to suggest that you had ever been to Texas before this last trip, or that you would have had time to do so.

"So, my apology, Sheriff. But understand, that is my apology. Not to be mistaken as an apology from the marshal's service. To convince the men in Washington might not be so easy. You have shone the light of the law on a couple of deputy marshals of some stature. One of those men is still in prison here in Denver, mostly at your insistence."

Rory spoke for the first time, asking, "So where do we go from here? For my part, I have every intention of riding out in the morning."

"And I'm asking you to delay for a day or two. I know we have your written report on file, but I'd like to address a couple of things in person. And that's better done in the office where we are sure of not being overheard."

Rory turned and looked at Cap, trying to find a message in his stoic countenance. All he saw was something that might have said, 'you're the boss.'

Rory stood and walked across the hotel lobby. He stood in front of the big window, looking out on the darkened street, seeing mostly the reflection of the room behind him. He was considering the work yet to be done in the gold town of MacNair's Hill. There was work to be done in Stevensville, where both the marshal and deputy sheriff were burned out of their holdings. There was work to be done on the bank matter. And there was a new wife at home who he missed terribly.

He turned and walked back to the meeting place. Holding a firm eye on the marshal, he said, "One day. Then we ride. We left a lot of unfinished business at home. We can't leave it any longer."

"Fair enough. Come to my office at nine tomorrow morning."

8

THE QUESTIONS WERE ALL ASKED, AND THE ANSWERS GIVEN by noon the next day. But Oliver Staveley insisted Rory accompany him and Block to the city holding cells. There they confronted, one by one, Webster Cunningham—who had charge of the Big C brand of rustled cattle in Texas—and Glover Harrison—the senior marshal who tried to prevent the Texas search and whose name Rory had found on the list of associates involved with the stolen strong boxes. Neither man was very welcoming to the county sheriff.

Deputy Marshal Staveley arranged for the use of the jailer's private office, and each prisoner was interviewed separately. In Rory's mind, it was all a waste of time since none of the talk brought forth new evidence. And nothing at all that wasn't included in Rory's rather lengthy report. But perhaps it was important since, to Deputy Marshal Staveley, it was confirmation of both Rory's and Block's reports. The man was going to have to return to Washington with his own written report. He needed it to be complete.

When Staveley boarded the train, he would be boarding with the two federal prisoners, well-cuffed and guarded by other marshals. Rory silently gave thanks that he wouldn't be joining them.

The sheriff and the senior marshal parted with a handshake. Hoping to have it all behind them, Col. Oliver Staveley grinned and said, "It's possible we in the marshal's service are going to have to work on our people skills."

9

AFTER A TWO-DAY RIDE, RORY AND CAP RODE DOWN THE muddy, single-business street of MacNair's Hill. A stop at the marshal's office found it to be empty. The street was teeming with activity, as were the trails through all the mining country. Rory grinned as they were approaching the town, wondering if Cap was going to twist his own neck off, turning from one pick and shovel operation to another and then studying on a couple of larger operations.

"Ever seen anything like it, Cap?"

"Never did. Don't know if I like it either. I'm kind of fond of the land as God created it. I know the nation needs these minerals to exist and prosper, but most of these diggers won't find anything. They'll dig, smash, and move on, leaving broken rock and dead trees behind them. And a hole in the hillside that will still be there when their grandchildren's grandchildren are running the country. I've ridden a good part of these western lands. Seen mountains and running streams, grassland to the horizon. I've also seen overgrazed grasslands that might never grow anything but weeds and cacti ever again, with smashed-down creek banks and drying and dying waterways. It's a wonder what man can do when he's using his energy but not his brain."

Rory had never heard the deputy express himself in such a way. All he could think to say in response was, "When you're right, you're right, Cap."

They found Deputy Buck Canby behind the counter at the mercantile store. Buck hollered a greeting to the visiting lawmen and asked the young lady Rory knew as Gloria to take over the customer he had been helping. Buck walked to the end of the service counter and beckoned Rory and Cap to follow him. He pulled away the canvas curtain that hung between the store and the storage room and living space behind. The men entered, and Buck let the canvas fall back into place. He led the way through the storeroom and into the small kitchen. It was only then that he turned and shook hands with Rory and then Cap.

Rory made the introduction. He then grinned and said, "Was that Gloria I saw in the store?"

"That's Gloria, all right. I coaxed her away from the diner. Coaxed her to marry me too."

Buck's smile looked like it was about to split his face.

All Rory could think to do or say was, "Well, congratulations! That should help with the 'lonelies' on the long winter nights. I don't know what it does for the peacekeeping, but I'm sure you can make it work."

"The spring has been pretty peaceful so far. Nothing more than a few fistfights and the normal run of drunks. But the summers are short, as you well know. The men need to take advantage of the opportunity. Most have no time to waste. They dig, they eat, and they sleep. The riffraff is soon pushed aside. I picked up another deputy, as you suggested. Otto Helm is his name. Says he mined out last summer. Gave 'er up. Came near to starving in a shack back south somewhere. Came asking for a job in the store. Didn't need him in the store, but he jumped at the chance to sign on with the county. Good man, I'm thinking. At least he appears so, this far into the season."

There was more talk as Buck filled the coffee pot with fresh water, but Rory could see no problem in the arrangement he had left in the gold town. If the town grew with good strikes, there would have to be a more formal system put in place, but that could wait until the claims either proved themselves or the miners moved on to other opportunities.

And there may come a time when the town would have to put their own marshal on staff.

A FEEDING at the small café put an end to the lawmen's visit. They were soon on the downward trail, now free of snow, but mud or exposed rock made the riding slippery, requiring caution. Rory took the time to show Cap around Kiril's abandoned buildings, including the trail behind the barn that led into Stevensville. He introduced the deputy to Ivan's family as they rode through the I-5 Ranch and arrived in town just as the sun was disappearing behind the Front Range. The available hotel rooms and the hot water baths were a welcome ending to a long, eventful ride.

Rory was ready to plunge back into the work left by the fire, but he wanted to keep his involvement short. It was important, too, that neither he nor Ivan, who were both county men, get involved in what was essentially town business.

Entering the dining room for breakfast, he was surprised to find Andy Speth sitting with banker Phil Canning. He invited himself to their table and took a seat.

Speaking to Phil Canning, he said, "You wasted no time getting here, Phil. And you've met Andy. How are you doing so far?

"Doing well," said the Denver banker. "We had a few hours last evening after the stage dropped me off. But Andy can tell you the rest. He's managed to do a couple of things."

As Rory turned his attention to Andy, the young banker said, "I've rented the space that phony judge was using. It's small, but we can make do for now. A couple of the men pulled the iron bars that had formed the jail cell out of the rubble. We were told about a new smithy up at the Fort. We've sent for him, telling him what we wish to do. I'm hoping he gets here today or tomorrow. We're going to borrow your old cell. I'm expecting the new marshal's office will want two or three cells, so the old one won't be much use. We're going to reassemble the cell with a good lock.

"Phil found a passably good, used safe in Denver before he left. It's coming down on a freight run in the next couple of days. We were first hoping the old safe could be brought back to life, but the fire damage was too severe. We figure if we put the safe inside the locked cell, there should be enough security until a new building can be put up. The town sent for the builder from the Fort. He came in with a wagonload of tools and such yesterday. He's already ordered bricks and what cut lumber will be needed. The town contracted for a new marshal's office too. Ivan talked them into doubling the size so the marshal and sheriff could each have an office and share the cells.

"We're hoping the builder can find enough men to work on two buildings at the same time."

Phil Canning smiled at Rory and suggested, "Have Andy tell you the rest. Probably the most important part."

Rory simply turned back to Andy and waited. Andy, looking a bit embarrassed, said, "Well, it didn't seem like such a good idea to have no access to banking. And I was concerned that the town might turn on me and the bank. So...I asked Mr. Browning to call a meeting. Enough folks turned up to kind of make it official. I told them their money and all the records were safe up at the Fort. That you had it all in safe keeping in the jail cell. That's where I got the idea for our temporary situation. I promised their money would be moved down here just as soon as we had the office ready. That seemed to satisfy most. But we need to move quickly. I'm not sure how long folks will wait."

Phil Canning slapped Andy on the back and spoke to Rory.

"That's not the half of it, Sheriff. This young man had the town eating out of his hand. He'll do alright. We just have to go over some details and explain the finer parts of financial control and how money moves through the system, and he'll be ready to be on his own."

RORY MET with Ivan for just a few minutes, explaining the recent happenings at MacNair's Hill. He then walked over to commiserate a bit with Tippet. The livery man was working day and night cleaning up his old space. He was filthy, black with soot and charcoal. But the space was nearly cleaned up. Rory couldn't see how this no longer young man was hoping to build himself a new barn, but he appeared to be determined, so Rory said nothing to discourage him.

RORY AND CAP rode into the Fort mid-afternoon.

10

THREE WEEKS AFTER THE FIRE, RORY AND JULIA RODE together to the Double J Ranch for a visit with family and then carried on to Stevensville the next morning. The change in the village was impressive. Tippet, indeed, had his livery laid out and a couple of walls standing upright. The bank building and the new marshal's office were both rising.

Gunter Stakes, the smithy from the Fort, was hard at work trying to keep the builder happy. Andy had decided that having the bank vault secured behind locked bars was a fine idea. He decided to incorporate the plan into the new building. With both structures requiring smith-work, Gunter was working long hours, and still, the builder was pushing him for more.

The bank was open in the small office beside Browning's mercantile. Deputy Sheriff Ivan had arranged an escort to transfer the strong box and the bank records from the Fort, and the bank was soon doing as much business as it had ever done. Phil Canning had stayed for one week and had returned once since. Satisfied with the acumen of the young banker, he left with the advice to call if he was needed.

Julia explored the shops while Rory visited the bank. When he was alone with Andy, he withdrew two hundred dollars from his personal account, a sizable sum in that economy. After the funds were counted out and lying on the counter, he said, "Put that in your pocket, Andy, and say nothing at all. When you get a chance, slip it into a box or jar of some kind and mark it for helping Tippet rebuild. Leave the box out on the counter where folks can see it and contribute if they wish. I'm sure he can use a leg up on the new barn."

Andy slipped the bills off the counter and nodded.

RORY STUCK his head in one store after another before he found his wife busy choosing some finery at the millenary shop.

"I'll be patiently waiting on the bench outside when you're ready to leave." There was, perhaps, just a hint of impatience in the words.

Julia laughed and continued her shopping. The lady owner of the shop very confidentially said, "That's why that comfortable bench sits out front. There's been many an impatient husband or father idling away his time on that bench."

When Julia finally came out of the shop empty-handed, Rory gave her a look that said, *'All that time, and you couldn't find anything you liked?'*

Julia picked up on the unasked question. Her response was, "She's holding it for me. I'll pick it up when we're ready to leave."

"I'm ready now."

"But, my dear, we've barely arrived. There's so much to see and many folks to meet. Surely, you're not in that big a rush."

"Once you've walked this boardwalk, you've about seen Stevensville."

"Perhaps, but the country around. You've told me about the river just to the south. I'd kind of like to see it. But what I'd really like to see is Kiril's cabin. You've talked about that too. It sounds mysterious and lovely all at the same time."

"It's an empty log cabin. There's nothing mysterious about it except, perhaps, how it is that Kiril managed to die sitting in his favorite chair with his rifle across his lap. It didn't look as if he had planned on dying."

"Does anyone ever plan on dying?"

To Rory's silence, Julia added, "Come on. You said it's not far. Let's ride up. I'm sure we can be back before dark, from what you said."

Rory fidgeted a bit on the bench. Knowing he had lost the contest before it had really begun, he still held back. Julia ended the discussion with, "I'll get the horses."

In spite of the years of riding, when the need called, and not having to answer to anyone, making his own decisions, Rory was not really unhappy with his wife's request. But he wasn't totally sure it was a good idea either. Wandering the hills with a beautiful woman at his side wasn't his idea of wisdom or caution. Still, there was every likelihood that the cabin was empty and that they could ride up, look around a bit, and ride back down, all without incident. Maybe.

It was common knowledge that Ivan had ridden to the cabin with Tempest Wardle without a problem. He was just working his mind through that fact when Julia arrived with the horses. She was already mounted. When she dropped his reins in front of him, he had little choice. He rose from the bench, stepped across the boardwalk, and mounted. He thought he saw a bit of smugness in his wife's smile, but he didn't mention it to her.

They stopped in front of the bakery. Julia went into the small shop, intent on purchasing a loaf of bread and whatever else caught her eye. When she went for the horses, she had walked to Browning's mercantile and waited while Browning sliced off several portions of smoked and cured ham. They would very likely be looking for a snack before they got back down the hill. She wished to be ready. Even a crudely put-together ham sandwich was better than going hungry.

Rory led the way along the familiar trail, stopping at the I-5 Ranch to introduce Julia to Ivan's family. Mrs. Ivanov gave her a grand welcome, insisting they come in for coffee and a snack. The men sat, more or less silently, as the ladies visited. Mrs. Ivanov stumbled over many English words and phrases, causing good-natured laughter between the women. When Julia asked how to say, 'we must go now,' in the Ivanov home language, her attempts at copying the older woman's words, getting the guttural sounds correct and the vowels in the proper order, brought them all to laughter. But finally, they made their way through the I-5 grass and onto the uphill trail.

The cabin came into view, with just a bit of the yard and some of the surrounding forest. Julia pulled her gelding to a halt. "Why, it's beautiful. Homey and cozy. And a lovely location."

Rory had no response. He simply urged her horse on with the flat of his hand across the horse's hip. When the entire small holding was visible, she stopped again. She took it all in as if it was somehow magical before saying, "It is lonely. But it's beautiful. So well thought out. The cabin, the chicken coop, the barn, all tucked into the forest with hardly a sign of other human activity."

She was just saying, "I want to see inside the cab—" when a rifle shot broke the silence. Neither of them was hit but as if the shooter had been either nervous, excited, or in too much hurry, the bullet threw up sod and dirt from beneath Rory's horse.

They wasted no time wondering where the shot came from or who stood behind the weapon. They both broke for the cabin. Another shot hurried them on their way. The second shot was accompanied by someone shouting, "You fool. We could have had them both if you had waited, holding to some caution, like you've been told many times."

Rory didn't know the voice, and he couldn't imagine who would have been lying in wait. There was no one he knew of that had a killing hatred for him, and certainly not for Julia. There were few men who would purposely hunt or shoot a woman. And no one could possibly know they were riding to the cabin that day. Rory hadn't known himself.

They ducked behind the cabin and jumped off their horses. Rory signaled Julia to stand while he looked in the cabin window. He eased along the wall and, with his hat in his hand, took a quick look inside and then a second, longer look. Seeing nothing, he again signaled Julia to stand while he eased around to the front. There was still no one in sight. He whispered, "Come," and ducked to the door. They were both carrying their carbines, and Julia had her .32 tucked into a pocket in her jacket.

Once inside, Rory went quickly to the stove and

pulled the wood box away from the wall. There was enough space for one person behind the safety of the big kitchen range.

"Quick, duck in here. Stay put but keep your eyes open. I'm going on the hunt. When I return, I'll call out before I open the door. If you don't hear my voice, shoot anyone trying to enter. And watch that side window. I'll be back."

Julia had said nothing. Was it fright, nervousness, or excitement? Whatever it was she was feeling, it seemed to cause her to hold her words to herself. She would trust her husband, who had much experience in these matters.

It was true that she had managed to survive the attack on her family's ranch home, as two fugitives had burst in and demanded food and horses from her parents. But she wasn't sure she wanted to repeat the experience.

The two men had beaten her father almost senseless and slapped her mother into submission. They were totally at the men's mercy until Deputy Sheriff Rory Jamison, a stranger at that point, had knocked on the door, pretending to be a neighbor coming to take Julia for a buggy ride. Much had happened in the next ten minutes, as Rory and Julia escaped into the darkness, that caused the rancher's daughter to feel the first inkling of affection, if not outright love, and left both men dead or dying. One died the next day from a beating Julia's mother had laid on him with a stick of firewood. The other had been laid low by Julia with a single blast from a shotgun.

Now, huddled behind the stove, she didn't have the shotgun, but she was a good shot with her .44-40 and a reasonably good shot with the little handgun. Cramped in as she was, secured behind the heavy metal stove, there would be very little maneuverability with the long gun, but the way she was situated, it covered the back half of the cabin. If anyone tried to climb through the small openings or even attempted to shoot through one, they would be within her sight. Her view of the front door was mostly blocked by the iron stove.

11

Rory slipped into the forest and around the back of the cabin. The shots had come from behind the cabin and across the uphill trail. Arriving at a position that gave him sight of the shooter's likely stance, he stood absolutely still, as protected as possible by a large spruce tree. He saw no motion, but the earlier shooting and subsequent shout of anger indicated that these impatient men were off to the south and, perhaps, a bit further up the slope. But, in any case, they were not far away.

He couldn't see the front of the cabin, but no one from the south could reach the door or the big window without breaking cover and coming into his view. It was doubtful if either man would try to ease through the bush to come up behind him or the cabin, but he couldn't be sure. Still, both horses were tied on that side, and his big red gelding would surely blow a warning if anyone approached.

Rory was not a naturally patient man. His every nature told him to call the men out and get it over with. Charge in and see who was left standing at the end. The problem with that was that it might end with him lying dead. He could be patient, hoping to prevent that.

He had learned patience with his father on the gold creek as a much younger man. The first creek-washed pan didn't make them wealthy. Neither did the one hundredth or the one thousandth. But patiently, pan by pan, day by day, week by week, over two and one-half years, they had built up a sizable account in the Boise Bank. Since that time, and leaning on lessons learned, he had patiently hunted down his father's murderers and hunted several more felons after he was given the lawman's badge. Yes, he could be patient. But could the hunters? And who were these men? Having that bit of knowledge might make his job easier. It might also tell him why they were out there, hoping to bring him down. And why here, at Kiril's old cabin? No one knew he would be here. He hadn't even known himself until Julia came up with the idea.

There was a movement. A rustled bush...and then an oath from the same voice that had burst out in frustration earlier. Whoever these men were, their wisdom was giving way to carelessness.

Rory studied on the bush that had been clumsily brushed against by one of the gunmen. There was nothing human showing. Then, just as he was about to glance away, there was a boot sole. He couldn't imagine what position the man had squirmed himself into, to show the bottom of his boot, but there it was. Wishing to make something happen, Rory recognized his chance. He squatted onto his haunches and eased the .44-40 around the trunk of the tree. Then, knowing he would have to expose himself to get the shot off, he studied the ground around him to assure himself there would be nothing in his way as he pulled back.

The boot was still there. It wiggled a bit as if the man was seeking a better position. Before he had a chance to pull it away, Rory aimed and fired. The scream of agony, plus the writhing scramble in the brush, was evidence that the shot had gone true. Foolishly, the attacker rose and hopped on one foot as he tried to escape deeper into the forest. Rory hollered, "Stop and stand still. This is Sheriff Rory Jamison. You're under arrest. Now throw out your weapon and stand down. The other one with you too."

Instead of surrendering, the wounded man, in one hop, was turned to face the cabin. As he started to raise his rifle, Rory hollered, "Don't do it."

When the shooter's gun reached the aiming position, Rory shot him again. The man fell silently and lay there with his legs showing clearly.

An explosion of movement sounded from lower down on the slope. A running man emerged from the brush with his rifle held hip high. He levered off three shots in Rory's direction as he ran. A branch and some leaves floated to the ground behind Rory, but no other damage was done. As if seeking the protection of the heavy, trimmed logs of the cabin, the runner concentrated on nothing more than escape into that last redoubt of safety. He obviously didn't know that Julia was already there.

The runner was soon in front of the cabin and out of Rory's vision. Knowing Julia would be under the attacker's gun in a matter of moments, Rory broke cover and ran to the north side of the cabin, where the horses stood alert with their heads held high.

~

JULIA, still crunched behind the stove, had repositioned herself. She had laid the carbine on top of the wood box and gotten to her knees. From that position, she could look through the openings in the nickel trim that rose from the cooking surface of the stove in a series of fancy scrolls, eventually to support the warming oven at the top. From her position on her knees, she was able to rest her wrist in the spread-out fingers of her other hand and aim the .32 through one of the openings in the scroll-work. Her eye and the .32 were held unerringly at the door.

As she listened to the shots outside and the progression of the sounds, she knew someone was running toward the cabin. Was it her husband? She would hold her fire until she was sure. Rory had promised to call out if he was coming in. The heavy footfall on the door stoop brought no warning call with it. She tightened her trigger grip just a bit. When the door burst open, the sunlight was suddenly blocked by a man. A man holding a rifle at hip height. A man who was not her husband. She squeezed the trigger.

With her unexpected shot, the man tried to stop. But he was moving too fast. He fell to the floor face down. Immediately, blood was forming a pool beneath him, accompanying his groan of agony, almost like a serenade of pain. When he attempted to rise to his knees as if to get back up, Julia shouted, "You move, you die."

She could have never imagined using such words before the raid on the family's ranch. But desperation can cause a man, or a woman, to set aside all pretense of civility.

Julia held her shot as the heavily bleeding man suddenly rolled onto his back and, with a lunge, was trying for the door. He got halfway out when his forehead ran into the wooden stock of Rory's carbine. This time the fellow fell onto the steps and didn't move.

"Are you alright, Julia?"

"I am, but I'm not sure I want this as a way of life. I can't believe what all this crawling around has done to my dress. And it was my favorite too. I bought it special to come to town in. Now, look at it. I love these new style split skirts, but they cost a lot of money. This is ridiculous. It's never going to come clean."

She was talking, not even totally sure what she had said, as if the talk was expelling her pent-up emotions.

12

THE SHERIFF AND HIS NEWLY MARRIED SPOUSE STOOD IN front of the stove, wrapped in each other's arms. Rory had helped her rise from her hiding place and pulled her gently toward himself. She was more than ready for his comforting embrace. Rory held his eye on the wounded man the entire time.

After a couple of silent minutes, Rory dropped his hands to her wrists and eased her to arm's length. Grinning, he said, "You're going to keep us broke and hungry if you keep destroying your dresses this way."

She folded back into his embrace and said, "Oh, I was so frightened. And excited. And worried. And I'm so happy you're alright. But I've gone and shot another man. This can't go on. It won't be good for my reputation. And it's going to cost me sleep.

He grinned at her and said, "Well, this time, you only wounded the fellow. It's probably just as well. I need to talk to him. Find out who he is and what this is all about.

Julia didn't mention the other man, assuming correctly that he was beyond talking.

Rory took a bucket to the creek. Julia was determined to try to at least get the soot off her hands and face. Once outside, in the bright sunlight, she confirmed her original judgment, the dress was beyond repair.

Ivan had long ago determined that he, as Kiril's only friend, had a right to the cabin. To claim it as his own. He had left some bedding, a few dishes, and the box of cut and split firewood in place. And a wash pan with a bar of soap. There was a towel hanging from a peg on the outside wall, but it had seen much use. Julia would most likely choose instead to dry in the sun.

While she was attending to herself, Rory was hoping the injured man would wake before he died. He was losing a steady trickle of blood. There was little chance of his survival. Finally, the eyes flickered, and there was a twitch in the man's hands as he moved them toward what must have been a very painful wound. Consciousness brought pain. And fear. And awareness of the man studying his every move.

It isn't necessarily true that the brave face dying without fear. He may face the enemy. Face deadly fire. And do it with bravery and honor. But by Rory's judgment, a wise man or woman must fear death...and the afterlife. A man of doubtful judgment and purpose, a man of criminal character, especially, would be a fool not to consider his Maker at the time of his passing. The evidence for a Creator God is overwhelming. To live without considering that evidence is foolishness. To face eternity without considering it is beyond understanding.

The bleeding man lying awkwardly on the steps was surely feeling fear and pain. Or perhaps it was pain at first, but, more profoundly, fear. His eyes were crying for help. Help and mercy. But both Rory and the man himself knew that there would be no help. A .32 bullet is not large, but in hitting a vulnerable spot in a body, it can do enormous damage. Rory had no idea what might help or even ease the pain, and being miles from town, there was no use even thinking of riding for a doctor.

After giving the shooter a half-minute to regain whatever of his thoughts could be regained, Rory said, "I need to know who you are and why you were shooting at us."

The returned words were stubbornly pushed out between gasps of pain.

"You shot and killed our brother."

"I'm the county sheriff, and I've faced a few men intent on evil. Who was your brother?"

"Arch. Arch Majeska."

"You two are brothers to Arch Majeska? He lit half the town on fire and murdered the banker. What did you think we would do?"

"Don't matter what he has done. Brothers are brothers. We stick together. Deke and me, we had it to do."

"That's your brother's name, Deke? And what's your name?"

"Deke. I'm guessing he's dead. Shot. Too bad. Young. He was too young to know how life is. Addison. That's me. Should have taken better care of my two brothers. Pa made me promise. Couldn't do it. Wouldn't listen. Neither of them."

"So now you're all dead. Or dying. Doesn't seem to make much sense to me. Anyway, you couldn't have known we would be riding up here today, and yet here you were, hiding in wait. How did that happen to be?"

Addison was clearly dying. His voice was becoming weaker by the second.

"Weren't waiting. Heading to town. Surprised to see you. Trail down the hill. Behind the barn. No one knows about it. Going to get you in town. That deputy and you both. Clean getaway up the trail."

"I hate to disappoint you again, Addison, but we've known about that trail for a year or more. Walked it up and down myself. Arch had no chance, and neither did you. Now tell me where you live and where you left your horses."

"No horses. Better on foot in the brush. Arch, he should never have taken his horse. Him and those others. Ties them down. Better in the bush on foot.

"Cabin. Cabin up the hill some. No one ever knew we were there. Woman at the cabin."

Rory looked up at Julia, who had listened and taken it all in. Her face showed mixed remorse and relief. She wasn't happy that she had shot him, but she was happy it hadn't been the other way around.

Rory stood to his feet before speaking again.

"Addison. I'm going to leave you for a bit. You might want to take the time to consider what comes after death. You'll never get another chance."

Rory walked very carefully, with his carbine at the ready, as he approached the fallen brother in the bush. Even a seriously wounded man can still squeeze a trigger. But there was clearly no need. The man was dead. Rory stripped his Colt and holster belt, picked up the carbine, and left him there.

When he arrived back at the cabin, the third brother was dead, and Julia was weeping.

With his arm around Julia, Rory walked toward the brush behind the cabin. He found a grassed spot where they could sit and lean against a couple of aspens. They sat in near silence for several minutes, listening to the creek tumble past. Finally, Rory said, "You sit. I've got a couple of things to do."

As he walked away, he took the reins of his big red gelding. The stronger of the two animals. Julia knew what he was doing, but she wanted no part of it. She leaned back and wondered about some things.

When Rory returned, he loosened Julia's horse from the tie rail and said, "Time to go."

She rose and followed her husband to the front of the cabin. He had closed the little house and washed most of the blood off the wooden stairs and the floor inside with a rag and a bucket of water from the creek. And he had somehow lifted the two brothers and laid them on the gelding, one across the saddle and the other behind. They were firmly tied down. It was an ugly sight. One that Julia turned her eyes from.

Rory stepped into the saddle of Julia's horse, pulled his foot from the stirrup, and held out his hand to help her mount behind him. There were no words that would ease the situation. It was all done in silence.

When he nudged the animals into motion, he was driving his own mount ahead of him with its grisly burden. They arrived at the I-5 ranch late in the afternoon. A quick explanation brought the offer of the loan of a horse. Neither had dismounted. With her arms tightly wrapped around her husband's waist and her head resting on his shoulder, Julia said, "I'd rather stay right here if you think the animal can carry us that far."

There was no more talk. Just a brief nod of thanks from Rory, and they moved out toward the hill trail and town.

13

WHEN IVAN HEARD THE STORY OF KIRIL'S CABIN FROM THE sheriff, he was intrigued. He had been raised on the I-5 Ranch, which extended into that same area. He had felt no real desire to ranch himself. There was a decent living to be made with cattle and a fair to middl'n lifestyle to enjoy, but still, to tend the brutes in good weather and bad, with never a day off, held no attraction for him. With his father and older brother more than able to handle the work of the I-5, he had been free to wander. And wander he did. He thought he had sought out almost every nook and cranny of the forested hillsides for miles around. He knew there were too many folds and twists in the mountains for any one person to know them all, but he had examined every area where there was any sign of human activity. Never had he seen a cabin such as Addison Majeska had mentioned.

With no other emergencies demanding his time, he had ridden to Kiril's cabin and left his horse in the corral, which was heavy with newly grown grass. He half-filled the wooden trough, carrying buckets of water from the creek. With that few gallons of water, the animal would be good for a couple of days. Then he set out on foot. He had been a pretty good tracker before, but after spending a couple of months with My Way, the Blackfoot warrior who had attached himself to the Wardle family and followed them south to Stevensville, he felt he could find the mysterious cabin. Immediately after thinking that, he grinned to himself, remembering that neither My Way nor he himself had been able to sort out the trail of the gold thieves. That thought was not enough to discourage him from continuing, but it embarrassed him a bit. He had built up an urge to locate the cabin, shack, or whatever it was. He also felt that if there really was a woman there waiting for the brothers to return, someone needed to inform her of the deaths of the last Majeska brother. And perhaps escort her out of the country and to a better life.

The trail through the woods was easy enough to find, beginning at the spot where the shooting had taken place. But from there, most of the grass had returned to its upright position after being trodden on, and few of the shrubs or brush showed any signs of disturbance. The men had been on foot. If there had been horse hooves stamping the grass down, the trail would be much easier to follow. But here and there, after turning back and starting again a frustrating number of times, he would find a broken branch. A turned-over rock. A footprint in a soft area. When he found recent footprints of two men following along the bank of a small trickle of water, he was able to hurry along. The stream led him behind a large growth of aspens, around a small moraine made of broken boulders that had slid from the overhang above, and into a small valley he had never seen before. The closer he got to the fallen rock, the more trampled the grass was. This had to be the place.

In his caution, feeling that this surely was the enclosure Addison Majeska had spoken of, he stopped and slid behind a larger pine that seemed to grow right out of the center of the aspens. It was more likely that the aspens had grown up around the pine, given the comparative life cycles of the two trees. He wasn't even sure why his mind went to the question, but he was brought back to the hunt when he heard the 'thunk' of an axe striking wood. He had still seen no sign of a cabin or shack, but the builder, whoever he was, might have tucked it into the forest to hide it from a casual hiker.

Using all the caution he could muster, Ivan worked his way toward where the sound had come from. He thought he was doing it in total silence until a woman's voice said, "Addison, don't you be trying to sneak up and give me a fright. I'm just liable to put a load of pellets into your worthless hide. Don't rightly know why I haven't done it before this time. You, and your even more useless brothers, too. Anyway, you've forgot everything you ever knew about keeping silent, if you ever did know anything. A rutting moose would make less noise."

"Now, you're just plain exaggerating, woman, but I must say, you've got ears."

"Yes. And I've got my shotgun too. And you're not Addison, nor Deke either. With Arch being dead, that makes me wonder who you are and what you're doing here. You might just as well come out and show yourself. You ain't going to come to no good hunkering down behind that pine. Probably call yourself a woodsman, but you ain't no such a thing. My old pappy would have caught you and skinned you out a half mile back, all the noise you're making."

"All right, I'm coming in. I mean you no harm, so you just keep that shotgun aimed at the ground. Or the clouds. Anywhere but at me, lest there be a misunderstanding."

"My shotgun will be where I want it to be. Take your choice. Come in or turn around and get gone. It matters no which way to me."

Ivan said, "This is Deputy Sheriff Ivan Ivanov. I'm coming in. I've got news."

Emerging from the bush and walking to within easy talking distance, the two came into sight of each other for the first time. The woman said, "You're that youngest son from the ranch down below. The one that was too lazy to work the ranch. Never seen you up here before, heard about you, though. Spend your time now a-sett'n on yer butt on a half-barrel chair down to the town. I seen you there the one time I was down that way. You said you have news. Spit it out, and then you can get gone."

"Woman. I've never triggered a gun on a woman but don't think I won't. I've told you already not to point that thunder-stick in my direction. Now put it down."

The practiced voice of authority may have caught the woman's attention, but whatever it was, the muzzle of the weapon slowly dropped.

"Good. Now let's try again. From what you said earlier, I'm assuming this is the Majeska brothers' cabin."

"It is. Or was. Until Arch went to meet his maker. Now there's just the two of them. And me. Are you going to tell me what happened to Deke and Addison?"

"I am. And it's not good news for you."

"I'm guessing they're dead. Elsewise they'd be home, and you'd be sett'n on that chair I mentioned."

Ivan could find nothing to say. The message was so

simple there were no further words needed. The woman hadn't shown any emotion at the news. She appeared to be in no need of comfort.

Knowing the question would have to be asked sooner or later if his hike up the hill was to have any meaning at all, he asked, "What about you? Will you be staying on here? Is there anything I can do to help you? Right now, I mean. I'll be heading back down directly."

"No. I don't know why I stayed this long. The boys needed a cook. I was down to my last dime, and I needed shelter and food to survive the winter. I wasn't drawn to the choices offered to a woman up at the gold camps, so the offer to come as a cook held some attraction, even as sparse and crude as this setup is. And it was nothing more than that, so don't you be letting your mind wander into deep water."

"None of my business. And I have no intention of making it my business. Do you want to know how the boys died?"

"I'm sure it was by the gun. Shoot-crazy. All three of them, although the two youngest were the worst. It was bound to happen. Heard no shooting after they walked out. Sounds don't somehow make it through all these hills and corners of rock. Near silent up here all the time. They went hunting the sheriff. I'm assuming they found him."

"Correct. They died down at Kiril's cabin, if you know where that is. Buried in town, down below. The little bit that was in their pockets I have here with me. One of them mentioned a woman and a cabin. I've been the whole of the day searching these hills for you and the cabin. I don't know who you are, but I thought you might have use a bit of traveling money or food money. Whatever. I'll leave the sack right here on this stump and be gone. I wish you well. And I suggest you'd be better off where there's people around. Good people. No telling who might wander down this way, catching you unprepared."

As Ivan started to back away, the woman said, "Might just as well come in for a feeding. The one thing I'm good at is cooking."

"Alright. No tricks with that shotgun. You've been warned. Once should be enough."

"No tricks. My name's Harriet, if you were wondering. Just Harriet. No need for more."

Ivan followed Harriet across the small yard, around an overhanging rock slab that was bound to fall to the earth someday, and into the cabin. It was surprisingly clean and neat, considering it had been housing three bachelors. Assuming she was the cook and cleaner, clearly the woman had earned the food she consumed.

There was little in the way of furnishings, and most of those were handmade and crude. But someone had hauled a small sheet metal stove through the woods and set it up in the shack. It would keep the place reasonably warm in the winter while providing a fair to middl'n cooking surface.

The woman went right to work after washing her hands, an embellishment on much of hill cabin, rough and ready, take it as it comes life—that pleased Ivan. Taking a more detailed look, Ivan decided she was a pleasant looking, but not beautiful, young woman. She couldn't be any older than her early twenties, perhaps even less. The food she prepared must have been adequate over the winter. She was carrying enough flesh to provide a show of strength while keeping a distinctly girlish figure. He could see why Addison would have to keep a close eye on his brothers if he was to fulfill his promise of safety in exchange for cooking.

Soon the pleasant odor of frying beef steak and onions filled the room. Speaking over her shoulder, Harriet said, "Don't drink coffee. Boys made their own. Tea. I have tea enough to share. That do it for you?"

"Tea might make me appreciate my coffee more next time it's available. Sure, I'll have a cup."

Ivan couldn't find one simple thing to talk to Harriet about, but he found himself wondering about that beef. He had seen no hide, showing a brand, lying over the corral rails, nor tacked to any wall, but he couldn't help but wonder. Before he had even thought it all through, he heard himself asking, "Is that I-5 beef?"

"I never knew, and I never asked. Best you don't think of it. Lots of things in life are best if they're let be."

"What were the brothers doing up here? There doesn't seem to be much point in it all unless they were hiding from the law. And how did Arch get tangled up with the others? Crain, Stanley, and Adams?"

"I never knew the other's names. I made a point of it. Fact is, I stayed out of their way, especially when Addison wasn't here. There weren't none of them much good, but Addison, he was the best of the bunch. Made me a promise that I'd be safe here, and he kept that promise, no matter what else he done.

"As to why they were here in this shack, I'm sure they were hiding alright. But mostly, they were lazy. Just bone lazy. My old Pa would have shot them just to improve the countryside. He was strong on his opinions of folks; my old man was. Course, Pa, he ended up being shot himself. He was some surprised, judging from the look on his face when I found him dead down by the creek. He seemed to never think that a gun can shoot in any direction it's pointed at. Left me alone, anyway. Must have been some neighbor, or perhaps even the law, that took exception to one of Pa's actions. There was nothing to save on our place, nor much to sell. I wandered off with the few dollars Pa had in a sugar bowl in the closet, and here I am."

Harriet seemed to feel the need to talk, so Ivan remained quiet and listened. Perhaps she could never talk or exchange stories with the three brothers. She continued on with her life story as if there had been no pause.

"Left me alone with my own brothers off and wandering. No way of knowing where they managed to get themselves off to. Good boys. Workers. And honest. They'll be doing alright wherever they are.

"Course, Ma, before she died, she was a good woman. And a teacher. I don't mean no schoolmarm. No, she taught her boys, and then, later, me, at home. Taught us right from wrong. Taught us from the Bible and from what her own Ma had taught her. Taught us to be good folk. Pa, he was good folk too. All except he believed he knew who was improving the world and who were otherwise. Took it upon himself to sort of balance the scales, you might say. Ma, she worried every time he left the cabin tot'n his rifle. Worried that she'd never see him again except in his bury'n clothes. But by the time those clothes were needed, she was gone. It was me that had to work his dead arms and legs into the heavy wool suit. Dug the grave too. Then toted his body over and rolled it onto the blanket I'd laid on the bottom of the hole. Wasn't no way strong enough to lift or carry him. Anyway, that was two years ago.

"Spent a whole year look'n for one brother or another. Then, when I was down to my last thin dime with winter com'n on, Addison, he saw me in need and bought me a meal. Made the offer to come cook for the brothers with the promise to leave me alone, like I already said. That sounded better than asking for a job in the saloon up to Idaho Falls, so here I am."

She turned to the silent Ivan with pleading in her eyes. Pleading for understanding, it seemed. And belief. Finally, she blurted out, "I'm a good girl, Sheriff."

"Alright. I believe you. And, judging by smell alone, I believe those steaks must be about ready. Whether it's I-5 beef or not, I'm hungry."

The two strangers ate in silence except for the sound of the knives and forks working on the metal plates.

When Ivan finally pushed his plate away and allowed Harriet to refill his tea mug, he said, "I've been thinking. You say you're a cook. Clearly, you can't stay here. Or at least it would make no sense. How about you come with me? I'm going to ride up to see the deputy working MacNair's Hill. Good fella. More or less under my oversight. Went and married up with the cook and server at the dining room. MacNair's is an up-and-coming town. There's a pretty good chance you'll find a cooking opportunity there."

Harriet looked around the little shack, unconsciously moving her arm as if assessing the surroundings and wondering how she had ever fallen to that point.

"I ain't got much. But I'll put my few things together in a tow sack and leave all the rest of this junk for whoever comes along."

"Did the boys have horses? I haven't seen any."

"You walk up the trail alongside the corral. Just a short distance. Small circle of rocks up there, holding plenty of grass. Boys strung a rope corral, and moved it from time to time."

~

WITH NO COMMENT on what Harriet had stuffed into her tow sack and with four horses saddled and ready, Ivan followed Harriet's lead out of the forest. Ivan, when he first looked at the gathering of horses in the rope corral, figured the Majeska brothers had one horse each, and the other three bank robbers had one each. Ivan and Rory had gathered up four animals after the robbery. The four in the rope corral would be what the other two brothers rode, plus one for Harriet and an extra. Not that it really mattered. It was simply Ivan's habit to try to sort things out. Curious about the deputy's actions, Harriet asked, "Why did you saddle all those animals?"

"One for me. One for you. The others because I suspect they're stolen. I might be able to find the owners. And I can't just turn them loose in the hills. Anyway, saddles cost money. Couldn't see leaving them behind."

After a short ride, they came to the well-marked uphill trail. Rory had mentioned having never seen a worn track leading off the uphill trail, making the location of the cabin an ever-bigger mystery. Ivan had been wondering about that too, until he saw that the two trails joined over a large, more or less flat, rocky surface. A surface that wouldn't show hoof marks unless an iron shoe slipped, leaving a slight gouge. Even then, the mark would weather out in a matter of days.

Ivan moved ahead of Harriet and turned down the trail, pushing the loose horses ahead of him. Harriet aimed a curious look at him. He had talked about riding uphill, but she said nothing. The ride down to Kiril's cabin was short. As Ivan was opening the corral gate, Harriet said, "I was down here one time. The old man gave the boys eggs until he died. Shared a haunch of beef or two with him."

Ivan mulled on all of that while he saddled his own horse and unsaddled the bunch he would be leaving there. Clearly, there was more to Kiril than anyone had ever suspected.

On the slow ride to MacNair's Hill, Ivan asked, "The boys ever say where they wintered their horses? That patch they were on wouldn't hold them."

"You ain't going to like me saying it, Sheriff, but they pushed them down to the I-5 upper pasture after your cattle were moved down below. Horses, they can scratch for their feed. Snow ain't a big problem to them. Get their moisture from snow too. I expect it didn't hurt the I-5 none too much."

Ivan took all that in with a silent shake of his head.

AFTER A COUPLE of hours of sometimes difficult uphill riding, Ivan led Harriet to the dining room in MacNair's Hill and introduced her to Mila, the owner and cook. Mila had looked her over and asked, "You telling the truth? Are you a cook?"

"I can cook anything you can catch or kill. And make folks come back for more."

"Alright, git yourself down to the tent hotel and have yourself a good cleaning up. If you don't have any new clothes, you'll find some at a fair price at the general store. You be here at six tomorrow morning. Clean, neat, and ready for work."

Knowing Harriet had enough money to care for herself until she earned her way, Ivan left her like that and went in search of Deputy Buck. He stayed one night and rode down the hill the next morning, turning in at the trail to the Majeska cabin.

Harriet would have no use for a horse, so he drove the one she had been riding back down to join the others left at Kiril's cabin. In any case, it would go hard on the woman to be caught riding a stolen animal, which the horses he had impounded almost surely were.

He hadn't wanted to do it with the woman present, but now he literally tore the place apart, looking for whatever it was that had kept the three brothers there. Or perhaps it was something they were hiding.

14

JULIA HAD RECOVERED ENOUGH FROM HER RIDE TO KIRIL'S cabin to enjoy life again and to return to the saddle shop to work. Mr. Sales had asked her about her time away. When Julia expanded her answer to include the happenings at Kiril's cabin, leaving out the part about her having shot one of the men, the old man laid down his tools and gave her a questioning look.

"Are you alright after that?"

"Yes. I am now. Took a day or two, though."

To try to lighten the moment, she said, with a grin, "Bought me a brand-new dress to replace the one I ruined, hiding behind that stove. Bought it with my very own money that you paid me. Do you have any idea how expensive dresses have become? You really should give me a raise in pay to cover it all."

"You didn't ruin your dress working here. If that ever happens, I'll reconsider your wages."

Julia was contentedly familiar with his gruff exterior, so she only grinned at him and got back to her work.

~

RORY AND CAP watched Ivan slowly ride along the main street at the Fort, wondering why the deputy was making one of his rare trips north. They wondered further at the five horses he was driving ahead of him. When he got close enough, Rory stood, walked toward the livery, and then to the center of the street. He would turn the horses toward the livery before the animals took it in mind to go somewhere else.

A minute later, he was closing the gate to the corral, and Ivan was unsaddling, with his gelding tied to an outside rail.

"What brings you way up here, Ivan?"

"Brought you some horses and some news."

"Tell me first about the horses."

"You look at those brands. They're all different and all strange to me. These are the animals the Stevensville bank robbers were riding. Them and the other Majeska brothers. Tippet is coming along with his new barn, but it'll be a while yet before he can stall anything. Thought to bring them here. You can list the brands in the paper from here. Might find the owners. Could even learn something about those boys if any owner does show up. It would be good, maybe, to follow their movements based on where these horses came from. Anyway, I needed to talk to you."

The three county lawmen, Rory, Ivan, and Cap, moved into the office where they would be out of the sun and away from listening ears. They took seats, pushing their chairs into a semi-circle. Rory didn't bother asking any questions. Ivan would speak when he was ready.

"Curious about some things, I rode up the hill. Left

my horse at Kiril's corral. Searched out the walking trail those brothers left the other day. Found it and followed. Went maybe about one mile. Not far from the I-5 upper pasture. I've been all over those hills. More than once. No idea how I've missed it before. Small shack hidden in some slid-down rock slabs where the forest thins out before a bit of a clearing gives way to the aspens. Almost missed it. There was a woman. Young woman. Perhaps twenty or so. Named herself Harriet. It was the sound of her chopping wood that led me to the shack. After we sorted out who was boss and where our guns should be pointed, we got along alright. I gave her the news about the brothers. She wasn't too surprised.

"She couldn't stay there by herself, so I took her up to MacNair's. She's a cook, she says. Anyway, Mila gave her a job in her eating place. I expect she'll make do. She rode out on one of the horses. I brought it back down to gather with the others. Wouldn't do for her to be found riding a stolen horse."

Rory, knowing there was a lot left out of Ivan's telling, let it go. If it was important, Ivan would eventually add it in. Instead, he asked about Deputy Buck and the general situation in the gold country.

Ivan answered his questions before saying, "There's more. More about the Majeska cabin."

With that bit of information, he reached into his jacket pocket and lifted out a small canvas sack with tie strings pulled tight at the top. Sliding his chair closer to the desk, he poured the contents of the sack onto the cleared space between two stacks of paper. Rory and Cap stared in disbelief.

Cap, who spoke little and seldom, said, "You might want to correct me, but I'm going to guess that's gold."

"And you'd be absolutely correct to guess that Cap.

Mostly small sharp-edged chunks, probably broken out of quartz. Plus a few nuggets and flakes, as if someone was panning somewhere."

Waiting for more that was slow in coming, Rory finally said, "Might be helpful if you were to expand on that information just a bit."

"I thought you needed a moment to kind of stare on that bit of loot before we carried on to the question I'm working toward."

"That gold does carry some mystery with it, but I think I can handle a bit more information now if you roll it out slowly."

Ivan grinned at the sarcasm. But he soon made his proposal.

"I'm thinking two things. One is that there is a need for a thorough search of that shack and the area around it. I went through it pretty well, but I'm not satisfied. That sack of gold I found behind some dishes on a shelf in the cabin was for sure stolen. So were the horses. I'm guessing those boys weren't there for the view or the sunsets, which would take place on the other side of the mountain anyway. I'd like to spend some time up there. See what I can find.

"The other thing I was thinking is that Cap is wasting away up here, with nothing at all to keep his mind active. Next thing we know, he'll be taking a siesta like our Mexican friends love to do. How about you release him for a few days to ride along with me?"

Rory looked over at Cap and waited for the deputy to speak. Cap was looking from Ivan to the little gold stash and back again. Rory could see the thoughts written in his eyes but couldn't interpret them. Finally, Cap turned his eyes to Rory.

"What do you say, boss?"

"I say if you two can't find whatever the Majeska boys stashed away, no one can. You might want to take a pannier or two in case you need to haul something down. I suppose you could take a packhorse, but then, it's not that far to the I-5 if you need an extra animal.

"Ivan can share the house with you for one night, Cap, and you can get an early start in the morning. You'll want to keep your eyes open. We've been assuming the Majeskas didn't have other partners, but that might not be true. If someone should come along, you don't want to be surprised."

15

Marshal Wiley had been away for nearly one week. His leaving had been sudden and secretive. He had simply left a note on the office desk, weighted down with an old, rusted-out Colt Rory had picked up along the trail and kept for some reason he couldn't rightly sort out.

He had become a collector of handguns and their accompanying belts and holsters. For the past year or more, he had kept the weapons of every fugitive he had brought to trial. Or death. He had the names of the previous owners written in ink on the insides of the belts. They were unloaded, hanging from wooden pegs on every wall of the small office. He had sold the long guns, rifles, shotguns, and carbines for the benefit of the county bank account.

Since the beginning, it had bothered Rory that there were no rules or guidelines for either the marshal's or sheriff's positions. The towns and county were, he assumed, satisfied that they had a fair return on the wages they paid out. Still, Rory fussed that he might be overlooking something. He had been elected to a huge county, split between flat grasslands lying at about the six-thousand-foot level and tiered mountains, rising to the glory of the Rockies, and named locally as the Front Range. Travel was slow, and communications even slower. The closest railway was at Cheyenne, offering no service at all to Rory's areas, except a through train to Denver that bypassed the towns. There was continuous talk of the telegraph, but so far, there were no poles rising nor any wire being strung. Unless he intentionally planned a circuit, it could be years between visits to outlying areas. Should he be concerned about that?

Adding to his concerns was the fact that the county to the east was uninhabited except for the occasional rancher. By agreement with the state people in Denver, he agreed to extend his peacekeeping efforts into that vast area as well. He had much to think about. Thankfully, there had been no call for his services that would drag him away from town again so soon after his marriage...and after the last call to Stevensville that had led to Julia joining him for the ride. He and his bride both needed some time to settle themselves after that excitement.

STICKS WILLOUGHBY WAS PUTTING the roof on the new brick building that would house both the sheriff and the marshal. In the lawmen's eyes, the builder had earned their respect by building a new home for Rory and Julia.

In the design of this building and the new bank building that Sticks was also constructing so soon after the big fire, prevention of another disaster was uppermost in everyone's minds. Brick walls, both inside and out, would prove adequate for the job. But what of the roof? Shingles, the normal rain shield used in the area, would burn as easily as they had before. It wasn't until Ivan, Cap, and Key rode with Sticks to the cantina at the south end of town, seeking lunch, that they all had an epiphany of sorts. There, lying close to the earth it was built from, rose the adobe structure. And hanging over it, like a low-sloping canopy, was a roof of dull red clay tiles. Sticks pulled his horse to a halt, staring hard at the structure. The other three pulled up beside him. He pointed with his chin. Grinning, he said, "Have a hard time burning that down."

The three men sat their mounts, chuckling at how long it had taken to figure out the obvious answer. But, as northerners, they had seen little of clay tiles. It would take a while to have tiles wagoned in, but it was worth the wait.

～

IT WAS midafternoon before Ivan and Cap pulled into the yard of the I-5. Ivan's brother greeted him with, "As often as you turn up here, a fella could start to think you miss the old stand."

"Not so much that I want to come back permanently."

Ivan said, "Pavel, I wish you'd say hello to Deputy Cap Graham. Cap, this is my father, Grigor Ivanov, and my brother Pavel. Ma's most likely at the house. With any luck at all, she's putting together enough food so that we don't have to wrestle Pavel to the ground in order to get ahead of him at the feed trough."

"We'll put in the night here if that's alright, Pa. We're riding uphill in the morning."

Knowing the request to spend the night needed no response, Ivan expected none.

~

AFTER A BREAKFAST that would hold them over the day and into the next morning, the two lawmen rode to Kiril's holdings. Ivan told Cap as much as he felt would be helpful as they rode along. Feeling Cap should know about the downhill trail that arrived on the level behind Tippet's barn, the two men walked to the barn, where Ivan explained about the wall that moved and the bushed-over walking path.

By noon, they were dismounting at the crude cabin Ivan had led Harriet away from. As he stood at the entrance, with the canvas door hanging loose, the tawdry excuse for living quarters looked more forlorn and desperate than it had when he had first seen it. The absence of human habitation removed any leaning toward decency or even a semblance of welcome from the shack.

Cap said it all when he had looked around and, without turning to Ivan, said, "It's a wonder how low some folks will fall through laziness or desperation."

There was no need for a comment.

Ivan, who had never smoked a cigarette or a pipe, or chewed the plug, leaned against the doorpost. His eyes seemed to take in every square inch, although he had rummaged through it all before.

"I don't know for sure, Cap, but I suspect this is the time a smoker would lean against this here doorpost, pull out the makings, and slowly contemplate his next move."

Cap leaned against the opposite side of the door.

"I've enjoyed a cigar or two and could roll a paper about as round and firm as those rolling machines folks are raving about—and do it while riding a horse—but I doubt as how it would lend any wisdom to what you have planned here."

"What I have planned, my smoking friend, is to pull everything out of this place and stack it in a pile where it can be burned when we're finished. We'll pull it apart piece by piece, checking everything as we go. There could be nothing, and there could be almost anything. We'll examine every piece of paper for writing that might guide us. We'll feel every seam of every piece of clothing and turn out every pocket. Anywhere and anything that might be hiding something, we'll tear apart and study.

"When we get the shack emptied out, we'll examine every inch of the floor and every crack and crevice in the rock walls. Then we'll pull down the roof and dump it on the pile for burning. That will leave us the corral and the lean-to shelter to investigate."

Cap was looking at his partner as if the man had taken on a fever. He was just sorting out his words to make a response when Ivan added, "That will leave us the rocks and any holes in the trees to study."

Cap wisely kept his thoughts to himself, seeing Ivan's determination.

But after a half hour of toting and tossing, Cap asked, "Is your determination partly because this all took place so close to your family's ranch?"

"Some. Other than beefing an I-5 steer, which I guess the ranch won't miss too much, so far as I can tell, they did no real harm to our land claim. But I'd still like to know what kept them here. I feel clear down inside that they were hiding something."

What about your friend Kiril? Did he have truck or trade with this bunch?"

"Harriet said they got some eggs from Kiril, but she mentioned nothing else. Mind, she wasn't here all that long. There's no telling what went on before she arrived. She did say that no one left this place all winter. That could mean they were lazy to the bone. Or it could mean they had what they wanted and planned to pull out for faraway places when spring came."

"That doesn't somehow fit with the raid on the Stevensville Bank."

"So many questions, Cap, and so few answers."

16

ALL THE SMALL MOVABLES WERE DRAGGED OUT, EXAMINED thoroughly, and added to the pile. The furniture came next. The bench, the table, the four chairs, and the cots. Even though it was all made from solid wood, crudely hand-hacked out of the surrounding forest, leaving no possibility of well-disguised openings, every piece was broken apart, the joints carefully studied.

The sheet iron stove was pulled from under the metal pipe that fed smoke to the outside world and set aside. There was value in the thing. They would leave it under the rock shelter when they were done. It would still rust, but slowly, away from direct rain and snow. Someone may find it and put it to use.

The shack was essentially gone. Everything that could burn was piled in a heap. Looking into the sloping rock walls of the hillside, two almost shear rocks facing each other at something less than parallel, Cap said, "I hold no truck with folks such as y'all ran into up here, but you'd have to admit what they did with this shack was pretty creative. I'm not at all sure I would have seen these rocks the same way."

Ivan agreed but had nothing to add. Stretching to straighten the kinks out of his back, he said, "We've got three choices. We can ride back down to the I-5 for the night. We can ride down to Kiril's cabin and at least sleep inside. We'd only have what grub we have in our saddle-bags. Or we can roll our beds out right here and finish this up in the morning."

Cap looked at Ivan, back at the pile of junk, and again at the bare rock walls.

"It would appear that we've about done it. But if you're determined to keep at 'er, I'd vote for staying right here."

"I was hoping you'd say that. We can fire up that sheet iron stove. It needs no chimney out here in the open air. We can at least have coffee."

THEY MADE their pot of coffee, dug around in their saddlebags for whatever they could find to eat, and rolled their beds out deep into the aspen grove. It was not impossible that some friend of the Majeska's would arrive on the scene and find them sleeping. The closeness of the aspens, combined with the bed of dried leaves, would give ample warning of a visitor, even if the horses did not.

With their last cups of coffee, they leaned against a couple of trees and visited the light away. With darkness, they rolled into their blankets and thought their own thoughts. Ivan's last thoughts, when he could pull them away from Tempest Wardle, anyway, were of finding the prize. Anything that would prove their work to be something other than a waste of time. If it was as he had thought all along, that the Majeska brothers were first-class crooks and thieves, there was still the possibility of finding a stolen and well-hidden treasure.

～

IVAN WOKE EARLY, aroused, as much by excitement as the early dawn light. He had a fire in the stove and coffee water in the pot by the time Cap struggled his way through the close-growing aspens. They had not been disturbed during the night.

As they had done with the last of their coffee the night before, they again took their cups and sat looking at the rubble pile and the little hollow in the rocks the thieves had transformed into a hideaway. Cap had commented on the bareness of the rocks the night before. Now, Ivan watched as he studied them anew.

"So how do you see them now that they're bare, Cap? If you were hiding something, something that wouldn't melt or break down in the cold or wet of winter, where would you dig, burrow, or climb."

As if his own question to Cap had opened a whole new world of ideas, a thought broke through to Ivan. Ignoring his own question to Cap, he said, with considerable expression, "Climb! Why didn't I think of that? I had my mind fixed on burying, looking for disturbed dirt and all that. But these folded rocks hold endless possibilities for climbing and tucking things away."

Without waiting for Cap to respond, Ivan walked to the side, where he thought he saw an easy path to the shelf above, where the roof of the shack used to be. Cap didn't follow, but he watched every move his partner made. Ivan disappeared behind the uplifted rock that formed most of the roof of the shack. There was no sound until his voice shouted out, "Cap, you've got to see this."

"I've always been more of a flat-ground guy, but hold on, I'm coming."

Cap barked his shin when his slippery-soled riding boots slid on the smoothness of the rock. With a 'yelp,' he rolled over and sat for a moment. Ivan was so preoccupied with what he had found that he hadn't noticed his partner's shout of pain.

"Cap! We found it, Cap! You come here and pull some of this out. My, this slit in the rock is deep. You've got longer arms than me. I'll go down and get that pannier we brought with us."

He turned to climb back down and noticed, for the first time, that Cap had his pant leg pulled up and was mopping at the blood that was running down his leg. Ivan's normal compassion, which had never been a strong motive directing his actions, was overcome by his excitement. The best he could do was say, "You wait just a minute, partner. I've got a couple of folded cloths in my saddlebag. I'll grab one and the pannier and be right back."

In only a few minutes, Cap's shin had ceased bleeding, with a rag wrapped around his lower leg. "Appreciate the bandage. I was surely hating to run my still usable boot full of blood."

THE PANNIER WAS HALF full of unopened canvas sacks. The loot, which they had yet to see, amounted to considerable weight. A close examination of the close-by rocks led them to nothing but open cracks and niches.

Accepting that they had found it all, Ivan took up the pannier and, trusting his own grip and balance on the rocks, climbed back down.

After cleaning out the crevasse in the rocks, Ivan had insisted on examining the corral and the crude shelter built above it. He found nothing, even when he gingerly walked across the shaky roof to investigate the rocks above. He was finally satisfied that they had found all the loot. They left the shelter and the pole corral standing. It was doing no harm, and it could be handy even to the I-5 under certain circumstances.

When they were standing by the horses, looking at all they had done and thinking of all they had found, Ivan said, "Good work, partner".

Cap, a man of stoic countenance, merely nodded.

They turned to their saddles and were soon ready to mount and ride. Only the pannier had to be dealt with yet. Cap said, "I expect I'm carrying a little more weight than you, Ivan. That big black of yours could carry you and the pannier. We'll tie it on behind."

"Now, don't you be laughing at me, partner, but I'd as soon carry the thing right here on my lap, where I can get a firm grip on it."

After Cap worked the strange look off his face, he said, "Alright, climb aboard. I'll pass it up to you."

Mounted and ready to ride, Cap asked, with his thumb pointing over his shoulder, "What about that pile of scrap?"

"I'll come back up when it's raining or when the snow blankets the country again and light 'er up. We'd probably be safe enough even now. But why take a chance of fire getting away on us?"

With the pannier held in his firm grasp, Ivan led the way down the mountain. To hold the canvas sack containing all the small sacks was somehow a comforting thing to the young deputy. They rode along silently until they passed the deserted cabin and turned onto the trail to the I-5. Ivan commented, "We'll be at the house in no time at all. If we miss lunch, I'm betting Ma will fire up the stove again."

17

Two days later, after dealing with a couple of matters in Stevensville, they were hunched over the desk in the Fort Marshal's Office. The pannier lay on its side where Ivan had dropped it after lifting out the last small canvas sack.

"We didn't take time to open these sacks, Rory, but if they're all filled with gold, I'd judge, by weight, that there's a fortune here."

"Well, open one up, and let's take a look."

Ivan fumbled at the pull strings with nervous fingers until the knot finally unwound. He stretched out the top and poured the contents into the wash basin they had cleaned and dried for the purpose. As the shiny pieces caught the light from the window, they clunked down the sloping edge of the white, porcelain enamel-coated basin. The pieces were rough and of varying sizes, glittering as if they had just that morning, been released from the quartz that had captured them. The men gasped and leaned back in their chairs. No one spoke for a full half minute.

When the awe started to wear off, Rory said, "Don't move anything else. I'll be right back. Make some room on that desk."

He stood and left the little office. He walked directly across the street and then a few doors to the north, turning in where the sign on the door read 'Assayer.' Gill Trove found little assaying work. The Fort was a long distance from any established mines. He left his shingle hanging out though, in the belief that the mining would be moving north, and he would find his niche. In the meantime, he managed to hold body and soul together, writing and publishing a small local newspaper, funded mostly through advertisements from local retailers.

When the bell above the door tinkled, he looked up from his writing desk and said, "Morning, Sheriff. I'm hoping you have a story for me. I'm a bit saddle sore sitting at this desk, writing of the wonderful bargains to be had in the stores we all are so wearyingly familiar with."

"No story Gill. At least not yet. I want you to dig out your assay scale and come with me."

"That sounds delightfully intriguing. Did you strike gold building your new house?"

"Perhaps gold of another nature but no—no gold-colored gold. But come with me. You'll perhaps have your story yet today. Bring a chair with you. Ours are all in use."

～

IVAN HAD LAID a copy of one of Gill's advertising papers across the top of the wash basin. There was no particular reason for it, but he grinned at the possibilities when the assayer got his first glance.

Ivan and Cap moved to one side of the desk. Rory and the assayer set their chairs on the front side, where Gill could put his knees under the desk. He set up his scales and took a few moments to level them precisely. As he laid various weights of test slugs on the pans, he turned a little thumb screw at the top until the two pans leveled out, causing the pointer to center at exactly the mid-point. He then repeated the actions with a different set of weight test slugs. When he was finally satisfied, he rubbed his hands together and said, "Alright, what have you got?"

Ivan lifted the paper, exposing the pan's contents, to a satisfying gasp from the assayer. All was silent for a count of ten. Gill said, "Do I dare ask?"

Rory replied, "Gill, we're all lawmen, and we're in the marshal's office. And this stash of gold could not be expected to come into our hands out of the goodness of some miner's heart. Ivan and Cap found it a couple of days ago. Up in the hills, in a poorly built but well-hidden cabin. There can be no doubt that it was stolen. This is the only bag we've opened so far. We want an accurate record of each bag and its true value. We'll number the bags as we go along. And make a list.

Gill lifted the wash pan and carefully poured the contents into the wide-mouthed brass container he'd brought along. It was wide at the top so anyone pouring minerals into it would have a fair chance of not losing any. It was folded to a pouring spout at one end, much like a small coal scuttle, or a gravy boat, making it easier to dump the contents onto the weigh scale pan.

He very carefully moved through all the necessary motions and then passed the wash pan back to Ivan. It wouldn't be needed again.

When the first weight and value were called out and

written on the clean sheet of lined paper by Rory, everyone gasped. Ivan couldn't hold back his thoughts.

"If all these sacks are like that…"

~

THE WEIGHING and itemizing took up the full of two hours. But finally, it was done. The weights were totaled, as well as the values. Ivan, the most expressive of the group, whistled through his teeth and leaned back in his chair. "My friends, that's a big find. And a big loss for someone."

Rory said, "You're correct, except that my guess is that the loss is spread around several mine holdings. It's doubtful that any one person would have left this much lying around where it could be picked up. There're at least four different canvas sacks here too. Some of the canvases are a bit different, and you can see by the stitching that more care was taken on some."

Gill's work was done, but his questions were literally pressing against the back of his teeth, burning to be asked. He finally said, "I'm familiar with confidentiality. Most of my mineral work is done in secret. In my other life, of course, I am a writer and a reporter. How do we stand here? Can I report on this?

Rory spoke without consulting the others. "You can report that the sheriff employed you in the weighing of some impounded gold. Nothing more than that. We would be unwise, I think, to announce the quantity or value. We could start a stampede of claims."

Cap seldom asked a question. He asked one now. "Where are you going to hold this, and what's the next step in finding the owner or owners?"

"Good questions, Cap."

Knowing the lawmen no longer needed his advice or his presence, Gill was gathering his equipment under his arms, ready to return to his own office. Rory said, "One more thing to say in your article, Gill. Say that the gold is no longer at the Fort. It has been moved to safe storage in Denver."

18

AFTER THE GOLD-BEARING PANNIER WAS LOCKED IN THE cell at the marshal's office, Rory walked over to the saddle shop. He was greeted by his smiling wife, who asked if he had come to take her to lunch, an action that was not at all common between spouses but that the newlyweds had done several times.

"Not today, my love. I've come to tell you I'm riding for Cheyenne and then taking the train to Denver. I'll be gone for a few days. Also, I want to purchase the biggest set of saddle bags you've got."

Mr. Sales, the saddle maker, and Julia's employer, didn't usually welcome Rory's visits, feeling them to be an intrusion into Julia's work schedule. But at the mention of large saddle bags, he perked up and asked, "May I ask what you will be using them for?"

Rory answered without providing any details.

Mr. Sales said, "Julia, show him that set I made for old Wardle. It doesn't look like he's coming for them. Also, dig under that pile in the corner. You'll find an old Pony

Express bag that slips over the saddle horn to hold it with no fear of loss."

Rory gave the Pony Express bag a careful look over. Admiring the ingenuity of the thing, he asked, "Do you suppose this bag will hold together? It's a long way from new."

Sales stood and walked over to the counter. He ran his experienced fingers over every seam and flexed the two buckles several times. He tipped it every which way, studying it with eyes that had been looking at leather for many years.

"This will still be firm enough to hold your life's savings when you're old and squinting from looking into the sun for too many years."

"I'll take that as a 'yes.'"

With a mischievous grin, he asked, "Are you donating this to the betterment of law enforcement in the territory?"

The saddle maker, coming to enjoy the repartee with the sheriff, said, "Julia, take five dollars from the man and then get him out of here. Him and that dog, both."

Rory passed over the coin, and with his wife's quiet, "Ride carefully," ringing in his ears, he laughed as he opened and then closed the door, heading back to the sheriff's office.

The dog turned in a circle a couple of times and then settled down in front of the door.

RORY WENT BACK to the office and moved the gold sacks into the saddlebags. They bulged a bit, but he wasn't concerned about it. Many riders had saddlebags that bulged with spare clothing and camp supplies. His wouldn't look out of place.

With some spare clothing brought from home, Rory was ready to ride. He didn't know if there was an evening train to Denver, but if not, he would take a hotel room for one night and still have the saddle bags securely stored in the big safe in Hebert Tremblay's Rocky View Bank in Denver the next day.

Marshal Wiley insisted on riding along to Cheyenne. He claimed it was to visit the sheriff he used to work for and to reconnect with a couple of acquaintances. No mention was made of backing Rory up in the case of some threat. The two men rode from town with that fabricated story supporting Wiley's actions. But neither bothered to discuss or challenge it.

19

STARTING FROM STEVENSVILLE IN THE EARLY MORNING, Ivan and Cap were riding up the hill again. Cap said, "This is becoming a habit."

Ivan, his mind thinking ahead, was engrossed in the problems of sorting out miners that had suffered real loss from the ones who simply wished to profit from other's efforts, and paid the comment no attention.

This time, the ride was in search of miners who had reported thefts. They had the list of weights with them and a sample of the four different sacks that had been used. The gold had been moved into new sacks to provide the samples before Rory took it all down to the bank in Denver.

Their first stop was at the general store where county Deputy Sheriff Buck Canby was operating. The final disposition of the estate of MacNair, the town father who had owned and operated the business but had turned out to be a thief and murderer, had not come down from the Denver courts yet. In the meantime, Buck was quickly learning the retail trade, as well as keeping the law as his first responsibility. There was also the matter of his family's mine. Buck had considered his options during the snowy months and decided to turn the mine over to a knowledgeable manager. The returns from the mining efforts were showing the wisdom of that choice.

Gloria, Buck's newly married wife, managed the store while Buck was busy with his sheriff's duties. She greeted Ivan and explained that Buck was away. Ivan introduced Cap before asking where Buck was.

The answer was that Buck had ridden to the north end of town on some matter he chose not to discuss in any detail. Gloria was not, in any way, reconciled to having her husband face gun-bearing thieves that had been attracted by the shine of freshly dug gold. Buck had decided early on in their marriage that a secret here and there might ease her concerns.

But she was able to say that there had been reports of trouble at one of the diggings out that way, but Gloria didn't know if that was the issue he went to look at or not. She knew her husband wasn't in the habit of telling her everything he was involved in. She suspected he was trying to protect her, but that was not the way she saw it. She wisely didn't mention her feelings to Ivan or Cap.

There had been little mining activity to the north the last time Ivan had been in town. What had been there was proving the pick-and-shovel men's efforts to be justified, though. It was only natural that others would follow. Now it seemed the mineral discoveries were drawing men in that direction in large numbers.

AFTER GETTING as much information from Gloria as she
had to give, the two deputies mounted and turned their
horses north. It wasn't long before the thumping of the
ore crusher, or stamp mill as it was more properly called,
rattled their ears and caused the horses to pull back in
fright. When they had ridden to where they could hear
themselves talk again, Cap shouted, "All the gold in these
hills isn't enough to make listening to that contraption
worthwhile."

"Some folks must think it is."

Cap just looked at Ivan and shrugged.

Along the way, they passed several new diggings,
from one-man pick-and-shovel efforts to larger operations with hired workers, drills, and powder men.

"Every one of those one-man operations is hoping to
become profitable enough to attract the big money boys.
Then he'll sell out and live on the California coast,
drinking orange juice from his own trees and soaking up
sunshine."

Cap actually laughed out loud, a most unusual
response from the ordinarily reserved deputy.

They rode a bit further, leaving most of the mining
work behind them, before they heard shots. A garbled,
angry shout, followed by three fast shots, a pause, and
then a response of only two shots. The first fusillade
sounded like it came from a handgun. Probably, judging
by sound, a .45. The response had clearly been from a
.44-40 carbine, with its sharp, distinct sound, followed
by a whining, terrifying ricochet.

The shocking sounds had come from the uphill side
of the surrounding forest, not far off the trail. But no
hunter would shoot like that, so there was most likely
trouble. Both men immediately thought of Buck. Gloria
had said he rode out following a report of trouble of

some kind. The shots, no matter who was doing the shooting, were a sure enough sign of trouble. Whether or not it was at a claim or not, they didn't yet know.

The two deputies sat their saddles, staring off at the forest and the tangle of undergrowth among the fallen rock. As was typical of mining country. The forest grew among the weather-worn and broken rock upthrusts, and sometimes, it seemed, right from the rocky crevasses where a seed had been dropped years earlier. In the already shattered rocks, the crevasses were widening, and the rock splitting further apart as the trees grew. All of that, plus the boulders and slabs that had come down the mountain in years past, created a jumble of possibilities for mines. And for man hunting.

Another shot from the carbine whanged off a rock and went sizzling into the air, leaving behind it a harmless but fearful sound. There was no response other than another muffled shout from near where the deputies were sitting their horses.

"That shout was close by, Cap. I'm guessing just up by that big boulder. I'm guessing, too, that whoever it is will be snuggled down a bit behind the rocks. I'm going to approach it on foot. There's a very good chance Buck is involved in whatever this is. The shooter with the carbine is most likely somewhere in that muddle of rocks over there to the right. I'm prepared to guess that will be our deputy friend.

"You do whatever you think best. But stay to the north of my position. I won't shoot in that direction unless I have a clear view of the target."

Cap took Ivan's reins in his hand and led the animal across the trail and into denser forest. He tied both horses there, lifted his own rifle from the saddle scabbard, and disappeared into the forest.

IVAN CHECKED the loads in his Colt as well as his carbine before entering the rocks himself. Not knowing if he was approaching friend or foe, he went slowly and carefully. From the muffled sounds of the shots and the shouts, he figured the land must drop off a bit beyond the crest he could see just fifty yards ahead. The low ridge would form a partial blockage for the sounds. His approach and response would both be limited by the fact that Cap was within range of his weapon. He wouldn't be discharging any lead off that way unless the clear need was upon him. With any luck at all, his carbine would still be fully loaded when the fracas, if that's what it turned out to be, ended.

He crawled, duck-walked, and scrambled until he was behind the biggest boulder on the hillside. He turned his back to the rock and straightened his knees just enough to see over the dense undergrowth. From that position, he scanned the slope behind him toward the crude trail. He saw nothing animal or human. But then, as he looked off to the north, he was able to see Cap doing much as he himself had done.

Cap, a more experienced deputy, was now crawling, holding his attention directly in front and at the crest that lay ahead of him. Ivan was impressed by how Cap was able to squat to the ground and disappear into the underbrush with no, or very little, telltale signs in the shrubbery. He didn't see him again until he rose to his knees right at the crest. He had taken his hat off. The little bit Ivan could see of the man and his clothing, blended in with the surroundings until he was barely noticeable. Now it was time for Ivan to move forward too.

He didn't have as much undergrowth for cover as Cap had enjoyed, but there were broken slabs of rock lying at all angles among the boulders. He could use those for cover. When he reached the crest of the small hill, he was able to slide on his belly, over the top and into a hollow of rock, where one slab lay on another, leaving a space beneath that was high enough to watch through or crawl under if necessary.

Ivan took a half-minute to check his Colt and the rifle. The crawling might have clogged either weapon's barrel or mechanism with dirt, twigs, or grass. Content that both were in working order, he returned the Colt to its holster and pushed his carbine to arm's length under the top slab.

He saw nothing at first. But then, on closer examination of the rocks and forest close by, he saw three horses tied, half-hidden in the denser forest. They stood with heads up, staring at the area directly ahead and below themselves. Taking the chance that the three horses meant three riders, he could assume what he was looking at was not Buck's stand since Gloria had mentioned nothing about riding with anyone else.

From where he lay, Ivan could see nothing of Cap. All was quiet in that direction. He turned his attention back to the horses and the area around them, hoping and praying for safety for himself and the other deputies.

Buck would not be aware of their presence. Caution was in order. Ivan had no desire to be shot by a fellow deputy. Now he wasn't sure what his own next move should be. He could shout an introduction and threaten arrest, calling for surrender from the men below him. But he would have to expose himself to make that in any way meaningful. The men weren't likely to throw down their weapons for an unseen voice from the bush.

But time was moving along, and he had to do something.

Crawling under the raised rock slab, he had only enough clearance to use his elbows for propulsion, aided a bit by sticking his toes into the gravely soil. But inch by inch, he moved. Not fast, but surely. He crawled less than ten feet when suddenly there was an opening before him, and at the end of that opening, the sight of three men sitting with their backs to the rock, busy with talk. He couldn't hear the words or read their lips, but it was easy to see they weren't happy or in agreement. Their words came to him a low rumble, with most of the sound lost in the distance.

Perhaps this was the ideal time to introduce himself, and catch them while they were arguing among themselves.

Ivan crawled a few more feet, which put him right alongside another boulder. If he was forced to shoot, he could squeeze off his shots and then roll sideways for complete cover. This had to be the time.

He rose to his knees, partially visible to the men below. With all the volume he could muster, he shouted, "Men, you're under arrest and under my carbine, and I can't miss from this distance. I'd rather not shoot anyone, but I will if you turn a weapon my way. This is Deputy Sheriff Ivan Ivanov. Lay down your weapons and stand with your hands empty."

He thought they were going to do it. Clearly, the shock of discovery from his direction was total. He could see their stiffening and then their questioning of each other as they flashed their eyes in every direction, as if looking for a way of escape.

At the very most, they would be able to see little of him, and it would take a second or two to locate even that bit. If they turned with a threat, he would have plenty of time to respond. He hoped it wouldn't come to that. He was just thinking of hollering again when one man jumped to his feet and, with a shout of rage or frustration, looked up the hill and started levering .44-40 shots into the brush, starting ten feet to Ivan's left and working north, shot after shot as if he hadn't spotted Ivan when he rose to shout his warning.

Ivan, knowing he had no choice, and with the other two now getting to their feet, he swung his sight just a bit and squeezed one shot off. With that shot, the standing man threw his arms to his sides, dropped his rifle, and flopped backward across one of his partners, who was still on his knees. Both men fell to a prone position and lay still. The third man, now on his knees and in the process of rising, started swinging his rifle in Ivan's direction. Ivan put a stop to that with a shot through the man's upper thigh. He fell down with a scream.

"No more," shouted Ivan. "Whatever it is, it ain't worth dy'n over. Lay still, all of you. I'm coming down."

The shout from Buck's position was a welcome sound.

"That you over there, Ivan? I seem to remember you were nowhere near here. What's going on?"

"What's going on, my friend, is that we have us three men here. Two are shot, and the other is groveling in the dust. And you've got Deputy Cap Graham riding herd on you. Don't shoot him. Now, why don't you come over here and see what we've got? I'm getting kind of tired of doing your work for you anyway."

Buck shouted some response, but it wasn't loud enough to make out. Ivan figured it might be best that he didn't hear it.

Buck and Cap arrived together. They came to where

Ivan held the three under his gun and walked down the short grade together. The uninjured man had tossed his weapons to the side to prove his surrender. The man Ivan had shot in the thigh had pulled himself to where he could sit with his back against the rock, he was bleeding from his upper leg, but the loss of blood wasn't serious. He was cutting the pant leg away and mopping at the wound with his bandana. The wound was hidden beneath a pair of filthy long johns. But judging by the limited blood flow, Ivan figured it would be sore, and the man would have a serious limp while it healed, but it wasn't deadly.

The first man, who had been busy emptying his rifle into the brush, was clearly dead.

Ivan knew neither of them. Shooting, and especially killing, had always sobered Ivan, whether he did the killing or someone else. There always seemed to be something foolishly final about a shooting, whether it merely changed the victim's life or ended it.

Buck looked over the carnage, glanced back at Ivan, and said, "Thanks for the help. You hold these two but watch them. This isn't their first adventure. They've been raiding these hills since the first snowmelt. And perhaps before that."

20

WITH DETERMINATION, BUCK WALKED TO WHERE THE three horses were tied. Ivan watched as he went first to the saddlebags of a big sorrel and then to the others. He returned to the sorrel, untied the saddlebags, lifted them off, and walked back to the group. He dropped to his knees and opened the first flap buckle. He lifted out a small canvas sack with a string tie around the top. A single pull on the string loosened the opening. Very carefully, Buck poured a sample of the contents into the palm of his hand.

"Care to tell me about this, fellas?"

When neither man spoke, he said, "No, I thought not."

Holding his hand toward Ivan and Cap, he said, "Pretty smart, actually. But not quite smart enough. These boys have been doing a bit of mining alright. The problem is they don't own the claims they're working. By the looks of it, they've had good luck with the color. Sure beats pick and shovel, eh boy's?"

Turning his attention back to the thieves but still

talking to Ivan and Cap, he said, "A few of these one-man claims have struck good rock. These boys have been sneaking around, finding out where the good strikes are. With no banking facility in town, they mostly just hide the take under a pile of waste rock in the brush somewhere.

"I figure these boys wait till the owner is asleep from exhaustion and long hours of breaking rock. Then they sneak in and lift the accumulated take from other men's work. Cute. But not cute enough.

"One of those miners woke up and saw what was happening. He laid still lest he be shot, but he watched. When he came to me, he had the number of men, their descriptions, the colors and brands of their horses, and their camping spot all laid out.

"And the description of one man matched one I already had from another source. That all happened just yesterday. Things can work fast when we have the right information. And the right help. This little deal is all but wrapped up. All that's left is to hold miner's court, find these boys guilty, and shoot them."

The two living thieves shrunk before the sheriff at the mention of shooting.

Buck directed his next comment to the thieves. "You didn't know you'd been followed, did you? That miner wasn't a gunman, or you'd all be dead. But he was a good enough man in rough country to follow and spot your camp. Then he came to me. And here we are. Now go saddle your horses. This other fellas too.

"If you resist at any point or come up with a gun I somehow missed in your gear, I'll shoot you. I didn't like doing that at first, but I soon found it was easier than carrying you punks all the way to Denver for trial. Trial by Colt. That's much easier. And I sleep just as well of a night."

Of course, Ivan knew Buck had done no such things, but the story had a sobering effect on the thieves, so he let it stand.

Following his long-time practice, Cap searched the two men before they went to the horses, stripping a camp knife from each and a derringer from the uninjured man. He tied their unloaded rifles across the dead man's horse after the body was lifted to lay across the saddle. The gun belts were hung from his own saddle horn.

It was a short ride back to the sheriff's office, but they drew a lot of attention as they moved along the trail. When one miner made as if he was going to follow the deputies, Buck waved him off.

THE DEAD MAN was laid out in a shed behind the saloon, a small building used before for that purpose. After it was clear that Buck was shunning the task, Ivan stepped forward and went through the dead man's pockets. Buck didn't thank him verbally, but the relieved look on his face told it all.

The stash laid on the square of cloth Ivan used to wrap the loot in was all the ordinary things men of the wilderness tended to find helpful in their way of life. Probably the most valuable was a metal cylinder with a tight lid that held a small handful of matches. Then there were a few coins, a pocketknife, and a piece of paper. Ivan walked to the door and held the paper up to the light. He read for a moment and then said, "Well, well, well. Now, that's interesting."

Block didn't enquire about the paper, leaving it for when they would be back in the office.

Ivan completed his search, finding a plug of chewing tobacco in a shirt pocket and a short stub of a pencil. He pulled off one boot and tipped it up. With a small 'clunk,' a hold-out gun dropped onto the door slab that was passing for a workbench. Nothing else that mattered was found, and the two men were soon leaving the shed, much to Buck's relief.

"Tough job, Ivan. Thanks for stepping in."

"The first time I was shown how to clean a chicken, I rose no higher than Pa's knee. I told Pa I wasn't going to do any such a thing. Slit it open, put my hand in, and pull out the guts? No thanks. His response was simple. Even more simple coming from his native language, with its short, guttural sounds, in a culture showing little sympathy for disobedient youngsters. The clear message was that I would be standing right there until the chicken turned green and rotted, but it was my job to do. I resisted for a few minutes but finally reached for the knife. It was a lesson learned. Pleasant or not, the job has to be done. And done right. Might just as well get at it. I never forgot."

"I'll be sure to call you if there's ever a chicken that needs cleaning."

It was said half in jest, but Ivan knew the young deputy would step up himself in the future.

21

THEY JOINED CAP IN THE JAILHOUSE. ONE MAN WAS IN the small cell. The wounded man had reluctantly stepped out of his pants, showing shame at the condition of his long johns. One leg of the underwear had been cut off short. The tag end had been tossed into the wood box, all soaked in blood and useless for anything else. He was sitting on a chair with his leg extended, resting on a small wooden box that Buck had been using for holding kindling wood. Ivan looked and asked, "How is it, Cap?"

"Bullet went right through. Took a bit of meat with it, but no real harm done. I've washed it out as best I can. I was just going to pull a string and a piece of clean cloth through the hole. Like I do with my rifle. If you had a bottle of some kind of drinking liquid, I'd use it for a disinfectant. Failing that, I could heat up this fella's knife till it's red and sear the wound. Stinks a bit, doing that. We'd have to do it outside. Wouldn't want that stink in here. Whoever's on the receiving end usually manages to scare even the coyotes with his screaming, but it's all for the good."

Buck glanced at the terrified man's pleading eyes and said, "I'll wander over and get a little something of the liquid variety. Anyway, there's no fire lit. Be hard to heat the knife."

The wound was soon drenched in whisky. A bloody rag and a piece of string from the trading store had been thrown into the stove to be burned up when they next needed a fire. The man was stretched out on a bunk behind bars. The saddlebags had been brought in, and the contents, held in small sacks very similar to those samples Ivan had in his own saddlebags, were stored in three larger canvas sacks and carried over to the general store. There they were locked in the only safe in town.

Ivan looked at his pocket watch. It told him the time was midafternoon. His stomach told him they hadn't eaten since their early breakfast in Stevensville.

"Lunchtime, men."

❧

IT WAS the only invitation either Cap or Buck needed. Seated, with their orders taken, Buck asked, "What did you see on that slip of paper that so interested you?"

"We'll leave that till later."

After returning to the marshal's office, Ivan laid the paper in front of Cap with a grin. "Read that, partner, and tell me what you think."

Buck leaned over Cap's shoulder. "It's a list of names. Any of them mean anything to you?"

Cap lifted his eyes to Buck and then turned them to the men in the cell, who could easily hear every word. "Addison Majeska. Seems I know that name, fellas. Heard it first, just a couple of days ago."

As if the next move was his, Cap stepped to the bars and looked at the men with angry eyes.

"You men have just the one chance to keep me from getting fearful angry. Now you speak. And you speak clearly. And you speak the truth. Start with Addison Majeska and how he ties in with your thievery. But first, tell me your names."

They didn't want to do it, but their lives were coming apart already. Holding off or delaying wouldn't put them back together. And there was no telling what these three deputies would do if they were foolish enough to resist, causing one of the lawmen to open that door. They saw the steel bars as protection for them as much as anything else.

Cap pointed to the wounded man, "You first."

"I'm known as Swat Mallory."

The other man spoke without being asked again. "Pug Yale."

Cap said, "Good. Now the dead man."

"Alf Conklin."

Ivan was studying the slip of papers as the men reeled off their names.

"Fine. Now tell me, Swat, what do you know about Addison Majeska?"

"He thinks we should look up to him. Treat him as if he's boss. Sometimes we do."

"Boss of what?"

"Boss of this here secondhand gold mining thing we got going."

"Secondhand. That means you let others do the hard work. Then you take it from their hands into yours. Is that about right?"

Swat could only look at the floor. Cap waited an uncomfortably long time with his eyes glued to the thief before he said, "Might be a bit of shame left in your sorry life yet."

"Now, what about you, Pug Yale? Is Addison Majeska your boss too?"

Pug raised his eyes off the floor long enough to look at Cap and say, "I guess. When he's here anyhow. The real boss is lying in that shed over yonder."

"Alf Conklin was the real boss?"

When no answer followed, Cap let it go, asking instead, "And who else is in this secondhand gold business of yours?"

"Two other Majeska brothers. Some others."

"And is it possible that you've been doing this for some time? Not just this spring?"

"Little bit before winter closed 'er down."

As quickly as the words were out of his mouth, Pug said, "You can't tell no one that knows the Majeska's. They'd kill us for sure if they knew you had us. And knew their names."

"I wouldn't worry about that. The Majeska's, and as you said, a couple of others are no longer your concern. The brothers are dead, and the coupl'a others are in prison. Three, to be exact."

The news of the Majeska brothers being dead clearly shocked the prisoners. They both flopped back onto the cot and remained silent.

Not content yet to let it go, Ivan asked, "What else can you tell me about that group down at the shack? About Deke and Arch? Did they accept their brother's leadership? And what about Crain, Stanley, and Adams?"

Swat Mallory reluctantly said, "Addison, he was a terror with a shotgun. Far as that goes, the Majeska boys —they was all shoot-crazy. But Addison, no one could stand up to him. He held his leadership claim only because everyone else was afraid of him. But Arch, he was just plain crazy. Never satisfied. Always want'n to do another robbery. Talked all the time of shooting someone just to see him fall. Those other three, the ones you said are in jail, they followed Arch like pet puppies. Follow him anywhere he went."

Ivan said, "That pretty much explains the Stevensville Bank robbery. The bank held less cash money than you boys already had stashed away in gold. Stupid to risk it all on a tiny village bank."

"We wasn't there. But Arch, he wouldn't listen to no logic once he got the bit in his teeth."

To be free of the prisoners' hearing, the three deputies moved outside. Ivan was holding the paper so he could read it to the others. When he was done, he ticked off names from memory. With that done, he said, "There's a number behind each of these names. Strange numbers unless we take them to be fractions. Here, Buck, you've got the education. Add those all up and see if it comes to one hundred."

Buck's lips moved as he added silently. With a smile, he said, "You got it right Ivan. One hundred. Fractions. Must be how they planned to split the loot."

Ivan rose and went back inside. To the two men in the cell, he said, "I'd like you to tell me where you and the Majeskas kept all the loot. The loot you took last year or even before. And I mean all the loot. Every bit of it."

The fight had gone out of the two men. Resigned to their fate, Pug said, "Shack. Down the hill. The brothers wintered there. We expected them back a few days ago. Guess that won't be happening."

"You store stolen gold anywhere else? Don't lie to me."

"Nowhere else. Addison, he wanted it where he could lay hand to it in a hurry. And he didn't trust anyone else."

"Any others at that shack?"

"Woman. Was cooking for the boys in exchange for a winter's shelter. Swore there was nothing more to it than that. Addison, he protected her."

"Did you know her before? Have you ever seen her anywhere else?"

"She's here. Come in a few days ago. Cooking at the dining room."

"You've seen her?"

"Yes. She ain't seen me, though. Same girl. I seen her once down at the shack. She'd know me. That's why I'm staying clear of the diner.

Silently, to himself, Buck said, *'Oh, she saw you alright. And that's how I found you. But you don't need to know that.'*

22

Later, a long discussion was held in the back room of the general store. Buck had invited Terrence Climber to join them. When Sheriff Jamison first rode up to McNair's Hill and ran into Climber, he was more than suspicious of the man. He claimed to be a lawyer, handling matters such as the registering of claims. But there was so little of that work, he could not have been making a living. There had to be something more.

His insistence that he was, in fact, working with the federal marshals, investigating wrongdoing in gold country, was finally confirmed by the marshals, setting Rory's mind at ease. Rory had done nothing to expose the dual purposes of Climber to the public. Now Block, who had been told in confidence about the lawyer being an investigator, had suggested his presence at the meeting. The store was closed, and Gloria had retreated to the living quarters. The men were alone and needed to be for what they were discussing.

Ivan laid out the sample gold sacks brought from the Fort and explained about that treasure find. The list of names was laid on the packing box that was playing double duty as a table. One by one, Ivan went down the name list, making a point of showing the percentage numbers behind each name.

"Four of these are dead." He pointed to the four names and put a small X next to each name.

"Three are in jail." Again, he pointed to the names. This time adding a short dash next to each.

"And these are the two arrested here this morning." A circle was added to their names.

He laid out another piece of paper with a list on it.

"This is the itemized list of gold satchels taken from the shack where the Majeskas wintered. Now look here. On the list, there's a mark showing which of those sacks identified by the assayer, match the sacks I've shown you.

"And then there's this stash from this morning, handled so carelessly by those three. Hauling them around instead of finding a safe place to hide them away.

"Sheriff Jamison's goal is to return as much of the loot as possible, always being careful to prove owner-ship. At least as well as it can be proven. And that's no easy task. We can't advertise, looking for those that lost gold. Every man on the hill would make a claim."

Terrence Climber considered for a moment and finally asked, "What are you suggesting?"

"I'm not sure I'm suggesting anything at all. My head fairly buzzes when I consider this wealth and the tangle of trying to return it. We do have the list you've seen from the assay taken at the Fort. And we have the two prisoners here. We might enliven their memories with the threat of extended prison time. Perhaps they could name their victims and some indication of the loot taken from each. Both now, as well as before, the snow drove everyone off last fall."

There was a silent pause while each man considered possibilities. Then Ivan spoke again, saying, "What I'm further proposing is that we turn the investigation and the solution over to Terrence. He knows the hill and the miners better than any of us. Further, Cap and I have to get back to our other jobs. And I'm guessing one of those other jobs will be to escort those two over there to a cell down at the Fort. They have to face trial. It could be Rory will choose to stand them before Judge Anders P. Yokam at the Fort, or they may be taken to Denver. None of that is up to me or Cap. We have no facility for it up here on the hill, and they can't just be turned loose."

Terrence had leaned back against a feed sack. He sat easy, studying each man. He finally said, "I'll take that on with one condition. You allow me to bring Emmett Streetly into the circle. I know Rory didn't hit it off with the man. I know too, that he can grind on some folks. Some question his honesty too, or his motives in being here on the hill. But I've found that after I dug through the suspicions, he is what he claims to be—a businessman floating loans and advice to small miners and facilitating purchases when moneymen show up looking for a claim to purchase and expand. In short, no one knows the hill better than Streetly."

Cap and Buck, both new to the situation, looked to Ivan for directions. He returned the looks and then glanced at the floor, as if looking for wisdom in the dust of the warehouse planking. He finally took a deep breath and said, "You know, I'm wishing Rory was here. But he's not. In fact, he's in Denver banking that other stash of stolen gold. Or he could be on his way back home by now. But in any case, he's nowhere near to offer his advice.

"So, here's what I'm thinking. We'll go with Terrence's proposal. We'll leave the gold we found this morning here, under Terrence's safeguarding. We'll need to have it assayed or at least weighed. We'll hold off our trip down the hill by one day to give Terrence time to put the squeeze on Swat Mallory and Pug Yale. The only chance of knowing what mine showings they hit is to ask them. And Terrance, or perhaps Streetly, is the man for that job. Terrence can divide the responsibilities any way he wishes between himself and Streetly. And use whatever method they believe will work.

"The other gold is in the bank in Denver. But it can be brought back up easily enough. Terrence can send a message down to the marshal's office when he feels the time is right. The marshals can see to its delivery."

He again looked at all the faces in the small circle before asking, "How does that sound to y'all?"

When there was no dissent, Ivan said, "Alright then. Terrence, you have tomorrow. And this evening for that matter. The following morning Cap and I will escort the prisoners down to the stand before the judge."

23

SHERIFF RORY MADE A MISTAKE DURING HIS VISIT TO Denver. At least in his own mind, thinking of it later, it had been a mistake. Others thought it was as it was meant to be.

He had the gold deposited in safekeeping in Hebert Tremblay's Rocky View Bank. He had made his report to Oscar Cator, written on hotel stationery, before leaving the lobby that morning. Oscar and Rory had their usual visit over lunch, and then, on his way to catch the afternoon train, Rory decided to make a quick detour to the marshal's office to say 'hello' to his friend Block Handley. The two men had much in common and always enjoyed a few minutes when time permitted.

He had barely closed the door to the marshal's offices after entering when a voice from a small office at the far side of the bigger room changed everything and caused him to miss his train.

Deputy Marshal Col. Oliver Staveley called out, in a voice meant to command attention, "Sheriff Rory Jamison, Sir, I was, just a few minutes ago, trying to decide what the fastest way was to get a message to you. And here you are. Come to my office, if you please."

Quietly, so that only Block could hear, Rory said, "And if I don't please?"

"I'm thinking that's just a formality. A polite way of demanding your attendance. You're trapped, my friend. You might just as well try to get out of whatever it is without making the boss feel as if you're about to tear the entire federal government to shreds." Block was grinning knowingly as he said it.

Rory made his way slowly and reluctantly to the far corner office. There, Col. Oliver Staveley, the latest senior deputy marshal sent from Washington to what the easterners considered the unsophisticated—if not downright ignorant, far, far West—was impatiently waiting for him.

"Sheriff. I wish I understood your scheduling. You're in Denver, and then you're not. I'm told you are most likely back at this place you refer to as the Fort, so I sent a man there to find you and bring you here."

Oliver Staveley wasn't finished with his monologue before Rory interrupted with, "Perhaps I should rush home so he can find me."

"Yes, I suppose you could do that, but it would hardly serve the purpose, would it?"

"I have no idea what the purpose would be, Sir, so I can't comment on that."

"Mr. Jamison, in spite of you and I seeming to have reached a satisfactory accord on our last visit, I get the feeling that you are not taking the marshal's service seriously."

Rory tried to look contrite as he said, "Except for one or two local situations, I have yet to see the marshal's service solve an actual crime. And since I was of the understanding that solving crimes was their founding purpose, it leaves me wondering what all this railroading back and forth across the nation, chasing a crime that is as solved as it's ever going to be at this end of the world, is all about. It might drive a citizen to wonder if the marshal's service is a law enforcement operation or an arm of some political movement. Assuming the purpose is law enforcement, surely the crime in question now moves to Washington. There would appear to be more than enough evidence to make that assumption. I can't imagine what else there is to discover in this area."

"Let me assure you, Sheriff, we are very much a law enforcement service. The service of last resort in the nation, when it comes to that. But to think that politics never enters in would be naive. You are, of course, absolutely correct in that, Sheriff.

"Saying that the investigation must now move to Washington is also true. In fact, we are now making arrangements to move the imprisoned suspects back east. You will understand that there is considerable work in an operation such as that, guaranteeing their safety and the safety of the accompanying guards and the railway itself. But we are working on it. Both here and in Washington. But the kicker, as far as you are concerned, is that you and Deputy Marshal Block Handley are also wanted as witnesses. So, I am asking you, as a fellow law officer, to agree, without forcing the need of formalities, to board a train at the Marshal's expense and accompany Marshal Handley."

Rory held the eyes of this man he was coming to like, trying to think of a way to refuse without sounding as if he was refusing. He had long been in the habit of referring to things his father had taught him in his younger years. Among those things was the love of the language.

"Our nation's British heritage left us with some valuable beliefs and practices, Rory. Practices our nation can, and has used, in building what we now enjoy. The principal ones may be the practice of democracy, as well as law and order. But perhaps the most valuable and enduring is the English language. Other languages are considered more romantic or as having a more ancient foundation, but there is no other that can make a valuable point and make it with precision in words that the common man or woman can understand and use. Be careful with your use of words. This great, informal West, has allowed, and almost encouraged carelessness with the language. Don't you fall into that trap."

Rory tried now to think of a polite way to say no. He finally settled on, "With all due respect, Sir, I have nothing more to offer. I doubt that Deputy Marshal Handley has either, but that is his to deal with. I was elected by the people. The people of a large, although sparsely settled county. There never seems to be a time that my and my deputies' services are not needed. And we are sometimes stretched to the limit. I made the trip to Texas at the marshal's services' rather strenuous insistence. Along with Deputy Marshal Handley, we successfully completed the task assigned to us. Deputy Marshal Handley came near to losing his life in the doing of it.

"In that doing also, we brought you back strong evidence that this matter has wormed its way into the marshal's services. How deep that goes will be determined by others. I suggest the prisoners be put on trial in Washington, and the truth be determined. There truly is nothing else to be discovered here in the West."

"I take it that is a wordy way of refusing my request, Sheriff."

"Please take no personal offense. I know you have a job to do, and you are doing it in the only way the marshal's services leaves open to you. But no. I will not voluntarily leave the people who voted me into office and travel thousands of miles when I can do nothing there that I haven't already done here."

"Truthfully, Sheriff, that is the answer I suspected. Go home. Do your job. But don't be surprised when we call again."

"Thank you, Sir. I wish you every success in getting to the bottom of this matter."

24

IVAN AND CAP ARRIVED AT THE FORT, TIRED AND WORN but with Swat Mallory and Pug Yale in tow, equally worn and tired. They had been free to ride and guide their mounts down the steep, sometimes slippery trail from McNair's Hill to Stevensville and then the remaining twenty miles on the more level ground. Ivan's promise to shoot them out of the saddle if they made a move to escape, had been taken seriously. So now they would stand trial before Judge Anders P. Yokam. It would be the first time Ivan had called prisoners before the judge without Rory there to guide the proceedings.

Alf Conklin, the gold thief who had been shot and killed during the capture, had been buried in the small plot reserved for such use behind McNair's Hill.

Law on the early frontier could sometimes be a bit informal. Judge Yokam was normally of a mind to accept the word of the arresting officer unless the accused made strenuous claims of innocence. In the case before him, the judge took the word of Ivan and Cap, along with the document sent along with the itemized list of impounded gold compiled by Terrence Climber. When the accused made no strong plea of innocence, the case was all but over. There was a bit more discussion involving the dead partner in crime, and even more when the connection with the men the judge had sent down to the state lockup just days before was made. But in the end, the sentence of ten years was really decided as soon as the connection with Keith Crain, Vic Stanley, and Muir Adams was made. He could hardly sentence them any differently without showing great unfairness.

The next issue, as always, was the transport to Denver, where the local people would take charge of the prisoners.

"How do you feel about a train ride, Cap?"

"Truth be told, I'd just as soon stay put. But if the choice is between three days on a stagecoach or a few hours on the train, the choice becomes simple. When do you plan to leave?"

"I'm thinking we could make it to Cheyenne this evening if we leave now. Hopefully, there will be a train to Denver in the morning. It might be we could be back in our own beds within a couple of days."

AS IT HAPPENED, after an uncomfortable night in a cheap hotel as they guarded the prisoners, the north-bound train from Denver, arriving at noon, was unloading passengers, one of whom was Rory, while the two deputies and their handcuffed prisoners were waiting for the south-bound. The Cheyenne platforms were a shuffling, pushing, and impatient mass of passengers. The lawmen passed within a few feet of each other, but neither saw the other.

Knowing they would be late arriving, Ivan broke loose for a few minutes to send a telegram to Oscar Cator at the state office, informing him of their arrival and asking for a contingent of guards to take the prisoners off their hands.

After a very quick exchange of information and forms prepared and signed by the judge, before they left the Fort, Ivan and Cap succeeded in catching the same train, making its evening run back north. As tired as they were, Cap managed to say, "Still beats the stage, even with the coal smoke. Smoke or road dust. Those seem to be our choices."

ANOTHER NIGHT IN A CHEYENNE HOTEL, a better one this time since they didn't have the prisoners to guard, and by noon the next day, they were gathered in the dining room with Rory and Wiley. After a long lunch that allowed them all to exchange stories and bring each other up to date, Ivan left for Stevensville. Law enforcement in Northern Colorado was back to normal. So why was Rory feeling an inward unease?

25

About one week after Rory was last in Denver, a rider arrived in town with a document. He sought out the sheriff, holding the brown envelope firmly in his right hand. Without knocking, he pushed the town marshal's office door open. Town Marshal Wiley was seated behind the desk. The visitor looked at him and asked, "Sheriff Jamison?"

"No, that's not me. What do you want the sheriff for, and exactly who are you?"

Rory was seated in the other chair, but Wiley saw no reason to point that out until he knew more about the situation.

"Deputy Marshal Cob Robertson, Sir. I have information for the sheriff."

"That would be for me then, Mr. Robertson. What have you got?"

"Are you saying that you're Sheriff Jamison?"

"County Sheriff, to be precise. And I'm asking, again, what you have in the envelope."

Deputy Robertson, with a bit of a smug look on his face, as if he had just completed a difficult assignment, passed the document-bearing envelope across the couple of feet separating the two men.

Rory lifted out his belt knife. Deputy Robertson took a quick, single step backward, putting him out of easy reach of this sheriff he had heard so much about. Marshal Wiley noted his actions and grinned. There was no threat, however. Sheriff Jamison merely used the knife to smoothly slit the top of the envelope open.

Before lifting out or looking at the enclosed papers, he asked, "Would this, by chance, be coming to me from Col. Oliver Staveley?"

"I'm not at liberty to do or say more than I have already done, Sir. Except, that is, to see that you read the document and follow its orders. I am then to escort you to Cheyenne, under arrest, if that should become necessary."

The foolishly blurted-out statement caught both Rory and Wiley by surprise. Wiley sat spellbound while a small grin formed on Rory's lips before he responded, "I see. Well, they gave you quite an assignment. But you may find fulfilling that assignment to be not quite so simple as you have hoped it would be."

"Deputy Marshal Staveley suggested something of that nature could be a possibility. That's why I'm here alone. To impose on your reason and your loyalty to the good of the nation. The marshal is hoping that one message and one man will be adequate to see you in Cheyenne and on the train tomorrow."

Rory continued grinning at the man as he pulled the document out to where he could see and read it. Finally, he cast his eyes on the paper and looked at the heading.

'Subpoena of the Federal Court of the United States, Washington, DC.'

Rory let his eyes scan the document, knowing immediately what it was for and what it would be demanding of him. The situation in Denver and in Washington had been leading up to this moment. Everyone involved had known what was coming.

Still, if for nothing more than to delay and cause some unease in the young marshal standing at attention a few feet away, Rory leaned forward and passed the papers across to Wiley. "Here, Wiley, you've studied law. What do you make of this?"

It took no more than thirty seconds for the city marshal to scan the document, flipping through the four pages. He then smiled and said, "Well, my friend, without reading all the fine print, which is put in there to justify the lawyer's fees, it would appear that you are wanted in Washington. Perhaps you could look into the possibilities of running for president while you're there."

Rory took the document back, placed it back into the envelope, and threw it on the desk. With an aggrieved look on his face, he turned back to the marshal, who hadn't so much as shuffled his feet since handing over the papers.

"Why don't you unwind a bit, Marshal? Take a seat. You're among reasonable, friendly folks here. Sit and tell me what's happening and who all's going on this railroad excursion."

The young man reluctantly sat, his spine ridged, never allowing his back to touch the back of the chair. Rory and Wiley grinned at each other. Getting into the conversation, Wiley said, "Fresh from the East, are you, Cob?"

"Yes, Sir. I am proud to be from one of the oldest established families in Maryland, sr. And proud to serve my country."

"And you're doing a fine job of it too. I can easily see that. But tell me, is this your first trip West?"

"It is, sir."

"Actually, Cob, my name is Wiley. We're not much on titles out this way."

"Yes, sir."

"Hopeless", Wiley said under his breath.

Rory took up the opportunity to explore the situation.

"I believe I asked you who all is going on this east-ward excursion. That information will aid me greatly in my planning."

"I am not at liberty to tell you any more than you already know. And as for planning, if you could pack a carpet bag for your stay in Washington, there will be nothing more for you to plan or do. All will be taken care of."

"But Deputy Marshal Cob, I always plan. That's why I'm still alive. And if you wish to be alive five years from now, you will obey your superiors but always have your own plan in the back of your mind."

Clearly, that advice did not rest well on the Washing-ton-trained deputy.

"Now, Cob, understand this. I'll not be going anywhere or doing anything to aid your service in this foolish venture until I know what's happening and who is involved. You can either tell me that now or ride back up to Cheyenne to seek permission to disclose it."

The two men studied on each other for a full minute in a force of wills. Wiley could have easily predicted who would win out.

Deputy Cob was the one to break the stalemate.

"I could end up back on the payroll of my father's company, a position I truly detested, if my superiors read me out of the marshal's service for speaking out of turn."

"Think of it this way, Cob. You were sent here to complete a task. A task your superiors apparently see as important. If you have to bend some rules or shake the bushes a bit to reach your goal, then that's one of the things that makes law work successful. Thinking on your feet. Finding a way. Being creative. And in this case, being creative simply means telling me what's up and who's involved."

Looking on as the young deputy marshal struggled with his thoughts, both Rory and Wiley could see the conflict in the man's mind. To ride back to Cheyenne alone could be seen as Rory refusing the subpoena, which could land the sheriff in all kinds of legal trouble. On the other hand, the deputy very much needed to be successful in the task his superiors had trusted him with. He fully understood that he had been chosen because of his youth and his non-threatening demeanor. He had found that realization to be humiliating, but, on the other hand, if he could prove his worth by riding into Cheyenne beside the sheriff, it would be a feather in his cap that he may never earn any other way.

He had always seen himself as an Eastern marshal, if not a big city marshal, doing valuable police work among the masses of city dwellers. To find himself riding alone from Cheyenne to the Fort, through open, semi-desert country, with a critical task to complete, had been a mental and factual adjustment. And now, here he sat, only a few feet from the man he came to find. But that man, who had a great deal more experience than he himself had, was challenging him for information.

Logically, the information the sheriff was asking for would become clear anyway once the marshals assembled in Cheyenne, ready to board the train. What difference was it going to make if he answered the man's question now?

"Sir, I can provide you with an outline only. What the entire plan is, I don't know. I can say that Deputy Marshal Col. Oliver Staveley is returning to Washington. Two deputy marshals from the Denver office will be joining the group, along with Deputy Marshal Block Handley and yourself. Marshal Staveley is in charge of making arrangements and overseeing the transfer of the prisoners."

That statement got Rory's attention. He interrupted the young deputy's comments.

"Are you saying that Glover Harrison and Webster Cunningham are being transferred to Washington, and they're being escorted on this same trip?"

"Yes, sir. They will, of course, be under the marshal's guard the entire time."

"And there will only be two men, besides Block Handley?"

"Yes, sir. Two deputies from the Denver office, and myself, returning east."

"And who all knows about these arrangements?"

"Why. I don't know. There have been telegrams flying back and forth for a couple of days. I would think the arrangements are well known."

There was silence in the little office as Rory worked this over in his mind. Wiley looked on, knowing Rory would not get involved in anything so important yet so poorly planned.

Rory finally said, "Cob, why don't you and Wiley walk over to the dining room and get yourself some lunch? I'll go home and pack that carpet bag you mentioned earlier. After saying goodbye to my wife, I'll join you for a quick snack, and then we can get underway."

Not waiting for an answer, Rory rose and left.

26

AFTER RETURNING COB ROBERTSON'S RENTAL HORSE TO the stable and making arrangements for the boarding of Rory's animal, the two men walked to the Cheyenne Hotel the others were registered in. The group of marshals was gathered in the busy lobby, talking as if making final plans for the morning. No handshakes or other greetings were offered. Rory wasn't exactly sure how to take that. Nor did he know what to make of the fact that Deputy Block Handley was not among the gathering.

Deputy Marshal Col. Oliver Staveley almost acted as if Rory was on par with the two prisoners.

"Did you find your room, Sheriff?"

"Yes. Or at least I have the key. The porter took my bag up."

"I see you are still wearing your pistols and carrying your carbine. Is that really necessary?"

"Except when I'm sleeping."

Rory, as he often did, was wearing his hip-length tanned hide, beaded coat. It was perfect for concealing his Colts, except when the front ties were undone. They were undone when the marshal noticed the gun belt.

When the marshal remained silent while he studied the sheriff, Rory asked, "Are you telling me that you and your marshals are not armed, sir."

"We remain armed but prefer not to make a show of it."

"Well, I have found that the bigger the show, the more likely an enemy will think twice before starting something. And the less likely I am to get shot myself. I shall remain visibly armed."

The pursing of the marshal's lips displayed his disapproval, but he said no more.

As it was evening and time for dinner, Rory said, "It was a long ride for Deputy Robertson and me. I believe I will have something to eat and then ready myself for an early night."

"Deputy Robertson may join you. The rest of us have taken our evening meal."

"And the prisoners? How are they secured, and where are they?"

"That is not your concern Sheriff. I assure you they are under our guard and will remain so."

"If you say so. But I have found the local sheriff to be most accommodating. I have housed prisoners behind his bars several times. I'm sure he would make the same accommodation to you."

"It won't be necessary."

RORY AND COB took their time over their dinners, visiting and relaxing. Having completed his assigned task of serving the summons on Rory, the young man appeared to be much more at ease than he was down at the fort. He was full of questions about the West and curious about how a one-man, or one sheriff and one deputy police force, managed to keep the peace in such a huge country.

What had been kept secret from Cob on the ride north, and what was still being held secret, was the fact that Cap had swung his horse a bit to the west to follow Rory and Cob to Cheyenne. He was bunked down in the same hotel but took his evening meal a block away in a small eating house. He had purchased his train ticket and would be watching happenings from a distance as train time came in the morning and then as they clicked and clacked their way east.

Rory had used county money when he passed several gold coins to the man. Cap had purchased new clothing and even a new hat. He thought about shaving off his mustache, an action he had never before anticipated, in the hopes of staving off recognition by the marshals, but decided against it. His one vanity would remain in place.

He was wearing his gun belt and carrying his carbine, the same as Rory had done.

AT BREAKFAST THE NEXT MORNING, several of the deputies were yawning and having trouble keeping their eyes open after alternating guard duties on the prisoners during the night. Rory was careful not to get into their conversations, lest he let slip that the local lock-up had been available to them. Having deputies casting doubt on their leader, with many more days and nights of guard duty ahead of them, would not be a good way to begin a long train journey.

Avoiding the deputies' talk on a range of topics, Rory completed his meal before most of the others. A dining room waiter came from the kitchen carrying a large tray with two complete breakfasts on it. Oliver Staveley looked around the bunch and said, "These meals have to go to the prisoners. Do I have a volunteer?"

Rory stood, relieved the waiter of the tray, and left the room. He climbed the stairs to the third floor, turned left at the end of the short hallway, and walked to where a deputy was seated on a chair with the front legs hanging above the carpeting as he held the back against the wall with the balance of his weight. The man looked to be ready to go back to bed rather than riding a train for the next three or four days.

"Morning, Deputy. Can you unlock the door? Breakfast for the prisoners."

The young man stood and reached in his pocket for the key without questioning Rory about why he was doing the delivery. Silently, Rory thought, *careless*. He followed the deputy into the room only after he had instructed the two prisoners to walk to the opposite side of the room and turn their backs to him. One had been standing in sight. The other walked from behind the door. The shame on the deputy's face was easily interpreted. Not wanting to make the carelessness worse than it had been, Rory simply said, "Never trust."

He laid the tray on the bed and backed away. With no explanation or instructions, he left the room and waited for the deputy to do the same. He then said, "Go down and get your breakfast or you'll miss out. The train leaves in less than one hour. Tell the Colonel that I've got the door."

∿

CAP PEAKED through the crack in his partially opened room door, watching until Rory was alone. He then eased into the hallway, fully dressed for the trail, with a small pack thrown over one shoulder and his carbine swinging easily from the opposite hand. Standing in a way that would allow him to begin walking away if someone came down the hallway, he spoke quietly to Rory.

"Four hard-cases at the station. I was just down there. Standing apart as if they don't know each other. Eastern by dress. Western hats. They're uncomfortable with the headgear. Keep touching it and adjusting it. Certainly not from around here. Skin white, like as if they don't ever see much sun. Armed with shoulder holsters. Watching every move anyone makes. I'm thinking the Colonel is walking into trouble."

He turned to walk away, leaving just four more words behind him.

"I'll be standing by."

Good man, Rory thought.

When the marshals came for the prisoners, they came in force, looking every bit the part of a professional organization. The men were soon handcuffed, searched again for weapons, and led downstairs and out the door. The walk to the station was about three city blocks. A chill wind enveloped them. The threat of rain hung over the western mountains. People moved off the sidewalks to give them room. There was no end to the curiosity, with morning walkers watching every move the group made. The thinness of the air at the elevation of Cheyenne was clearly having an impact on the breathing of a couple of the easterners, but they moved right out anyway, taking heavy breaths.

Rory had passed the entourage and moved on quickly

to the station. With his carpet bag in one hand and his eyes casting in every direction, he looked every part the anxious traveler. Although not always approved by other travelers, men carrying long guns were not unusual. No one challenged Rory with his carbine.

Turning to his left, toward the outer corner of the platform, he saw Cap leaning nonchalantly against the freight shed wall. His hat was tipped down, and he was rolling a smoke. He had raised one foot, propping it against the wall behind him, a move common among riders. No one was paying him attention.

As Rory gazed about, holding his eyes on Cap for a few seconds, the man's hand, the one holding the small sack of tobacco, moved, pointing toward the bench alongside the station wall about twenty feet away. Then, as Rory continued to watch, Cap's fingers spread. The thumb moved to a position behind Rory. The middle finger pointed toward the train, sitting idle as the engine puffed and blew smoke into the air.

Loading wouldn't begin for another quarter hour. The crowd was growing, active and anxious. There was an undercurrent of whispers and quiet talk as folks had their last-minute conversations and their whispered goodbyes.

Traveling by locomotive was still unfamiliar enough for most folks that the mixed smiles and anxiety was a normal departure pattern.

As if he was simply taking in the windy beauty of the morning, Rory slowly turned to where Cap's fingers had pointed. There, up against the stove-wood shed wall, opposite the baggage shed that Cap was leaning against. A tall, thin man wearing an Eastern suit. City shoes. New western hat. A bulge under his left lapel. Hands that fidgeted, never seeming to be still. Eyes casting in every direction, taking in everything. That's one.

There, on the bench. He could have been twins with the man leaning against the shed, except for the difference in height and the color of their suits. That's two.

Both men were studying the crowd, not attempting to use their hat brims to hide their faces. Rory would know them when next he saw them.

He continued the study, now made more difficult by the restless surging of the crowd. There. The man, dressed the same, was studying every passenger as they boarded. That was three. Cap had been correct in his judgment; these men had no familiarity with Western hats and looked distinctly uncomfortable wearing one. The man who was mingling with the crowd kept touching his hat, a sure sign that it didn't fit well.

At the foot of the steps, he had just laid into place stood the porter, one of two Rory had spotted. He was a black man, as was his partner. He was handing the ladies and lifting the smaller children onto the train platform. Beside him stood the conductor, diligently watching everything. This was his train. He was responsible. Rory was wishing he could speak with the man, but that was impossible. Any contact that couldn't be hidden from the crowd would only serve to point him out to the watchers. That would help no one.

Rory casually turned back to Cap. He adjusted his hat with three fingers splayed. His little finger was folded into his palm. Cap blew smoke into the air and nodded. With a push on the boot, he had raised against the shack's siding, he stood upright and moved easily through the crowd. Rory let him go without trying to follow his movements. Cap would be where he was needed.

The marshals, with their prisoners, were holding back, standing on the end of the large platform, waiting for the crowd to thin. There was no fear of attack with the prisoners virtually surrounded by marshals. When the crowd thinned, the marshals and their prisoners would be guided by the porter to the rear section of a half-filled passenger car, the last one on the train. They would have to walk the length of the train to get to their reserved sleeping rooms or the dining car, if there was one. Most trains didn't attach a dining car west of Omaha.

Rory waited until the very end. The three men he was watching had, one by one, several feet apart, already boarded. The fourth man hadn't been seen. He must have boarded the next car. Cap was nowhere in sight.

When the conductor sounded serious with his loud shout of "Bo-o-or—d," Rory stepped forward and swung up the stairs.

27

As if he was lost or looking for a satisfactory seat, Rory walked to the front of the train, passing through four cars to get there. Along the way, he studied each face, spotting all three of the men he had seen on the platform, all sitting in separate cars. Satisfied, he turned around and returned to the last car, the one the marshals and the prisoners were on. He still didn't see the fourth man. Or Cap. But the train was moving, picking up speed. There was nothing to be done.

He made his way to where Deputy Marshal Col. Oliver Staveley was seated. He was in the last row, sitting alone, his eyes alert. In the row in front of him, the prisoners were handcuffed, each one to a deputy marshal. Those two marshals had turned in their handguns to prevent any attempt from the prisoners to get a grip on one.

When the prisoners, Webster Cunningham and Glover Harrison, saw Rory approach, their looks alone would have killed him if such a thing were possible. Rory ignored them and bent to speak quietly to Deputy Staveley.

"Walk with me, please, Colonel."

Staveley, who had barely spoken to Rory since their last visit in Denver and was totally ignoring him on this trip whenever possible, studied him now.

Not being able to pin down any other reason for the marshal's attitude, Rory figured he was upset by the way his Denver subordinates, a short while before, had spirited the prisoners away from Cheyenne and back to the lockup in Denver. He was tempted to explain that the action had nothing to do with him. It was entirely the deputies' doing. On a quick second thought, he let it go, not wishing to dredge up more hard feelings than were already in evidence.

Finally, making a decision that the sheriff might have valuable news, the marshal stood, picked his hat off the seat beside him, and placed it on his head, adjusting it carefully. Only then did he step into the aisle. They were halfway down the length of the car before Rory said, very quietly, "Sir. You have enemies on this train."

Staveley stopped walking and burst out, "Impossible. My men..." Before he could say more, Rory said, "We need to keep that to ourselves, sir."

As if coming to an understanding, Staveley nodded, started walking slowly again, and said, "I'm listening."

To anyone watching, it may have appeared as if two old friends were talking about something as innocuous as a child's birthday party. But Rory was talking about life and death. And careers that could easily be sidetracked or ended if something went wrong on this trip. He said nothing more until they were standing in the passageway connecting the two cars. There they stopped.

Rory had to speak loudly to rise above the outside noise, the clanking of the wheels, and the flapping of the shrouding protecting the passengers as they moved from one car to another.

"Four men. Eastern. Armed. Western hats. Eastern suits. Shoulder holsters. Dangerous men."

"How do you know that?"

"Let's say I'm just guessing. But to be wrong could carry a heavy price. I know where three are. The fourth, and my man, have disappeared."

"Your man?" The volume rose too much as he spoke.

"You really must hold it down, Colonel. Now, in each of the next three cars, there is one man. You will probably pick them out from my description. I'll not be walking with you. It's best if we are not connected on this trip. Each of those men is a danger to your prisoners and the deputies. I'm thinking it would be best if they didn't know you had identified them. If it were me, I'd look but not be obvious about it. Or you could simply arrest them and let them holler about it."

"Young man. The marshal's service trains its deputies very well to create a professional force. I'm sure we can figure out how to safely ride a train."

"I'm sure you can too, sir. My concern is for the lives of the deputies and yourself. If I may be bold, sir, the marshals have had their eyes so fixed on Texas and gold coins that I fear you may be missing the fact that others don't want you to sort that all out. Those men in their new western hats would gladly shoot any one of you, but their real target will be the prisoners. Someone doesn't want those men to arrive safely in Washington and be able to testify in court. At least, that is the premise I would be working on if I was in charge of the operation."

While the marshal was studying him as if trying to

sort out how to respond, Rory said, "I'll be leaving you now. But I'll be around if you need me."

~

ABOUT ONE HOUR LATER, Col. Oliver Staveley walked slowly past where Rory was seated. A slight hand motion indicated that he was to follow. Rory waited a couple of minutes before he rose and nonchalantly followed. He walked past the prisoners and their guards and stepped through the door, taking him to the platform outside. There was no connecting car. Only the caboose rode behind the one that the prisoners had been assigned to. They stood, holding the guard rail with one hand and their hats in the other, lest the wind or a curve in the track cause one of them to lose his balance. Or have that same wind grab a hat, where it would flutter in the air before falling, to eventually become one with the Nebraska sod.

Over the clank of steel wheels and the whistle of the wind, the marshal said, half shouting, "Now, young man, tell me everything."

"I've told you the important part. This is my world, sir, this West. Just as Washington is yours. I will be as out of place in the big city as your eastern deputies are out here. Again, if the operation had been mine to organize, I would have used the Denver deputies who are well familiar with the West."

After allowing a few seconds for that remark to sink in, he continued, "Those men I pointed out to you are Eastern. They've fooled themselves into thinking they look Western because they bought new hats. But there's a lot more to it than that. To say a man is Western means he has a look, and a way of walking as if most of his time

163

is spent in a saddle. It means his skin is sunburnt, his eyes familiar with squinting into the horizon against the brightness of the sun. It means he eases into a chair rather than folding down, pulling his pant knees up to preserve the press. It means he gives deference to the ladies, doffing his hat as a natural gesture. It means many things, sir. Things I failed to see in those men I pointed out to you.

"And that means you have enemies on this train. I watched them as they were waiting to board. They tried to look uninterested, but every chance they got, they took another look at you and your group."

Deputy Marshal Staveley interrupted with, "I believe you said, at first, that there were four men."

"I did say that. But on the train, I only saw three. One is missing, as is my deputy. But Cap is a good man. He'll be where he can offer the most help.

"I'm told, sir, that telegrams between Denver and Washington were numerous over the past few days. That means everyone in the country knows your plans. And has known them from the start. And since this is very clearly politics you are trying to deal with, the problem and the eventual solution will be political, a subject I know little to nothing about. What I do know is criminals. I deal with them regularly. I find there is no conscience among the group. It shows in their eyes and in their swagger and demeanor. We have enough paid killers here in the West without importing more from the East. But that is exactly what those four men are. I stake my reputation and possibly my life on that assessment.

"The bank box robbery a decade ago has little or nothing to do with this. That money is spent, and the thieves have moved on. It would be a small note in history, except that someone at the top was involved in the theft and is now afraid that they will be caught out. We know that from the list of names I captured on the trip to Texas, where we arrested Webster Cunningham. I'd suggest there is a powerful man, or men, in Washington who want the witnesses dead. They want all memories of the bank box theft buried and forgotten. They may very well want Deputy Block Handley and myself dead, as well.

"I'm also suggesting that they sent men west days ago to watch for your arrival in Cheyenne so they could board the same train."

As Deputy Staveley thought that over, both he and Rory turned their eyes to the roof overhang above them. A sound that at first was muted turned into three or four quick footsteps. The sound neared them, and then a short sliding motion was heard. A voice hollering, "Halt. Halt, I say," covered the grunt of lost breath as the walker flopped onto his belly, blindly sliding and wiggling backward to the edge of the overhang. As the lawmen watched, one foot and then the other dropped from the roof. As the man on the roof slid downward, he somehow managed to stop and peer over the edge, as if to see what he was dropping onto.

Rory laughed and said, "Come on, Cap. I've got your legs. I'll guide you down."

Cap, letting go of the overhang more quickly than Rory really expected, was soon in Rory's strong arms. With the federal marshal steadying Cap with a grip on his shoulder, Rory eased to bended knees, setting Cap's feet on the steel plate of the platform. Cap grabbed for the steadying railing, waited while he took a deep breath, and said, "Thanks, fellas."

Another sound from above caused the three men to

glance upward. Peering over the edge of the roof was a florid-faced railway worker. He was sputtering in anger, trying to get words out even as he was sizing up the situation.

Finally, he managed to ask, "Who are you men, and what are you doing on my train?"

Col. Oliver Staveley stepped to the edge of the platform where he could be easily seen. He spoke with authority in his voice.

"I am Federal Deputy Marshal Col. Oliver Staveley, sir. On federal business. These men are lawmen working with the marshals. We have prisoners in this last car. Your conductor and porter are aware of the situation. We mean no harm to you or your train, I can assure you of that. We are simply discussing our plans. We believe there are certain men on board that mean harm. Harm to our prisoners and quite possibly to ourselves. We will handle it. You needn't involve yourself."

The face disappeared, and a moment later, a few retreating footsteps were heard until the wind and the noise of travel drowned out the movements of the railway worker.

The three men on the little platform took a few moments to gather their thoughts. The silence was broken when Rory, with an audible chuckle in his voice, asked, "Where have you been, Cap, and what were you doing on the roof?"

"It was the only way I could think of to get from the engine to the car I knew y'all would be riding on."

"You were on the engine?"

"Well, when a man needs to disappear for a bit, it's good to know your way around. Riding the engine with the hog head and the ash cat proved to be a good escape plan a few times in my life. Of course, it helps your welcome if you don't mind taking a turn on the shovel."

"I assume you're referring to the engineer and the fireman."

"Good men, those boys. Met more than just a few of them over the years."

Leaving the subject of the moment for just a bit, Rory smiled and said, "Why do I get the feeling there are things you haven't told me about yourself, Cap?"

"Generally, tell what needs telling."

"And you're right again, Cap. So, I'll tell you that the marshal and I were just discussing the possibility of danger from those easterners in the Stetson hats. You indicated that there were four of them, but I only spotted three on the train. Sitting apart in three different cars. But I didn't see a fourth, not if he was dressed like the others anyway. Do you know anything that needs telling about that?"

"He decided not to catch the train. It was a last-minute decision. He didn't have time to inform the others."

The look on the marshal's face indicated that he was wondering if these local lawmen were talking in some kind of code.

Rory ended the conversation, leaving the marshal's questions unanswered.

"We may just as well move inside. I'm getting a bit tired of shouting over the wind and the rattle of the wheels. You men take a seat. I'm going for a stroll."

28

AT A SMALL TOWN IN NEBRASKA, THE TRAIN PULLED ONTO a siding to allow the westbound to pass by. It was a planned, scheduled stop, timed to give the crew the opportunity to top up the water tank and for the passengers to de-train. Anyone could easily learn of the stop by simply referring to the printed schedule.

Passengers could crowd toward the old railway car that had been lifted off its wheels and set on some timbers to be used as a diner and coffee stop. Although the diner staff served the crowd as quickly as possible, the scheduled stop was short. Some passengers would be re-boarding the train unfed.

The rail crew had their own entry to the diner at the end of the old car, guaranteeing them fast service so they could get back to work. Passengers would take their chances as the crowd surged forward. The diner staff had mountains of sandwiches ready to take back to the train, and gallons of coffee for anyone with a way of carrying it. Many quart-size canning jars of the hot brew were purchased to wash down the cold beef sandwiches.

With no dining car on the train, the passengers were expected to fend for themselves. Many brought food along for the trip. Others knew of the quick stops along the way and hoped to take advantage of them.

A kind word from Rory, along with an extra coin pressed into the porter's hand, would guarantee food and drink for the prisoners and the lawmen.

Three of the deputy marshals had, with the marshal's permission, de-trained to stretch their legs and get a breath of smoke-free air. And, perhaps, a sandwich. That left one deputy, plus Cap, Rory, and the Colonel guarding the prisoners.

UNSEEN FROM WHERE the prisoner waited, the three men wearing their new Stetson hats rose from their seats, joined together, and pushed their way down the aisle toward the last car.

Before the three attackers reached their destination, shots were heard from outside, along with screaming and shouting of terrified passengers, spoiling their attempt at surprising the lawmen.

From the platform, a half dozen shots were heard, answered by a fusillade of answering shots, sounding as if they came from lighter arms. The marshal rushed to the windows to see what was going on.

Although their timing was thrown off by the shots from outside, the three assassins sent to take the lives of the prisoners burst into the car, shooting as they entered. The passengers remaining in the car either cringed against the windows or dove to the floor.

The assassins were clearly professionals. Their shots were going true. One of the first shots hit Webster

Cunningham in the shoulder. It was, undoubtedly, meant for his chest or head. It was only that he was beginning his dive to the floor that the lead missed its original mark.

The marshal was quick to pull his weapon, shooting from the side of the car, where he had been staring out the window. Rory and Cap's side-by-side position beside the prisoners, and a bit to the front, blocked further the view of the handcuffed men. The air was soon full of the roar of shooting, the whine of lead, the sound of breaking wood as shots thunked into the framework on the carriage, and the less solid, more terrifying sound of lead striking flesh. And over it all, the stink of burned powder.

From the corner of his eye, Rory watched the Colonel drop, first onto the seat beside him and then sliding onto the floor. Standing beside Cap, Rory watched as the young deputy was taking careful aim. The movements of the assassins made for western-style shooting; fast and from the hip, more appropriately. Still, the deputy's marshal's lead took a toll on one of the shooters. The man didn't drop to the floor, but he was turned around, cringing in pain, giving the deputy time for a second shot. That time the shooter did drop.

Rory and Cap, both holding .44-40 carbines at hip level, poured lead into the remaining two men. One, hit dead-center of his chest, stood for a slow second, lifeless on his feet, before falling sideways onto a woman who had laid down across the seat. Her muffled, hysterical scream added an exclamation mark that signaled the end of the gunfight.

The third assassin was sitting on the floor, holding his hand over his belly, his eyes glazing over. He offered no more threat.

The young deputy took a few quick steps and was soon bending over his boss, Deputy Marshal Col. Oliver Staveley. He was unceremoniously tearing the man's jacket and shirt apart to get to the upper chest wound. Rory glanced his way and then ran to the center of the car to see to the woman who was frantically trying to push the dead man off. Rory had her freed and standing when Cap turned away to see to Webster Cunningham.

That man, the boss, and manager of the Big C herd in Texas, was hurting and bleeding but would recover. Cap was sure of that.

Before he did anything else, Cap checked the handcuffs on the two prisoners and sat them back upright on their seats.

"Shooters are dead, fellas. No more danger for now. Sit up here where I can keep an eye on you."

As Cap turned away, Cunningham whined, "What about this wound? Hurts like nothing I ever felt before. You gotta do something."

"What I've gotta do is see to those boys outside. The shooting's stopped, but that might not mean it's ended. You sit tight. You get up and run, I'll find you and shoot you dead, and don't you disbelieve me."

The deputy had the marshal sitting in the seat. He was bleeding, but the younger man didn't seem to be panicking, so Cap left him to it.

Rory had ushered all the passengers forward, into the next car. A porter immediately ran to the weeping woman, who was now trying to brush the blood off her clothing. Knowing she was in good hands, Rory turned back to his own car.

He was just closing the door again when the conductor, who had been seeing to matters outside, leaped onto the metal platform between the two cars. Not sure who the bad guys were and who Rory was, he acted suspicious. To set his mind at ease, Rory said, "Sheriff Rory Jamison here, sir. The trouble is ended in this car. I don't know about outside. Come in. You can see for yourself.

Rory stayed with the man until he could see that everything was under control and then turned to join Cap on the wooden planks surrounding the station house.

THE MILLING PASSENGERS and most of the crew had fled from the deck, taking refuge behind the station. With only the dead and wounded lying on the boards, and the living standing guard over them, it was easy to see that the deputies had prevailed. But they had paid a price. One deputy, still on his feet, was holding a folded cloth pad, perhaps his bandana, against his upper arm. The pale blue pad beneath his pressing fingers was turning red with blood. He still held his weapon in his hand, holding his eyes on the men on the deck while also glancing around to watch for new threats.

The second standing deputy appeared to be unhurt. He stood in ridged guard, holding his pistol on the one attacker who was still alive. At his feet, lying in an awkward pose, another young deputy lay dead. Rory bent to see who it was. With his dead eyes staring back at him was Deputy Cob Robertson, the young man who had hated working for his father. Even after seeing too many deaths, Rory never hardened to that reality, caught his breath, and felt a wave of sadness pass over him.

Believing it was all over after searching the area with his practiced eye, Cap was walking from the freight shed, pulling a wagon behind him. Guessing at his intent, Rory joined him, easing the heavy cart over the uneven boards. Then, solemnly and wordlessly, they lifted the dead assassins onto the cart. At Rory's wordless direction, they then eased the cart to the door of the last rail car. It took little time to drag the three dead assassins from the car and drop them beside the others onto the freight cart. It was a grim load that Rory and Cap steered into the freight shed, out of sight from the passengers.

The dead deputy was carefully lifted and laid onto the rear car platform. Rory and Cap then climbed aboard from the other end of the car. Walking through the car, they glanced at the two wounded men. The colonel was sitting on the seat. His eyes showed pain and weariness. It appeared as if the deputy had the bleeding under control. When Rory approached, the deputy said, "He'll be fine. Needs some treatment, though."

Col. Oliver Staveley slowly turned toward Rory and spoke his first words since the fight. "They were waiting for us!" There was a wall of disbelief in his voice. He then turned his head back to the window, saying no more.

The two prisoners hadn't moved. The wounded Webster Cunningham still sat, holding his hand over his wounded shoulder. His face was pasty white, not from loss of blood but from pain and fear.

As Rory and Cap shouldered their way back into the car, carrying the dead deputy, the marshal, showing more agonizing sorrow than Rory had ever seen before, struggled to rise, and then stood to ridged attention. His lips were working a silent prayer. It was as if his every breath accused him, saying, *this is your fault. This is your fault.*

They gently laid Cob Robertson's body onto the floor ahead of the front seat. Rory took a blanket left there by one of the passengers and reverently covered the young man.

Asking no questions or permission from the marshal, Rory took charge of the next steps. He located the conductor and said, "Get the people back on the train. No one is to enter the back car. The porter can see to the moving of the belongings left there. Then shuttle this train however you must but get that unused freight car off that siding and tie it in front of the caboose."

"I have no authority to do anything of the sort. We'll have to wire for permission."

"Believe me, sir, when I tell you that the marshal's service will see to all permissions. Now get to it."

With ten seconds wasted in studying the sheriff, the conductor turned on his heels and went to see the engineer. With much puffing and blowing of black smoke, along with the clanking and banging of the hitches, necessary back-and-forth movements were completed, and the empty car was connected between the last passenger car and the caboose. Rory and Cap, now aided by one of the porters, wheeled the cart with the bodies on it to the freight car.

Although he felt the shooters actually deserved no respect at all, Cap said, "Easy does it, boys. Good or bad, they were made in the image of God. We'll respect that, if nothing else".

～

BEFORE THE TRAIN was again underway, the young deputy who had been ministering to the marshal, came to look at Webster Cunningham's shoulder. The bleeding had stopped. The drying blood was forming a clot. There was no exit wound. And there was no possibility of removing the bullet with what was available on the train.

Intent on at least cleaning up that wound, as well as the colonel's wound, the deputy went for a bucket of water, hoping also to find some clean cloths and a wash pan. He met the helpful porter along the way. Explaining his needs, the black man said, "You go back and comfort the wounded. I'll be there in a few minutes with what we have available."

As the deputy was cleaning his boss' wound, the colonel said, "Deputy Grandby, you work as if you have had some training in medicine."

"Nothing formal, sir. My father is a physician. I've aided him on occasion, is all."

"And yet, here you are in the marshal's service. Did you feel no attraction toward following in your father's footsteps?"

"He wanted me to. Still does. And I thought about it. I may go back to it one day, but I wanted to try something on my own first, where I knew he was not standing there with a safety net in case I fell."

"Every man should try his wings. I pray you will find where yours are leading you to. I can see that you have both a feel and knack for medicine, though."

"Thank you, sir. I'll remember your words when the time for a decision comes."

Deputy Grandby went next to Webster Cunningham. He cleaned and wrapped the wound, but the man was going to need much more than that. As the porter came to see if there was more the men needed, he asked, "Where is the closest town where we could find a competent doctor?"

"Why, sir, I expect that would be in Fort Kearney.

These small settlements along the way ain't likely to have what these men need."

"When will we be reaching this Kearney place?"

"The schedule says ten this evening, sir. We'll be stopping there for food for the passengers and a crew change. And to water up the engine. Scheduled to be back on the line at eleven. Be full dark by then."

Cunningham had listened to the conversation. Thinking of another eight or nine hours without surgical help drove him into despair. He turned his head to the side, away from the young deputy and Glover Harrison, and pulled the blanket up to cover his shoulders. He closed his eyes, although it was doubtful that he would sleep.

Deputy Ren Grandby—with nothing more to do that would aid either the prisoner or the marshal, turned to where the two surviving deputies, who had been in the fight on the platform, sat.

Reb Collinga, the unwounded man, was attempting to comfort his riding partner, Con Hewson. His arm wound wouldn't be serious if he got immediate attention, but he too, would need the services of the surgeon. The bullet, deeply embedded against the humerus—the upper arm bone—would need the hand of a skilled man to be removed. Deputy Grandby did what he could with lukewarm water and a clean rag and the suggestion that the deputy try to get some sleep.

29

It was perfectly clear to both Rory and Cap that the Colonel had no desire to talk. Except for the normal noises of a moving train, the ride to Kearney was long and silent. Deputy Ren Grandby, on occasion, moved from one wounded man to the other, silently checking the condition of the wounds. Each man was hurting, even more so as time moved slowly on and the train puffed its way across the miles. Kearney, in the minds of the wounded, couldn't turn up on the horizon quickly enough. But until then, there was nothing more to be done.

As the sun set behind them and the light in the car diminished, the porter came through, lighting lanterns. As he approached the set of seats Deputy Marshal Col. Oliver Staveley was seated in, he was brushed away with a single, off-hand sweep of Staveley's hand.

Rory thought earlier that he had seen tears in the Marshal's eyes. Perhaps the sorrowing man wished for darkness to hide his emotions.

At Kearney, the Colonel was informed by the train

conductor that the train could not possibly wait while the surgeon treated the wounded. They would be moving on just as soon as the marshals and the prisoners vacated the car. The porter had quietly cleaned up the car as they crossed Nebraska. It was ready for a new crew and for those passengers now waiting on the station platform.

Oliver Staveley demanded that the freight car holding the bodies of the assassins be removed from the train and held ready for when the lawmen were again prepared to move east. Through much grumbling and demands, the marshal had his way. Only then did he join the other wounded men, along with Deputy Ren Grandby, handcuffed to Cunningham, as they wagoned to the surgeon's small office.

Prisoner Glover Harrison, with Deputy Reb Collinga in charge, was held in a small room in the station house. Rory and Cap, who had both caught some sleep on the ride to Kearney, sat beside the deputy. Cap had moved a chair in front of the door. No one was either coming in or leaving the room without his knowing.

With deputy marshal Staveley no longer within hearing distance, Harrison began to speak to the young deputy who had so recently been under his command. Whether he was about to make excuses for his actions and plead innocence or use some other wile to free himself would never be known. He didn't have more than three or four words out of his mouth before Reb Collinga held up his hand.

"Stop. No more. Save it for the Colonel. Or for the courts. If I had my way, I'd drag you out into the wasteland and shoot you. Leave you lying there."

The room fell to a deathly silence.

Rory's feeling toward the marshal's service was

improving as he watched the young men in action and away from the stifling presence of commanding officers with little or no field experience.

WITH THE SURGERY completed and the men fed and given the opportunity to rest, the remainder of the trip east lay before them. They had no choice but to wait for the next train, which was still hours away. Following that, there would be an interminable series of trains, stations, shuffling of cars, and weariness before Washington hove into view. To simplify matters, the bodies of the deceased were transferred to a freight run. Deputy Reb Collinga was assigned to ride the same train, overseeing the transfer of the car through its many stops before it reached its eastern destination.

Temporary wooden coffins were provided by the railway. The weather was warm but not hot. The bodies should arrive in fair condition without driving the freight hands off with disturbing odors.

ON THE LAST leg of the trip, Deputy Marshal Col. Oliver Staveley recovered enough from his wound to interrogate each man. He stationed himself in a section where the seats faced each other. Drawing Glover Harrison aside first and inviting Rory to sit in, he pinned the prisoner to his facing seat with a stare. He spoke after holding that pose for a half-minute, "Harrison, you are a disgrace to everything that matters; your family, your uniform, your country, and to yourself. It troubles me to even have to sit here with you and look at you. Now, you talk to me. What are you mixed up in, and who's at the top?"

Harrison appeared to be trying with every bit of strength and determination in his body and mind to look the marshal in the eye. He couldn't do it. He held the pose for no more than a few seconds before his eyes dropped. Was it shame or, more likely, fear of exposure and prison? When he spoke, he offered nothing helpful.

"The answer to both questions is I don't know."

"You're going to have to explain that."

"I don't know enough to even explain it. I do know that it started out as one thing, and somewhere along the way, controlled by people unknown to me, it became something else. It was all well underway before I backed into it, not understanding in any way what it was about or what would be demanded of me and others. The marshal's service was infiltrated by people unknown to me, all based on what turned out to be lies. I thought we were protecting the government. Then it became apparent that we were protecting a powerful politician. By that time, I couldn't get out."

"You're lying. Assassins aren't used to shut down people who know nothing. Now speak to me. You've directly caused the death of a fine young deputy. You owe it to him, if not to your own conscience, to come clean. You're going to prison. There's no escape for you. But you might still preserve whatever is left of your honor and dignity. Now come clean."

"All I can tell you is that there are people at the top who have much at stake. Powerful people. Political people with great ambitions. I don't know a single name. I was always treated as if I didn't exist, except when I said I wanted out. Then the threats started."

"Give me one name. Who did you tell you wanted out?"

"They'll kill me if I answer that question."

"They have already tried to kill you without you answering any questions. And the courts might well hang you if you don't. I'm holding that fine young man's death directly against you."

There was nothing more to gain, so the marshal moved on to speak with the living assassin. He gained little there. Only the information that, on occasion, they would receive a package in a mailbox. A package with no return address, containing names and a wad of cash. No further directions were necessary. The named person was to be eliminated. The only other piece of information the man offered was that never before had they ever suffered such losses. It was a bitter lesson learned.

Webster Cunningham, of course, as he had already confessed to Rory and Block on the Texas trip, knew nothing beyond what it took to put the Big C brand together and hold them to some unknown future. He speculated that his task was to prepare a ranch for someone unnamed, almost on a whim, as if the unknown person saw something romantic or otherwise special about owning a western ranch.

30

NEAR ENOUGH TWO THOUSAND MILES TO THE WEST, IN the little town everyone was calling the Fort, Town Marshal Wiley Hamstead was seated on his half-barrel chair in front of the combined office and jail, a position that signified that all was well in the little town and there was no immediate threat to the ladies who were going about their normal shopping routines.

Shortly before, a heavily laden covered wagon had pulled up in front of the mercantile with a sweating, four-horse hitch now standing at rest. A bull-shouldered man and a woman wearing a split riding skirt climbed down from the seat and stepped toward the mercantile. The man's self-important swagger was either the mark of 'somebody come' or of a fool. The woman walked with hard heels, showing no daintiness at all. A not uncommon posture of frontier women who were familiar with working alongside their men.

Two town ladies who were visiting as they strolled along the boardwalk were forced to stop while the two newcomers, ignoring everyone and everything in their path, pushed their way into the store. Once inside, the man stopped and said, "Alright, you've got you one-half-hour. No more. Get what you need and have it packed out for you. I'll get that horse shod and be back."

With that, the fellow turned on his heel and stomped back outside. Again, he ignored anyone standing or walking between him and his wagon. He stepped to the rear of the wagon and untied a beautiful bay gelding. The high-stepping animal showed its pride, with his head raised and his neck slightly bowed, as he was led across the street and along to the south just a bit, to arrive at the livery.

Kegs was enjoying a quiet morning and a rest after caring for the animals in his charge and then cleaning the big barn. He watched the horse approaching, ignoring the man. He noticed the slight limp, with the gelding favoring its off-hind foot.

"Animal needs a shoe."

Those were the gruff words that came from the mouth of the man. There was no show of respect or friendliness.

"Can see that." Kegs pointed his thumb over his shoulder as he said, "Take him around to the back. Smithy back there."

When the man moved toward the barn with the intent of leading the horse down the central aisle and to the rear door, Kegs said, "Just now cleaned the barn. Go around. I'm pretty sure I mentioned that."

"Shorter this way."

"You go in there, you'll get no shoeing done. I'll see to that. But you suit yourself."

The two men entered into a brief, foolish staring contest which Kegs won with little effort. The difference was, of course, that Kegs had all he needed at the moment, while the horse still needed a shoe. Since most of life is driven by wants or needs, the victory, such as it was, belonged to Kegs.

Gunter Stakes, the smith who rented a small space from Kegs, was busy fitting an iron tire to a large wagon wheel. The tire had been made and rough-fitted before being removed and laid into a ring of coal fire Gunter had been stoking for the past half hour. He was carefully shoveling the hot coals over the steel to bring it to a uniform high temperature. His son, fourteen-year-old Peter, was standing by with a pair of tongs in hand. When the time was exactly right, Gunter would grab a pair of matching tongs, and together they would lift the red-hot iron and lay it on the wooden wheel. The smithy would then very carefully hammer the tire into place, leaving it to cool. The wooden spokes and rim would creak and snap a bit as the tire cooled, shrunk, and tightened. It was a process that couldn't be interrupted without having to start over, something Gunter was not likely to do.

"Need a shoe."

"Tie your animal to the fence. Come back in an hour."

"Can't wait."

"Then go somewhere else."

The now angry man led his gelding back to the front of the barn and spoke to Kegs.

"Need another smith. Where will I find one?"

"Only one in town is right where you just came from."

"Stubborn fool sent me away. I'm in a hurry here."

Kegs, still sitting in the tipped back chair, leaned his head back against the unpainted barn siding, and lifted his hat brim just enough to get a better look at the demanding man. He grinned just a bit of a grin, shook his head, and said, "Fella. This here is a big country. I don't know where you're heading to, you and your lady. But that four-horse hitch of yours, the ones you ain't fed, watered, nor paid any attention to their comfort since you trotted them into town, won't miss the one hour it would take to just be patient. Maybe go for lunch after you care for the animals. I expect Gunter will get 'er done, by and by, and you'll be no worse off for the downtime."

"I told you I'm in a rush here, old man. Now you get off that chair and direct your man to get at this shoe."

"Ain't my man. Ain't my issue. I guess you got it to do, fella."

Unnoticed by the horseman, but watched by Kegs, Marshal Wiley was approaching from his office. There was another man. A stranger. Walking across the dusty road with a carbine cradled under his elbow. Kegs had taken notice when the fella had parked his two-horse rig behind the big, covered wagon the complainer had parked there. It was no fancy rig such as that already there. The box was smaller, although still heavily loaded. There were no hoops nor any white canvas top. There was simply a ground sheet stretched across the back to protect the goods from the dust, the direct heat of the sun, and the scattered rains that blessed the country.

Along with the man, a woman, and two young girls had been sitting on the seat. A boy, a bit older, judging by looks and size, had ridden alongside on a ten-dollar horse. There was no sign of wealth in any of the setup. The woman looked weary and trail worn. The girls looked mystified, covered in dust, hair a tangle of dust and days-old braids. One of the girls didn't look quite right, but Kegs couldn't sort that out from the distance. The boy on the horse sat tall in his saddle. At least as tall as a thirteen-year-old can sit, studying everyone and everything in town from that high vantage point, as if he had assigned himself the task of keeping watch over his family. *Going to grow into a man, that one,* Kegs thought, as he studied the boy, the rig, and the people.

When Wiley came within talking distance, he asked, "What's happened here, Kegs? I'm hearing shouting. Got no real patience for shouting on a nice day like this. Almost always leads to something else that, in turn, leads to me having to get out of my chair and do some work. Too nice a day for that. Day for enjoying life and letting others do the same."

Now speaking directly to the man who was grasping the lead to his gelding with a fierce, knuckle-whitening grip as he attempted to hold back his anger in the face of a visit from the marshal, Wiley asked, "What's the big hurry here, fella. And all the shouting?"

The second man who had been crossing the road spoke up, entering the conversation with, "I can tell you what the man's hurry is. Needs to get on his way, hoping to not be found again soon. Running, he is. Him and his woman.

"This man and his woman are thieves. Stole from me. And from who knows how many others. Broke into the cabin while we was out fighting fire. Stole our little bit of savings the wife kept in a sugar bowl in the cold pantry. Stole a hanging, salted, and smoked ham from the smokehouse. Two sides of bacon wrapped in cheese-cloth. Stole what-all I couldn't just exactly tell, what with all the mess he made in the cabin, tearing 'er apart searching for treasure, which we don't have any more of than it takes to keep body and soul fed and clothed. Stole my Winchester .44 Henry Yellowboy carbine. Stole a double twelve shotgun and a box of shells."

The man holding the gelding was bursting with indignation. Whether real or feigned, Wiley couldn't tell. But he finally burst out with, "Them there is all lies. I never seen this man before, nor do I have any idea where this cabin he talked about is located. We're just traveling through. Sold out in Oklahoma. Moving on to Arizona. Prescott, to be exact. I get a shoe on this horse, and we'll be gone. Anymore rough talk from this man, and I'll have my say. And I'll say it with my Colt. Ain't anyone ever successfully argued with me after that."

Wiley was looking at the two men and listening carefully. When both men seemed to have spoken what was on their minds, Wiley suggested, "Why don't we go over to the wagons and just take a look? It's hard to identify a ham or a side of bacon. And savings from the sugar bowl would look like any other money, I suspect, unless there was something different in the coins. But that Henry might be right there, ready to tell us a story. Or the shotgun. Let's just walk over there. But maybe first you tell me your names."

The accuser said, "I'm Trev Haraldson. Wife goes by Trix. Sometimes Trixie. Boy is Kreg. Girls are Willa and Eugenia.

Wiley shifted his attention to the belligerent man. He had shown signs of turning and leaving, but Wiley never took his eyes off him. "And you, sir?"

He turned back and said, "Not that it's any of your business, but I'll tell you if it means I can get this horse shod, and we can get back on the road. Names Tattersley. Felix and Charity Tattersley. There's just the two of us."

With doubt written all over his face, Wiley asked, "And have you ever used any other names, Mr. Tattersley?"

"Name's just what I said it is."

"Alright, lets us go over to the wagons and take a look."

"You ain't look'n in my wagon, Mr. Lawman. You got no right."

"Oh, but I have. There's been a serious complaint made. Neither of you are leaving town until we sort that out. Kegs, would you mind taking the man's gelding around to the smith? He might just as well do up that shoe while we're all working this through."

Reluctantly, Kegs dropped the front two legs of his chair onto the ground and rose, easing his weight carefully onto his work-weakened knees. He took the lead from Tattersley's hand, only because the marshal had asked, and headed down the center aisle of the barn. Tattersley watched in frustration, remembering that he had been sent around the outside. It wasn't really something to choose to fight about, but it dug at his pride just the same.

Trev Haraldson led the way to the wagons. Both women, having completed their shopping, were standing beside their own rigs several feet apart. There appeared to be no communication between them. Perhaps there was a hint of hostility in the air.

DURING THE STOP, Kreg Haraldson had led the team to the town water trough and pumped it full while the horses drank. He then cared for the gelding he had been riding and the other, part Appaloosa, that had been trailing the wagon on a lead. With that done, he had moved the wagon again, right behind the Tattersley rig, close enough that Tattersley would have trouble gaining access to the tied canvas flaps at the back. As he sat with the reins in his hand, the pettiness of the move rang an unwelcome bell in his youthful mind. As quietly as he could, he tugged gently on the reins and said, "Back, team. Back, you horses."

Reluctantly the animals moved the wagon back until there was a five-foot span of clearance. The distance opened just in time for the marshal and the two wagon men to step into the space vacated.

As the men stopped, standing in a rough circle, the two women and the young girls moved a bit closer. The women were still keeping a discrete distance from each other. The girls were huddled close to their mother. Kreg, the son, sat on his horse, moving his eyes from one person to another, finally focusing on the marshal. Wiley, like Kegs had a few minutes before, noticed there was something wrong with one of the girls. Reverting his eyes to Trev Haraldson, Wiley said, "Alright now, with everyone else keeping quiet, tell me your story. Then we'll hear what Tattersley has to say.

"But first, I'll have your guns. Lay them right there on the boardwalk. Carbines and pistols. Whatever you're carrying."

When Tattersley jumped in with an objection that sounded like a threat, Wiley calmly said, "Mr. Tattersley, you can either peacefully lay your weapons on the boardwalk where we can all see them, or I'll take them from you. And put you in the cell, to boot."

It took only a moment for a sneer to form on the big man's lips. Then, as if speaking to an inferior, he said, "You think you're man enough to do that?"

With almost no visible effort, Wiley swept Tattersley's feet from under him with a sweep on his own foot and a slight shove on his shoulder. As Tattersley began falling, he reached out for the tailgate of his wagon, seeking support. Wiley had lifted his Colt as he was swinging his foot. He used it to tap the grasping fingers, and the bull-shouldered man let go, falling into the dust. Immediately, Wiley partially bent over him, holding his Colt just a foot from Tattersley's head. With his other hand, he lifted Tattersley's Colt from his belt and dropped it on the boardwalk.

"Mr. Tattersley, I asked you nicely. My only wish is to keep the peace and find out the truth. But I'm surely beginning to believe you have much to hide. Now, I told you I would put you in the cells if you didn't do as I asked. I'm going to do that. You can plan on it. And I'll keep you there as long as I feel the need. But first, we'll hear two stories. You can stand if you wish. I'll cuff you if you stand. Or you can stay there. You have just those two options."

Tattersley stood, not believing the marshal of this tiny town would have the courage to put him in the cuffs, but he was wrong. While he was still gaining his full balance, getting back onto two feet, Wiley snapped a cuff over his wrist. As quickly as that was done, the other cuff was snapped onto the metal handle on the back of the wagon. The handle that was meant to be an aid in climbing into the rig. A great howl of protest drowned out all other nearby noise, but Wiley was unimpressed and unrepentant.

When all was again settled down, Wiley felt his teacher-training instincts rising in him.

"You see, Mr. Tattersley, there is nothing to be gained by being belligerent. Now, I'm asking you again to be still."

Speaking to Haraldson, Wiley said, "Now, sir, your story. Make it short, and don't tell any lies."

"There's no need for lying or exaggeration, either

one. The simple truth is that this man and his woman took advantage of our busyness to steal from our cabin and smokehouse.

"You can see from our rig and animals that we ain't no wealthy folks. Had some hard times. Droughted out in Oklahoma. Grasshopper'd out the first year in Kansas. Then the Kansas drought took another crop. Decided to try 'er once more. Had a good crop showing until a grass fire, starting who knows how many miles to the north, driven by its own wind, and came swirling across the land. Burned out our wheat and what little bit of fence we had managed to build. Lost most of the crop to fire and half of our few cattle to fire and fear. Managed to round up a few head, but the others might have run till they were in Missouri for all I could tell. Might still be running.

"The thing is, our little girl there, she ain't just quite right. You can probably see that by looks. We spent near enough all we had, taking her to the big city doctors looking for help. It was not to be. You can tell without even a word from me that she would be a danger to herself if we took her out to fight fire. Fact is, the fire was too big to fight anyway, but we tried. We surely tried. But a hundred strong men couldn't have put down those leaping flames.

"Now Eugenia there, she has a special place in the yard she loves to hide in. And that's where she was, all the while we was out trying to save our wheat. There's a big ol' oak tree. The cabin was built some years ago in the shade of that tree. Built by someone before our time.

"I built a ladder that was easy to climb. I fitted a seat to Eugenia's favorite tree limb. She spent many an hour just sitting in that tree. Sometimes she'd sing at the top of her voice, and sometimes she'd sit still and quiet so's the birds would come close. She named a bunch of birds as if they were family.

"Thing is, that's exactly where she was sitting when these folks drove their wagon into the yard. We didn't get many visitors. Too far off any good trail, and too close to Dodge City. Most folks just went right on through, leaving us in peace. Perhaps these folks saw the fire and decided the cabin would be empty of people. And they were right to think so. What they didn't know was that our little Eugenia was sett'n right there in that big ol' tree, watching everything they did."

Wiley couldn't help noticing Felix Tattersley chewing the inside of his lips as he struggled to remain quiet while the story rolled out. Occasionally, he glanced at his wife, Charity, as if seeking comfort or some such. But Charity looked as if she was ready to run, except there was nowhere to run to, and the gathering crowd had encircled her, making escape unlikely.

The story continued. "We gave up the fight on the fire and knew we had to run for our lives, expecting we might even lose the cabin. Thankfully, that didn't happen, as the wind changed direction, but it was a close thing. When we saw what had been done to our cabin and fixn's, we loaded up just as fast as we could, gathered up our few cows and saddle horses, and lit out for Dodge, hoping to somehow find the thieves. We weren't no way look'n for such a wagon as you see here. We thought maybe some cowboys who had spent too much time tipping the jug. But when we were driving slowly down the main street of Dodge, Eugenia points and starts to scream and cry. She don't know too many words, but she knows enough to point out this wagon and Tattersley there and cry out, 'Bad man. Bad man.'

"I questioned her carefully if this was the man who

had come to the cabin. Again, she shouted out, 'Bad man. Bad man.'

"Tattersley, I didn't know his name until you got it from him, Marshal, he was just walking to the gun shop with my Yellowboy in his hand. Hoping to sell it off for cash, I'm guessing. Well, Tattersley, he heard the girl shouting and turned to look. Then he bellowed for his woman to get on the wagon. He ran to untie the team and stepped into the seat. He threw my Yellowboy into the back and drove off as fast as that team could run.

"I followed from a bit of a distance, losing ground every minute. You can see that my scrubs would have no chance of keeping up with a four-animal team on the run. We've followed by watching for tracks and camping spots. Caught up a couple of times, but they always outran us. Took a few shots at us a time or two, trying to drive us off. We was stuck, hoping to catch them camped out or maybe with a broken wheel or some such like that. They were avoiding towns, not that there's many to avoid between Dodge and here. A lot of country but not many towns."

Charity Tattersley, seeing the temper of the town moving toward the storyteller, eased back and took a step away from the crowd. Politely, the crowd, none of whom were about to lay a hand on a woman no matter what she had done, were making room. But Kegs had wandered over from his livery. He had staked out a position right behind the woman. When she began easing away, he said quietly, almost right into her ear, "Why don't you just stand by, lady? Hear out the rest of the story."

So quietly did she speak that only Kegs heard her when she said, "I guess the story's about come to an end."

Nevertheless, she turned back to the street and tried

to become invisible to the staring crown that had gathered. She ended up closing her eyes and shutting off her ears. She had heard enough and could guess the ending.

Thirty seconds, passing as if it were geologic time, waiting for the river to wash out the Grand Canyon while everyone stood still and quiet, left Wiley with little to say other than, "Well, Mr. Tattersley, or you, Mrs. Tattersley, do you wish to tell a different story? I promised you the opportunity, and this is the time."

Another long wait led to hearing Tattersley doing no more than shuffling his feet. Wiley said, "Mrs. Tattersley, I'd recommend that you check into the hotel. You're going to be in town for a while, and you won't have access to the wagon.

Mr. Kegs, I'd appreciate it if you would take this wagon and store it inside your barn. I don't want anyone getting into it. Mrs. Tattersley, you may go along and take out whatever you need for the next few days. Any food that might spoil too. Kegs will see to the safety of the rest of your belongings. And your horses. Your husband will be in the cell over at the office."

Kegs waited while Wiley unclipped the handcuff from the wagon before he took the lead horse by the bridle strap and led the rig across the road. There was no need to mention costs. Sheriff Rory and Marshal Wiley had worked out a system of sharing rewards and other funds coming in from the services of the lawmen. His costs would be covered.

31

With Tattersley safely stored away in the cell and Mrs. Tattersley shyly, reluctantly, and showing much embarrassment, asking for a room in the hotel, Wiley walked to Judge Anders P. Yokam's office. After being welcomed in, Wiley got right down to business.

"Sir, I need a favor, and you're the only one I can think of to ask. Both Sheriff Rory and Deputy Cap are away. I have a heavily loaded wagon impounded and stored safely inside Keg's big barn. The team is also under his care. The wagon belongs to an accused thief and his wife. When the accusations were publicly made, the accused had nothing to say in rebuttal. The case appears to be solid and difficult to defend against.

"Now, the thing is, I don't know what-all is in that wagon. I know what the accusations are, but I have no physical proof. If I search the wagon alone, I could be accused of planting evidence. I would very much appreciate you accompanying me as an observer."

The judge laid down his pen after wiping the nib, rose, and reached for his jacket.

"I seldom get a chance to escape this office, although there is little enough call for the services of the court. I am pleased to stand as an observer in this case. I remind you that in a big city court, with much more formality than we generally deem to be sufficient out here in what many refer to as the frontier, I could be seen as being in a conflict of interest. That would mean I couldn't sit in on the case. But we'll go take a look at the wagon and see where it goes from there."

~

WILEY LEFT the judge in Keg's care while he sought out Trev Haraldson. That didn't take long, as the services and security of Keg's wagon yard had been taken up as the Haraldson's home for the next few days. They would live out of their wagon, cooking outside, a safe distance from the barn and haystack.

~

THE JUDGE, Kegs, and Haraldson stood behind Wiley as he untied the bindings holding the rear canvas flaps together. Charity Tattersley had told Wiley she would prefer to clean up in the hotel and get a rest before going to the wagon.

With the flaps pushed back and tied off, allowing a bit of light in, the men stood four abreast across the tail-gate, looking in wonder at the accumulation of bedding, foodstuffs, both smoke-cured and preserved in glass canning jars, small items of fancy furniture, none of them seeming to create a cohesive pattern, as if the pieces had come from hither and yon as they became available. Two closed steamer trunks pushed to the front, close behind the driver's seat, hid whatever was inside. Other items in the jumble were difficult to identify until it was all pulled apart and sorted out. Wiley reached in and lifted a torn blanket. That act exposed a collection of weapons; holstered handguns, rifles and carbines, and two shotguns.

Trev Haraldson immediately said, "There's my Yellowboy, and that double shotgun with the scratched-up stock is mine too. They most likely ate the ham and the two sides of bacon. The money would have gone into their pockets. But those guns are mine, no doubt about that."

The men were silent for a few seconds as the implications of what they were seeing soaked in. The judge broke the silence.

"No normal couple would travel like that. There's hardly room enough to get in for shelter from the rain, let alone get a night's sleep. We could almost refer to the load as chaos. No system or sorting to it. I'm convinced you're correct in your suspicions, Marshal, and that you men can be trusted. Get a paper and pencil, Marshal, and make a list as you go through it all. Don't throw anything away, no matter what shape it's in. And make sure all those weapons are unloaded. I'll be available if you need further assistance."

Wiley stepped back to the dirt floor of the barn and re-tied the back flaps. Speaking to Kegs and Trev Haraldson, he said, "I'm going to talk with a certain young woman, and then I'm going to have lunch. I'd appreciate it if you could meet me here again in a couple of hours."

AFTER RECEIVING the room number from the hotel desk, Wiley climbed to the second floor and walked the length of the hallway to room 216. A knock on the door brought a quiet, "Who's there?"

"Marshal Wiley, ma'am. We need to talk. Open the door, please."

Charity Tattersley had taken the time alone to clean herself up and put on town clothing. The change was remarkable. She was really a very attractive woman, if a man could look under the sun-squint lines around her eyes. Her manner had also been adjusted. With a smile and a glad "Come in, Marshal," Wiley took a step backward. He wasn't a sophisticated man of experience, but he saw danger in the woman. His immediate internal warning was to stay away and out of the room.

"Ma'am, we must talk. We can't do it in your room. It wouldn't be proper. We can't do it at the office because your husband is locked up over there. My suggestion is that you accompany me to the dining room. We will take the corner table I often use and talk quietly. No one will overhear us."

SEATED IN THE DINING ROOM, the woman seemed almost eager to talk. Figuring something was amiss, Wiley decided to play along. For a while, at least. He took notes while the woman talked, blaming everything on Felix Tattersley while declaring her own innocence. At one point, she coyly said, "You know how it is, Marshal. A woman has no real rights. When her husband takes a direction, she has no choice but to go along, no matter how much she wishes to do otherwise. I begged Felix to stop what he was doing. I tried to tell him he was bound to get caught. I even threatened to leave him in Dodge, get on the train, and head home to Kentucky. He threatened me with harm, so I stayed, scared half to death the whole time."

Wiley slowly ate his lunch while he thought of ways to trap this woman in her own obvious lies. Laying his fork and knife across the empty plate, he studied the eyes that were staring at him. Then, thinking of the jumble of stolen goods in the back of the wagon and the folks those goods had been taken from, he began to feel a new anger. This woman was as guilty as sin, he was convinced of that. He was obviously young and unsophisticated in the ways of women and the world in general. And this beautiful woman was trying to play with him. Now, the question was how to turn that to his advantage.

"So, Mrs. Tattersley—"

"Please, call me Charity."

Stifling a grin, Wiley said, "Well, alright, Charity. I'm not sure that's the exact proper thing to do, but if you insist."

"I insist, Marshal Wiley. After all, friends should be open and honest with friends, don't you think?"

"I'm not quite sure what to think, Charity. But the important thing now is to sort out the truth about the wagon, horses, and the accumulation of stuff filling the wagon almost to overloading. I need you to start at the beginning. Is the wagon really Tattersley's, or is it stolen?"

That question brought on an avalanche of admissions and accusations, all blaming her husband and attempting to reinforce the innocence of Charity Tattersley herself. Wiley was buying none of it, but he took notes and listened politely while the woman talked of raiding ranches and homesteads while the folks were away or out working. The team and wagon were stolen. Wiley wrote down the name of the Texas ranch they had come from. The saddle horses had been stolen a couple of years before. She couldn't remember where they were from. On and on the tale of thefts went. And joining that tale were stories of sales made along the way. Most of the sales were guns, an easy sell on the frontier.

Their target for the remainder of the stolen items was Denver. They would sell the wagon and team there too. Then, with just the saddle horses and the wealth gained from their drive across five states, they would head to the gold fields and then the sunshine of the west coast.

Wiley shook his head as he listened and wrote. The daring and audacity of the whole scheme was new to his experience. That Wiley knew the woman was lying to save her own skin, he would hold to himself for the time being. He would need some supporting evidence before moving to laying charges and calling the judge. The telegraph. Sheriff Rory had made great strides in the use of the telegraph for law-keeping. There was no reason Wiley couldn't do the same. He would write out a wire and find someone to ride to Cheyenne. But first, another question.

"Charity, I really appreciate your forthrightness with me. And I'm sorry you felt trapped in your husband's scheme. So, just one more question. Is Tattersley your husband's original name, or has he used other names over the years, ending up with Tattersley?"

The question seemed to trouble Charity. She looked down at the table and fidgeted with her teacup. Finally, she raised her head and said, "Cowley. Felix Cowley. That's the family name."

With all of the Marshal's questions asked and Charity ready to go back to her hotel room, she first tried to outwit him.

"Marshal Wiley. I've told you all there is to tell. And this may be my one opportunity to escape the clutches of that awful man. I'm thinking you don't really need me anymore. If I could have my saddle and horse, I could get on my way. And—"

"Mrs. Tattersley. Or perhaps I should say Mrs. Cowley, I'd hate to have you try to run on me. I'm young and green at this job, but perhaps not quite as green as you think. You run, I'll catch you, and don't you doubt it. By all that's right, you should be in the other cell, next to your husband. I'm giving you a break by letting you stay here in the hotel. Don't do anything that you'll regret."

"Why, Wiley, I thought we had come to an understanding."

"We have. I understand that you are an accomplished liar and that you would sacrifice anything and anybody to save your own hide. Now go back to your room and stay there."

He stood and left her sitting by herself. She didn't lift her head to watch him leave, so she missed when Wiley spoke to the hotel manager. The hotel would be on extra alert during the woman's stay.

32

WILEY FOUND A RIDER TO DELIVER THE TELEGRAM TO Cheyenne for distribution, but somehow, he didn't think he would need it. He knew he had shaken Charity Tattersley to the bone when she had told her story so freely and was then summarily dismissed as an innocent party to her husband's thievery. The obvious truth was that there was a very good chance of them both going to jail. But what would the scheming woman do? That was the question. Wiley was alone. No Sheriff Rory. No Deputy Cap. That thought had repeated itself in his mind for hours. It was all up to him.

Finally deciding on a plan, he returned to the hotel and spoke quietly to the desk manager again.

"I'm taking a bit of a risk here, Sid, but I don't think there will be any violence. It's about Mrs. Tattersley. Tell your staff that if they see her walking around or sneaking out of the building, to just let her go. I'll be watching from outside."

Stifling the desire to ask further questions, Sid nodded and said, "Will do."

THE QUIET HOURS of late afternoon and evening passed uninterrupted while Wiley took some rest, advising Kegs to do the same. They would bank some rest against the hours of darkness to come. Hours when Wiley was betting there would be a need for the law to show itself in the little village known as the Fort.

With darkness, Wiley vacated the marshal's office, leaving the door unlocked but with the gun rack emptied of all but the gun and belt taken from Tattersley earlier in the day. And that gun was left unloaded. The cell door key was hanging from its normal wooden peg beside the desk.

At Wiley's request, Gunter Stakes would take a position at the rear door of the livery barn. He would be armed, but they all hoped to avoid a shooting. The door had been blocked so it couldn't easily be opened. Kegs would be in his own darkened room inside the barn, awake and ready.

Wiley had positioned himself alongside the shed the town wood seller had built years before to keep the weather off his product for sale. It was very close to the office and jail, a convenient location to watch and listen from. It provided a good hiding place and also good shelter if shooting began sooner than Wiley expected. Nothing could drive a bullet through a stack of firewood. From that position, Wiley could see the front street but not the doors of either the office or the barn. He would be depending on movement and the sound of voices or opening doors.

And so, they waited.

FINALLY, at what Wiley guessed was about two hours after midnight, a shadow, created by a runner sneaking through the light cast by the weather-worn lantern that hung on the outside of the barn, warned Wiley that it was time for extra vigilance. Charity Tattersley ran silently within a few feet of where Wiley was staked out. He heard the snick of the opening office door and then a whispered, "Good girl. Get that key but be quick about it. And don't make any noise."

It was only seconds before two figures made their way cautiously through the dark of the night to the livery barn door. There wasn't much light, but Wiley could see Tattersley quickly loading his Colt from the ring of shells on the belt.

Wiley thought, *'be careful, if nothing else,'* before he took a couple of steps away from the shed and watched as Tattersley opened the single door that was used when the big sliding doors were closed. It was meant for walkers but was wide enough to allow a saddled horse to pass through.

As the two thieves entered the barn, Wiley saw another movement. This time from the wagon shed attached to the side of the building. The lantern light said it was Trev Haraldson, armed and sneaking toward the barn door. He could ruin everything.

Wiley broke from his cover and ran as silently as riding boots and a dirt road would allow. Haraldson saw him approaching and was about to call out when he picked up on the meaning of Wiley's waving arms. Cutting Haraldson off before he reached the door, Wiley said, "You go back to your wagon. Stay there. You hear me? And keep your family quiet. No talk. Absolutely none. Now go."

Reluctantly, Haraldson nodded and turned around. But that unforeseen interruption had caused Wiley to lose track of the sounds from within the barn. He was left with no choice. He would have to enter the building before he had planned to.

Knowing the outside lantern was lighting the door opening, Wiley dropped to his knees and then his belly. He crawled, pushing his carbine before him, until he was through the door and off to the side, into total darkness. Only then did he stand again. He could hear some whispering from where the wagon was stored. Carefully, he eased forward, his arms out before him, hoping to feel any obstruction before he ran into it.

A whispered, "Get that money box from outa the wagon and be quiet about it. I'll saddle the horses. We ain't going to be able to move the wagon."

"How are you going to find our horses in this dark?"

"Leave that to me. You do as you were told. And if you can grab up that Yellowboy without making no noise, I'd like that too."

Wiley felt a big, loft-supporting post with his left hand. It wasn't quite wide enough to shelter him completely, but if he turned sideways, it would be close. Close enough. He had heard Keg's door open and knew he had backup.

"Stand down Tattersley. I've been wait—"

The voice, and any other sound, were overshadowed by the blast of a .45 Colt. Wiley could hear the 'thunk' of lead as it drove into the fir tree post. Even as he was levering his carbine, aiming at the gun flash, Wiley was thinking, *fast. That man is good with a weapon.*

Shooting at gun flashes in the dark, when you have no idea where the shooter had moved to or if the woman was in the line of fire, was a poor way to keep the law at the Fort. Wiley had been reasonably certain Tattersley would give it up. The chances of shooting it out with the marshal in the black of night, then finding and saddling two horses, and still hoping to make a getaway, was a bit of a stretch. But there had been no surrender or even the mention of it. Tattersley had turned and fired. The woman had screamed, and no doubt ducked out of the way. Wiley had no idea if he had hit anything. All this went through his mind in the flash of time. His thoughts were drawn to a close by a second roar of the .45. Again, he shot at the flashing light but heard no sound of lead on flesh. The thump of his bullet sounded more like it hit wood. Probably a stall partition.

Kegs—more mature, more hardened, and far more cynical than Wiley—let go with first one barrel of his twelve gauge and then the other, toward where he figured the wagon was stored, moving the barrel just a bit to the left, before he shot the second time. This time Wiley heard a shot hit flesh. There could be no doubt. That sickening sound was followed quickly by another scream from the woman, a Colt firing, and a body falling back onto a stall. The last shot showed the fire pointing toward the dirt floor.

Wiley hollered, "Enough. Everyone, stand down. There's no use in dying over a stolen gun. Now, stand down."

When there was no verbal response, Wiley said, "Mrs. Tattersley, call out. Where are you?"

The response was a sob, followed by a weak, "Right over here. By the wagon wheel. I'm shot."

"Where's your husband?"

"I'm not sure. I think that shotgun did it for him, but I just don't know for sure."

"Alright. Kegs is bringing a lantern. I'll be watching every move. Any attempt to shoot when the lantern brightens the room will result in me shooting you. I don't want to do that, but I surely will. You can plan on it."

Kegs walked out of his little living space with the bail of the lit lantern hung over the end of a broomstick, holding the light several feet from his body. It wasn't much assurance, but it was all he could think of on short notice. When there was no reaction from either of the thieves, he stepped more quickly along the alley, brightening the room as he walked. Wiley stepped away from the post where he could see Tattersley slumped against a horse stall with his chest and a part of his face punctured with shell shot. Much of his shirt and jacket were blown away. The remainder was a swamp of blood and gore. Charity Tattersley, who had scrambled to a standing position, took a quick look, screamed, and threw up. Then she sagged once again to the floor.

Wiley waited while Kegs hung the lantern on a peg at the top of another post. Then the two men approached with their weapons at the ready. A brief glance from a closer vantage point assured the men that Tattersley would not be firing any more shots. Charity was folded up on the floor, almost in a fetal position, sobbing and muttering unintelligible words. The way she was lying, it was impossible to see how much lead shot she had taken, although there was blood enough on her shirt, and some dribbling down her neck from a wound near her jaw.

Wiley lifted Tattersley's .45 off the floor and stuck it behind his own belt. He then walked to where Charity was lying.

"How badly are you hurt? Can you get up? Stand if you can, and we'll get you to the doc's clinic."

Unnoticed by either Wiley or Kegs, Gunter Stakes had made his way around the building and come in the front door. Beside him stood Trev and Trixie Haraldson. Trixie stepped forward, saying, "You men get yourselves gone. Let me see to the woman."

"Let's make sure she's unarmed first."

Wiley bent and felt all around and under the crying woman, finding nothing on the floor. He then said, "Mrs. Haraldson, you feel all around her clothing while I'm here. I'm not leaving you alone with her until you do. This is not a person you can trust."

Instead of the men retreating to the outside, they moved further into the building, where they were out of sight but still within easy range if Charity somehow was to cause a problem for Trixie. There was no need, as they knew soon enough.

Paying no attention to the men, the two women slowly walked to the front door, with Charity leaning heavily on the other woman. Trixie Haraldson now had blood on her clothing too. As they neared the door, Charity's knees folded, and she collapsed to the floor. Gunter Stakes said, "I'll get her to the docs. I'll want the woman and one man to come with me."

As he bent and picked up the still form, acting as if she was no heavier than a shadow, Trixie Haraldson said, "Trev, come with us. You might be needed. And you're not needed here."

There was silence in the barn as they watched the small group of rescuers moving along the slowly brightening road. It must have been further into the short early summer night than Wiley had guessed. The predawn light was well underway across the eastern flatlands.

Although no one had ventured outside, that Wiley

could see anyway, there were a few lights showing that wouldn't normally be lit for another couple of hours.

Kegs quietly said, "I'm guessing that about wraps that up."

"For you. But not for me. Not by a long shot, my friend. Not by a long shot. It proves guilt on both of them, but now I have a wagon to sort out and a woman to stand before the judge. I don't look forward to either of those jobs. Anyway, Kegs, did I thank you yet for the help? I don't believe I did. So, thank you."

Kegs, never comfortable with receiving thanks, grumped, "I have some coffee in the pot that might still be drinkable."

Wiley followed along. If nothing else, the coffee would delay the rest of the cleanup for a short while.

WHEN FULL DAWN finally arrived Wiley could no longer delay the miserable task of hauling Tattersley to the undertaker's shed. He borrowed a light wagon from Kegs and, with the livery man's help, managed to lift the heavier man into the wagon box. As Wiley was walking away, leading the single horse out of the barn, Kegs was kicking dirt over the mess left behind, where his shotgun had put an end to the exploits of one Felix Tattersley. Or, as Wiley had told him, perhaps it was Felix Cowley.

Wiley returned the wagon, unhitched the horse, and put everything back where Kegs normally kept it. He then went to the marshal's office, lit a fire, heated water, stripped off his now filthy shirt, and tried to get clean. He soon gave it up as hopeless. Putting a shirt on that had only seen one day's use and tucking a roll of clean clothing under his arm, he went to order water for a bath at the barbershop. He had breakfast at the small café a block down from the hotel while he waited for the barber to heat the water. He would face the big wagon later.

33

ONCE BACK IN WASHINGTON, DEPUTY MARSHAL COL. Oliver Staveley felt much more at home. He had said nothing to the others on the train, nor would he ever, but he had the deep-seated feeling that he was out of his depth in the matter of the tarnished gold coins...and all that led from it. Heading up a supply depot during the war was hardly qualification for a peacetime national police force. But he had been sheltered within the mass and hubbub of Washington. He sometimes felt like a make-believe peace officer. Still, he believed in the force, and in his part in it. He recognized that the training was lacking but that it was improving gradually as systems were put in place. No longer was learning on the job the order of the day. But that was for the new men coming in. By the position attached to his name and title, he was exempted for that training. That it was not required for the older serving deputies was clearly a mistake.

Now he was returning to Washington from his first out-of-office assignment with both dead and wounded men. The loss of the young deputy had hit him deeply.

Cut close to his heart. He couldn't imagine the hurt and despair the young man's family would suffer with the news. He would have to locate the wife—if a wife there was—or parents, and make a point of seeing them at the appropriate time.

But now he had a report to write and present, and a job to do. Washington already knew, from wires sent back and forth, that Deputy Glover Harrison had been arrested. There would be much interrogation on that matter. With Harrison himself, of course, but also with Staveley and Sheriff Rory Jamison. Washington's top man, Marshal Jeramiah Kootenay, would demand nothing less than the entire, truthful story.

THE TRAIN HAD ARRIVED in the evening, so after seeing to the transfer of the prisoners to secure federal custody, the deputies were released to their homes. Rory and Cap were shown to a hotel, convenient to the national marshal's office. Everyone would gather, refreshed, in the morning.

RORY AND CAP WERE FRESH, clean, and rested. It was a new day. A cloudy Washington day. While it had been early spring in Colorado, it was well into that season in warmer Washington. All around the town; the hotel, the restaurant where they had breakfast, the sidewalks connecting those two addresses, and further, to the Marshals' Office—the Colorado lawmen seemed to see walkers with an energy in their steps, as if they were anxious to get about their work. That the movements were more a duty than a pleasure, they had yet to figure out.

In the West they were familiar with, the energy was very much there, but it was a more subdued energy. A cowboy saddling his horse in the morning wasn't rushing into the task. He might look almost casual about it, but familiarity made the job easier. That same rider would swing effortlessly into the leather, lay the reins across the horse's neck, and roll a smoke as his animal jogged out of the ranch yard. What the unfamiliar watcher might not recognize was that the same horse and rider would carry the same laconic expression in looks and work until the sun was setting.

The shouting, anxious riders and drivers of wagons and carriages on the Washington streets, demonstrated none of the ease of the western cowboy. The contrast could be easily misunderstood.

When the first pedestrian bumped shoulders with Cap on the busy sidewalk from the hotel to the restaurant, he stopped, ready to offer a "'scuse me" apology. But when he turned to the man, all he saw was the back of a rushing walker. The man had clearly not taken note of the mild collision. Cap was bumped again as he stood watching the retreating form. He turned—this time to Rory, who had also stopped—as if expecting the sheriff to offer an explanation. But Rory was grinning at the sight. When they turned again to the eating house, Rory barely managed to sidestep as another walker, this time a woman, brushed past without seeing him. He was about to tip his hat, but the lady was gone.

～

FINALLY, seated, with menus laid before them, they stared out the window, watching all the activity. Cap, having thought out some of the activity, said, "You could add the entire fort to this one street, and no one would even take note."

Rory turned from the window and picked up the menu. "That's a lot of folks, for sure. Even makes Denver look small by comparison."

❧

DEPUTY MARSHAL COL. Oliver Staveley entered the office looking rested. His wound had much healing to do, but he managed to look reasonably dressed and groomed, even with his right arm hanging slackly in a sling and with that empty jacket sleeve pinned at the front so it wouldn't flap around. He carried his leather satchel in his left hand.

Several voices welcomed him home. One voice, that of his superior, was silent. But the thumb pointing over his shoulder to the big corner office told it all. He was to make his way immediately to the office of Marshal Jeramiah Kootenay.

Staveley removed his hat and tucked it awkwardly under his right arm. Then, standing as straight and tall as his aging body would allow, he moved to the office door and tapped three times with his knuckles. The response, "Come in," was returned almost immediately.

Managing the doorknob with the same hand that was holding the leather satchel was awkward, but he got it done. He stepped in and said, "Good morning, sir."

"Close the door and take a seat."

As Oliver Staveley eased into the chair opposite his boss, the head marshal said, "Welcome home, Oliver. I'm anxious to hear all about the trip. Perhaps, first, tell me what happened to your arm."

"It isn't really the arm, sir. It's the upper chest. Collar bone and whatever else God put there to make our lives easier."

"Right. But that doesn't tell me what happened."

"A little bit of a skirmish on the train, sir. And my small wound, which received adequate medical help in a town along the way, is the smaller part of the trouble. It hurts me deeply to report, sir, that we lost a man."

The Marshal said nothing in response, but his eyes and manner were saying, "Keep talking."

"It happened on the train. We had prepared well, I thought then, and still think. Even with the loss and the wounds. If there was any part that I was unprepared for, it was to be attacked right on the train."

Oliver Staveley, at his boss's insistence, continued with the long tale. Even after asserting that he had it all written out in his lengthy report, Marshal Jeramiah Kootenay wanted to hear it firsthand.

The telling was delayed just long enough for the marshal to walk to the door and beckon three senior deputies. He wanted them to be fully conversant with the matter. No one thought it had ended with the trip to the West. There would be work still to do. Much work.

As Staveley talked, all of the officers were taking notes. Scratching down names especially. When the story wound to a conclusion, the room turned to silence. Every eye was on deputy Marshal Col. Oliver Staveley. In discomfort, he tried to hide his urge to squirm in his seat.

Marshal Kootenay finally broke the silence, saying, "And now the two local sheriffs from this village you mentioned are seated in the foyer under supervision. Is that correct, Deputy?"

"Yes. I spoke to them as I entered. There is really no purpose in holding them under supervision, as you say, but which could as easily be called guarding."

The ex-supply officer had never spoken to a senior officer in that manner before. To some hard nose officers, his words could almost be seen as insubordination. He wasn't sure he cared any longer. He had trained originally as a schoolteacher. His qualifications could even take him to a college as a professor. The job was gaining in attraction day by day. Maybe. Perhaps his talents could be used in the new West. He would think of that and discuss it with his wife. In any case, the marshal didn't call him on it.

What the marshal did say was, "It's good you brought them along. One, at least, was in this thing from the beginning. I believe I would like to hear from them now.

A deputy was assigned to escort Rory and Cap to the Marshal's Office. Another deputy carried in more chairs.

34

RORY AND CAP MOVED INTO THE OFFICE AND TOOK SEATS where the escorting deputy indicated, which was unnecessary as they were the only unused chairs in the room. They lifted their hats off and balanced them over their knees. Rory had yet to untie his long, leather coat. As if it was some kind of conspiracy between men, Oliver Staveley said nothing, although he was sure the two Westerners were still fully armed.

Staveley himself made the introductions, simply giving the two names without signifying which man belonged to which handle. No one offered to shake hands or make any show of welcome. The surrounding faces were universally grim.

Rory grinned inside at the thought that these men were seeing them as small-time. Amateurs with little to offer. Men to be used for their information and then dismissed. The thoughts of others had never bothered him. He doubted that Cap noticed or cared.

Clearing his throat, Jeremiah Kootenay said, "Welcome, men. I'm sure you're anxious to return to your homes and families, so we won't detain you any longer than necessary. That you have information we wanted to hear firsthand moved me to wire Deputy Marshal Col. Oliver Staveley to bring you along. I am now told that you were of some assistance during the raid on the train. Again, thank you for that.

"Now, which of you was it that accompanied a deputy into Texas?"

Rory replied, "That would be me."

"And you would be," Kooteney referred to his notes, "Sheriff Rory Jamison."

Rory nodded and waited.

"Sheriff, I wish to know everything there is to know about that trip to Texas. I wish to know how Deputy Glover Harrison fits into the narrative. I also wish to know all you can tell me about a ranch referred to as the Big C and this Webster Cunningham who was overseeing it. And I wish to know where you thought you had received the authority to arrest one of my deputies. I'll hear that now, sir."

Again, Rory smiled inwardly, appreciating the voice of earned authority. He had no idea how the marshal had earned his position, but he was prepared to accept what was before him. He hesitated before he spoke, looking around the room at the solemn faces.

"I'd be happy to do that, sir. But I wrote it all out in detail. I had made the assumption that you would have been given a copy."

"And I was indeed given a copy, Sheriff. I have it right here in my desk. But I'm a good listener, so humor me."

"Alright, let me start at the end. Or near the end, in any case. I suppose I assumed the authority to arrest a crooked deputy when no one within your department appeared to be willing to do it. The evidence against the man is overwhelming. He did everything within his power to prevent me or any deputy marshal from examining the situation on the Big C Ranch. For my part, I felt the marshals had all the evidence needed to simply close my portion of the file. If they wished to dig further into the crime, it would be a federal matter, not a county matter.

"The original mystery was solved. The crime that impacted me and the people I serve was dealt with and put behind us, until it was shaken awake again by the marshals. I really didn't have the time to spare from my duties to ride to Texas, but at the special request of your Denver office, I agreed.

"Glover Harrison tried until the last moment to prevent anyone from riding south. He clearly did not want anyone locating the Big C Ranch or arresting and questioning Webster Cunningham. Finally, one faithful deputy, one Block Handley, challenged that restriction. The result was that it was just the two of us that rode south. Deputy Handley came very close to paying with his life for that loyalty to the marshal's service.

"Glover Harrison is a thief, a possible murderer, and a traitor to the service you all claim allegiance to. Coming out of that experience and other things that have happened along the way, my respectful question to you now, sir, is, 'Do you truly trust every man in this room?' We already know the marshal's service is compromised. To what extent, is your job to sort out? Now, I will continue with the story if you wish."

The silence in the room could be felt. With as solemn a look on his face, as any Rory had ever seen, Marshal Jeramiah Kootenay turned his eyes from man to man, not rushing, looking deeply. That he was troubled at the thought laid before him could not be hidden. What he was looking for in the men, Rory couldn't be sure. Was it fidgeting? Was it nervously wringing the hands? Was it the refusal to hold eye contact? Or was it something else entirely?

When the scrutiny was finished, the Marshal stood. He adjusted his jacket and then his tie. Only then did he speak.

"Men. We will take a break. I'm hoping someone thought to make a cup of tea. There will be coffee. That is beyond doubt. Sheriff, if you follow these men, they will lead you to where you can refresh yourself if you feel the need. Pour yourself a cup of your preferred drink. Then I would have you find chairs away from the others. Hold your silence until we are back in this room."

35

A SECRETARY POURED A CUP OF TEA FOR THE MARSHAL AND delivered it to his office, laying it quietly on the desk. Without a word, she turned and left. Rory could see part of that action through the glassed-in door. The marshal stood at the outside window sipping his tea. There was no real way to know, looking only at his back, but Rory thought he was looking at a troubled man.

A single glance toward the silent Cap confirmed that the deputy was missing nothing.

When the secretary was next seen, she was walking toward Rory and Cap.

"If you would follow me, please."

She took the empty cups from the men, set them on a nearby desk, and turned toward the marshal's office. When they were inside, she quietly closed the door. Rory and Cap were alone with Jeramiah Kootenay.

"Sit down, men."

The marshal eased into his big wooden swivel chair and leaned back with his fingers entwined over his flat stomach. He studied the two men before him as an eagle might study the grass hundreds of feet below, missing nothing. If the look was intended to unnerve these western sheriffs, it failed. Rory kept seeing a man with a problem he didn't know how to solve. They would have to wait to hear what came next before they could figure out their own next step.

"Men. We are, obviously, alone. And to set your minds at ease, be assured of a couple of things. First, I have read your report, Sheriff. More than once. I congratulate you on its thoroughness and completeness. It shows the hand and mind of an educated man. And a man I'm leaning toward trusting. Clearly, you are a man who likes to finish what you start. That was also shown in the report from some months ago, where you and Deputy Block Handley were successful in bringing a ruthless gang to justice. You might already know that Mr. Handley gives most of the credit to you, Sheriff."

Turning his head just a little, the marshal looked at Cap.

"Deputy Graham, I know very little about you. But that you are riding with the sheriff in a trust position is enough information for now. I would, however, like to know where you are from originally and where you stood as sheriff. If you would see my secretary on the way out later, she can note down that information. The other thing you need to know, men, is that you can trust me. I give you that word as a man of honor, serving his nation.

"Continuing in that vein, I will say that at this time, I trust the men that were in this room with us. But if there is a weakness in the organization, I intend to weed it out. I will excuse no one from that process or from my investigator's diligence. And, no, that was not a slip of the tongue. I have had an investigator working on this matter, behind the scenes, for a while now. That fact is known to the men. If that steps on toes, so be it.

"Now, talk to me, man to man, forgetting titles and positions. And to start that conversation, I have heard that you found a list. A list of the names of conspirators. I have yet to see that list. I rather thought you would have given it to Deputy Marshal Donavan Gaines to be included with his report."

Rory lifted the small satchel he had carried into the room and laid it open across his knees. Shuffling through several pages, he lifted one out. He leaned forward and set it on the desk.

"That, sir, is the list. I definitely gave a copy to Deputy Gaines. I kept the original for myself. That's it, lying before you. I have another copy for myself. I have no explanation for why it wasn't forwarded with the report. I'll assume it was an oversight until I know something to the contrary."

"Very diplomatic, young man. Let's hope you're correct."

The marshal took his time reading and then re-reading the incriminating list. His facial expressions varied as each name was settled into his memory. As the man read name after name, he wiped his brow occasionally and closed his eyes twice, looking grimly hurt, while his lips pursed.

He laid the paper aside and said, "Very sad, if this is what it is claimed to be. And all over such a small matter. So little money. Not small to the average man, of course, but small to a government the size of ours. Or even small when it's divided among everyone on this list, and perhaps others who are not named. Such foolishness to risk life and reputation with so little reward."

The marshal again sat silently while Rory and Cap

waited patiently. When the words came again, they were brief but hurting.

"But it wasn't money, was it? Politics. Politicians. The scramble for power."

The statement required no response. It had almost been as if the marshal was speaking to himself.

Then, as if he was making a major decision, the marshal hesitated, his eyes going from one man to the other. He lifted the single sheet of paper off the table and jiggled it, searching for his next words. They were, "Men, I need some time. You are free to go for now. Stay in town and close by. I will send for you when I'm ready.

"Washington is a beautiful city, alive with energy. New buildings on every corner, it sometimes seems. Fine eating establishments. Parks and greenspaces for your enjoyment. You may also appreciate a trip to the Capitol building. It is really quite magnificent. I would ask only two things of you. One, talk to no one at all about this matter. No one. And two, come when I send for you. Time is important in this."

36

THE SHERIFFS FROM THE FORT WERE SITTING IN A sidewalk café enjoying a lunch of food they had never heard of before. The young lady waiting on tables recommended the item. They were glad she did.

Cap studied on Rory while they ate. Finally, he said, "Your mind is many miles from here."

Rory grinned and nodded. "I have a new wife living alone many miles and days of travel from here. And a town and county that will be wondering where we are. And here I sit, facing a federal matter that is clearly over my head, wondering how things are at home."

RORY COULD HAVE no way of knowing, but at home, Wiley was having his own crises of decision-making. For only the second time, there was a woman housed in a cell in the little marshal's office. Charity Tattersley was slowly recovering from her wounds, which turned out to be more serious than Wiley had originally thought. The fight seemed to have gone out of her. It may have been the death of her husband, or it may be the obvious truth that she had little chance of avoiding serious prison time. Whatever it was, she was almost a model prisoner, if such a thing was possible. Her needs were being seen to by Birdie Stakes, the blacksmith's wife and the mother of the two kids sold by the orphanage the year before.

Charity had yet to make a confession beyond the obvious. That she and her husband had traveled across the country stealing from unoccupied dwellings could not be denied. Wiley and Kegs had torn the wagon apart. Other than clothing and food, everything else was valuable and saleable. Guns seemed to be of particular interest to Felix Tattersley. Small, heritage pieces of fine wooden furniture had also caught their eye.

Looking at the row of weapons laid out on the floor of the barn, Kegs said, "Good as money in the bank. Sell them anywhere."

Wiley found the cash box Charity was hoping to grab in their mad scramble for escape. The sum of money involved was considerable. More than most Western travelers had ever seen.

Wiley slowly, meticulously wrote a list of the items in his daybook before piling them back into the wagon. He walked to the jailhouse holding the book in one hand, laid it on the desk, and spoke to Charity.

"Ma'am, I have here a list of all the items in your wagon, a description of the horses and their brands, and the wagon itself. Now, I'm curious. Either I or the federal marshals will return as much of this as possible. That is, if the owners can be found and if the desire for their return warrants the costs and the trouble. But I need your help. You say you started in Texas and traveled through Oklahoma Territory and Kansas before arriving here. Is that true?"

"I already admitted to that. The wagon and team came from Texas. A remote ranch close to the border with Oklahoma Territory. We scooted out fast, knowing it was dangerous to hang around there any longer. We mostly crossed the Territory with few stops. We slowed coming through Kansas."

"How much did you sell along the way."

"Only some guns."

"Did the cash in the money box come from the sale of guns?"

"Mostly. We had some of our own when we left Arkansas."

The woman changed the subject, asking, "What are you planning to do now?"

"I don't exactly know. As far as I can tell, none of your crimes happened in this area. Except that Felix tried to kill me, of course. I take that quite seriously. But I can hardly charge a dead man with attempted murder, so I have little left to go on here.

"I'm sure our local judge would feel he has no jurisdiction over crimes committed in other towns and states. I've sent for the federal marshals. We seem to be involved in marshal's business too much lately, but I can't change the facts. Your thievery took place elsewhere. I expect the marshals will move you to Denver, where you can face federal charges. There is little doubt that you will end up in prison. For how long and which prison, I have no idea."

❧

THE RIDER SENT to Cheyenne with the telegram enquiring about thefts in eastern jurisdictions, returned several days later with a wad of answering wires. Wiley thumbed through them and set them aside. All the crimes reported along the trail Felix and Charity had followed were petty, and not worth the trouble of dragging the accused back across the country to face justice. If the owners of the wagon and team could be found, the story would be different. Now it was a waiting game with nothing more to do until the federals arrived.

37

In Washington, Rory and Cap started out walking after finishing their lunch. The sidewalks were even more crowded, with the warming day welcoming business-people and strollers alike. Men in business suits carrying briefcases and serious looks hurried past ladies in lovely dresses, with parasols resting on their shoulders, protecting their pale complexions from the sun.

The streets were busy with horse-drawn carriages and wagons of all sorts. Many men, and a few women, were riding saddle horses among the wagons. Pedestrians were darting every which way through the traffic in an attempt to cross the roads.

After several blocks of walking, Cap said, "There seems to be a livery barn on near-enough every block. Is there some reason we're wearing out our boot leather?"

Rory laughed, wondering why he hadn't asked himself the same question. Turning into the nearest livery, they asked about renting saddle animals.

"Well, son, unless them there duds you're decked out

is left over party costumes, I expect you can set a saddle without me having to run alongside to keep you safely mounted. Spect too that you don't want a itty-bitty saddle such as most here prefer. And you're in luck. Got me a selection of good working leather. You walk down this here aisle and pick the animals you want. I'll pull out a couple of good saddles."

After adjusting the saddles for stirrup length, the men were mounted and ready to venture out. The warning to be careful on the cobblestones was unnecessary. That they were slippery was obvious with even a casual glance.

After riding almost aimlessly for an hour, weaving here and there, as one of them saw something interest-ing, Rory slowed to a stop in the shade of a group of trees on the edge of a park. When Cap pulled up beside him, Rory said, "Ease your animal around slowly to where you're facing me. Don't study on the road or make any obvious signs of noticing anything."

The two men folded their arms on the saddle horns, sitting, perhaps, five feet apart. It was easy talking distance. Rory said, "Don't hold your eye on any one rider but take notice of the fella on the grey, wearing the bowler hat. He's sitting there as if he's not sure what to do next."

Cap made an obvious move to look toward the park, not at the man Rory had mentioned. Lifting his hand and pointing at a building rising from the ground on the opposite side of the small park as if pointing it out, Cap said, "Already seen him. Seen him when we were having lunch and then several times when we were walking. I said nothing. I thought you might have taken his note too."

"I did note him. But I thought it might be just because

we kind of stand out in this finely dressed crowd. But when he somehow turned up horseback, I took a closer look."

"He's been following us, there's no doubt. But is he the marshal's man or something else?"

"Let's move along. I can see the top of what they said was the Capitol Building. I might like to get a closer look."

Taking every opportunity to look behind them, without seeming to, the men kept track of the other rider. And then he was gone. They hadn't seen where he went. He could've turned down any corner. But, in any case, there was no sign of him.

Sitting their rented horses across the road and a half block away from the Capitol Building, Rory and Cap sat in awe. Neither had ever seen so large or so fine a building. It was a sight to look at and remember. Rory thought he might try to find a photo to take home to Julia.

Grinning in delight at his discovery, Cap said, "Let's ride off to the right. That same fella is sitting there in a buggy. It might be fun to ride right past him as if we're paying him no never mind, just to see what he'll do."

Making up their thoughts as they rode, expounding loudly on the wonders and grandeur of the big building, as if they were in a practiced stage play, the two lawmen rode very close to the buggy without even looking at the man holding the reins. The poor fella was frantic to avoid recognition, but it was too late. At the last possible moment, Rory looked directly at the man, lifted his hat just a bit, and said, "Good day, sir. Fine afternoon for a ride." With that, they were past the buggy and on their way back to the livery.

They were safely out of voice range when Cap said,

"I'm thinking you may have put a damper on his afternoon's plans."

THE EVENING WAS WARM AND MUGGY WITH HUMIDITY. Rory and Cap returned to the same café for dinner, again taking seats in the outdoor area. The staff had changed, but the new waitress turned out to be as helpful as the one at noon. She pointed at the menu and described the four choices of beef, expounding on the wonders the chef was able to perform with a simple cut of beef steak.

As a way of explanation, Rory said, "At home, we just fry 'em up, smother 'em with onions and lay 'em on the plate with potatoes fried in bacon grease."

The waitress appeared to be appalled, but perhaps she was just going along with the pointless jargon. In any case, the men ended up with a delicious plate, followed by a slice of apple pie, and to be expected, several cups of coffee.

Restless, and weary of what seemed to be their futile trip east, the men again went for a walk. The warm day was turning into a cool evening. They found the humidity to be not to their liking. Nevertheless, they kept their jackets on and the thongs tied together at the front. They had discussed the possibilities of danger, but neither had any real confidence in their understanding of the city—or of the politics and politicians driving the crime—that seemed to have no end to it. No end yet, at least. What had started out as a simple question of a tarnished gold coin had all but consumed Rory's life for far too many months. His only desire, after all those months, was to leave it to the marshals and return home.

The fort sheriffs admitted to themselves that they were unsophisticated in their knowledge of big cities and the ways of big city men. The time spent in Denver had helped. Experiencing Denver had also opened Rory's eyes to the fact that trouble could arise quickly, and from the strangest corners of town. So, as they walked, they kept their wits about them.

Neither of the men were drinkers, but they dropped a dime each for a stein of beer in two saloons just to watch and read the gathering of men. No one seemed to have a weapon in sight, but there were a few ominous bulges in poorly fitted jackets. When they left, their steins remained full.

They found themselves a half mile from their hotel when darkness descended over the city. The poorly lit streets that had so recently been alive with walkers were now empty, or nearly so. The cafés, taverns, and theaters were crowded. It was almost as if those who had so recently been outside had all moved indoors.

Shadows cast from the streetlamps struggling against the night were only partially successful, making it difficult to sort out everything within view for the western visitors.

When trouble presented itself, it was Cap who first sensed it. His warning to Rory was a halted step and a tight grip on Rory's sleeve. Silently, the two men stood their ground, waiting. Had something, or someone, moved in that darkened entryway in front of a closed and locked store? There could be some doubt of that, but there was no doubt about the rushing footsteps from behind. And then, as if answering a signal, the shadow they had been studying did move. It moved very quickly and divided into two. Two men. Armed, for sure. Whether or not they had guns could not be seen, but the clubs held half aloft were a certainty.

There was little time. The men were moving fast, and as silently as possible, closing with those coming from behind. Rory spun on his one foot to meet the two running up on them. One man hesitated for a fraction of a second while the other stepped a bit to the side to get a better swing at his prey. It was a mistake. The move brought him within arms reach of Rory. The sheriff simply grabbed the attacker by his coat front, ignoring the club that was meant to bring an end to the fight, and perhaps to the sheriffs as well.

Using the attacker's own momentum, Rory turned him in a half circle to where he could get his other hand gripping the man's leg. He lifted and spun the man off the ground, letting go when he was facing the brick front of another store. The attacker hit the wall. His head snapped back against the brick with a sickening crunch, and he fell to the sidewalk. He didn't move.

Rory bent, picked up the dropped club, and spun back toward the road. It had all happened so fast that he caught the second man still hesitating. Swinging the club sideways with all his strength, Rory caught the second man completely exposed. The club took him full across the belly, leaving him breathless and gasping, lying on the sidewalk.

Rory was in time to turn and see Cap fend off one

attacker, but the other was already swinging his club. He was close. The club was shoulder high and descending. There was no doubt he was going to lay Cap out. Cap's response was to grab his iron and squeeze the trigger just once. The man stopped all his actions as if he had been hit by a train. The club fell from his hands, and his eyes closed. He crumbled at Cap's feet and lay still. Whether he was dead or not, neither man took time to check.

The fourth man had dropped his club and run off. With three attackers laid out and possibly two of them dying—or dead—it was time for Rory and Cap to be somewhere else.

There was a narrow alley. Right there in front of them. They had run a half block from the site of the attack. There had been no sounds of alarm. No shouts. No tweeting police whistles. No sounds of approaching horses or running feet on the sidewalk. It was as if the town had suddenly become deserted.

They turned into the alley and stopped in the darkness. Rory leaned out just far enough to look in both directions. He leaned back and said, "Nothing. No one. It's as if everyone suddenly decided they had to get to bed. I wonder who those guys were. They were dressed like the ones on the train. Had the same look about them."

Cap held out a pocketbook he had grabbed from the man he shot.

"Fell out of that fella's jacket pocket. It might tell us something if the sun ever rises in this town again. Or if we can find a lamp."

"Good man. Put it back in your pocket, and let's get out of here."

By a series of roads, alleyways, and a couple of trails

through undeveloped land, the men finally located their hotel. The foyer was brightly lit, and the adjoining bar was loud and in full swing with music, laughter, and the clinking of glass on glass.

Cap listened and said, "It's like nothing else ever happened. That's how life is. A woman's giving birth, and close by, a man is dying. And one knows nothing at all about the other. There's three men down and one running, and no one here knows anything about any of it, or cares."

Sobered by the happening of the past hour, Rory said, "I'm for getting my key and calling it a day."

The desk clerk lifted the keys from the brass hooks they hung from and passed one to each man. He offered a quiet, "Good night." Rory answered with a nod. Cap ignored him.

39

THE RUNNER FROM THE MARSHAL'S OFFICE ARRIVED AT what, to an easterner, was an early hour. He half expected to have to knock on a couple of doors to arouse the sheriff and his deputy. But following the desk clerk's direction, he found his prey in the dining room, taking in one more cup of coffee after breakfast and wondering what to do with their day. The expected repercussions from the evening before had not so far shown up to spoil the morning. The messenger stood at the dining room door, wondering just what time these men had arisen on a day when they had no responsibilities. A short glance, and he approached their table.

"Good morning, men. You're the only ones in here. You must have almost beat the cook getting to the door."

Without waiting for a response, he continued, "The marshal wants to see you. Just as soon as possible is what he said. That was late last evening. I got up early so's to get you the message before you got out on the town. Off on some looking around, don't you know. If you're finished up here now, you could crowd onto my single buggy seat and save the walk."

~

A SHORT FIFTEEN MINUTES LATER, they were seated with Marshal Jeramiah Kootenay. The office door was closed. The secretary, the only other staff in sight, brought them all coffee mugs and a silver pot of coffee. She poured the coffee, left the half-empty pot sitting on a silver tray, and quietly left the office, pulling the door closed behind her.

Rory assumed the other agents would file in within the next hour.

They sipped their coffee while the marshal studied the men sitting before him. It was a long study. Rory was tempted to think he saw the beginnings of a slight smile on the man's face, but finally decided that was unlikely.

"Sheriff, Deputy, how far off would I be to suggest that you had an interesting time last evening? I'm an early riser, men. But even earlier are a couple of local newspapers. There were several interesting items this morning. Among them was a short report of injured men found by a passing waggoner. Two appeared to simply have the kind of injuries that can result from any face-to-face fight. One was shot. Not dead. But struggling to hold on to the vapor of life that we all treasure.

"Is there anything you would care to mention or discuss? Perhaps something that happened while you were out strolling, taking in the beauty and the drama of our city?"

Rory took another longer drag on the coffee mug. Cap deferred to Rory for any response.

Rory set the mug back on the tray and reached into the inside pocket of his leather coat. He lifted out the billfold picked up by Cap the evening before. Leaning forward, he laid it on the desk.

As if talking about some totally unrelated incident, he said, "There could be some helpful information in there. We found it on the sidewalk. Name and such, in case you might feel the pocketbook should be returned, or some such thing. We got pretty well lost finding our hotel, after being out for several hours taking in the city. Darkness caught up. Can't say with any clarity just where we were."

"Should I even ask how this came to be in your hands?"

"Just found it lying on the sidewalk."

The marshal flipped the billfold open and read the information on the paper that was inserted into the interior pocket. He then thumbed through the other pockets and folders in the piece. Rory and Cap had done the same while they were waiting for their breakfasts. Rory had also copied the name and other information into his own notebook. There was considerable money enclosed, along with some other folded papers, most of them old and worn and probably irrelevant. One was new, with the ink still bright; a few more names, which he had also copied down.

As if mumbling to himself, the marshal said, "Hamish Blain. That's a familiar name. Can't place it right now, but it will come to me. A couple of other names on this piece of paper too. New. Freshly written. I know those ones too. Could be good for me. Bad for others. And dumb, no matter how you look at it, carrying this around with him and then losing it. It's as if no one has a memory. Or perhaps the names were of men recently met, with no one having the time or familiarity to take the names to remembrance.

"But this, gentlemen, might be the connection that has eluded us. This leads directly back to a gang of thugs that have been operating for some time. Men with no softness to them. Available to do another's dirty work so long as the money kept flowing. We've suspected that the incident on the train was the work of the same gang. We've been well aware of their existence but, so far, haven't found anything we could pin on them.

"It's interesting that this fell into your hands. Coincidence, I would suppose."

Neither the sheriff nor the deputy chose to answer.

"Changing the subject just a bit, fellas, there's been another development. Ex. Marshal Glover Harrison has decided to be more forthcoming about his involvement. I believe he told both you and Col. Oliver Staveley that it was worth his life to speak about his involvement or how it all came about. But now, something happened that changed his mind. Perhaps it was the realization that he couldn't outrun this thing and the marshals were in the best position to protect him.

"In any case, he had a long conversation with our lawyer last evening. Named names. Gave some details. I am not free to discuss all that with you, but I can say that he confirmed Mr. Webster Cunningham told you the truth. He really has no in-depth involvement. He was simply hired to do a job. That job was to build a ranch in a new country.

"With millions of acres either open for development or that will soon be open, that decision was questionable, from my Eastern perspective. But in any case, it confirms your work, Sheriff. Yours and Deputy Marshal Block Handley's.

"It also means that there is little reason for you to remain here. With Glover Harrison's testimony, we can move ahead. In point of fact, if Harrison had come clean earlier, there would have been no need for you making this trip.

"I, and by extension, the country, thank you for your diligence, your sacrifice, and your loyalty. If you will attend my secretary's office on the way out, she will reimburse you for your expenses and forward the costs of your return journey."

The marshal stood, adjusted his waistcoat, and held out his hand.

"If there is ever anything you need in aid of performing your home duties, please be assured that I have instructed the Denver Office to provide all assistance. Again, thank you. And I wish you safe travels."

Their dismissal had come about so quickly that neither Rory nor Cap could find anything to say. They shook hands and left, but not before seeing the secretary who was entrusted with the financial matters of the Washington Marshal's Office.

40

RORY AND CAP HAD CHECKED WITH THE FRONT DESK AT the hotel. They had the railroad schedule available, confirming an afternoon run. Deciding to risk the availability of seats, they packed their few things, picked up their carbines, and checked out of the hotel. Their intent was to hail a passing hack and head out to the station.

They had no reason to take note of the enclosed carriage sitting at rest beside the walkway two doors down from the hotel. It was just one of the many carriages on the roads. But when the carriage driver immediately urged his team into a slow walk as they came out into the sunshine, Rory did take note. Not that it was particularly suspicious, but it was movement, and to stay alive in the peacekeeping business, it was best to note new or unusual movement or activity.

The timing was near to perfect. As they stepped to the edge of the walkway, intent on hailing a hack, the carriage stopped right beside them, blocking their access to the road. Instinct told both men that this was not a hack for hire, nor was its presence a coincidence. They were immediately on guard, so when four men stepped up beside and behind them, they were not taken completely by surprise. The voice came from beside and slightly behind Rory.

"Just stand still, fellas. We'll make this easy for you. Pass over those rifles and don't turn around. You turn around or make a fuss, and you're dead. Be good boys now and do what I say. We wouldn't want to raise a ruckus on a public street now, would we?"

Without even glancing at Cap, knowing the man would do what was necessary, Rory shifted his feet and turned his shoulder just a bit, as if to give the carbine to the man. Instead, with a motion that involved all his considerable strength, he drove the bit end of the weapon into the mid section of the man who had been speaking.

Cap, just a split second later, as if he had been waiting for Rory's lead, became a ball of furious action. Before there was even time to think or react, two men were down and gasping for breath. The man who had been directly behind Rory wheezed out a startled response to the happenings and was reaching for his gun when the barrel of Rory's carbine connected with his right ear, changing his plans for the afternoon and his looks forever. Cap had simply balled up his big fist and laid out his assailant with a thundering left hook.

Knowing the recently moved carriage was somehow involved in the attack, Rory immediately took several steps and grabbled the bridle cheek strap of the curbside horse. Cap, at the same time, perhaps remembering how effective his actions had been with the wayward stage driver back at the fort, leaped onto a front wheel spoke and reached for the driver's coat lapel. The man cringed back in fear.

Cap settled for a grip on the man's belt. With a fierce yank, he stepped down, dragging the terrified and screaming driver along with him. When they were both on the sidewalk, he let go of the man and climbed nimbly onto the driver's box. It took him a moment to settle the team with Rory's help.

With Cap in control of the carriage, Rory went quickly to the carriage door. The single passenger was intent on escaping the melee, but Rory caught him with his feet still inside, although he was half out, leaning most of his weight on the carriage door. For some reason, the thought flashed through Rory's mind that if he had taken to the other door, the man would have escaped into the crowded road traffic.

Rory pushed the man back inside with the warning to sit and not move again. The ever-ready carbine pointing his way seemed to convince the well-dressed city man that the advice was good, and healthy, considering the alternatives.

Rory then bent to the ground and grasped the man he had struck with the butt of the carbine. He was just trying to rise. Since he had been the spokesman, demonstrating some leadership, this was the man Rory wanted. With Rory's help, aided by a firm grip on the fella's collar, he was soon on his feet. Very quickly, knowing the need for a clean escape, Rory flashed his hands over the logical places where the man may be carrying a weapon. He felt a shoulder holster, and the .38 pistol was soon in his own hand.

"Get in and sit. If you move, it will be your last."

Rory jumped in behind and took the front seat, with his back to Cap, who had the reins at the ready, with his foot on the wheel brake, prepared for release. Rory turned and shouted through the small opening behind him, "Move out, Cap. Take your time. We need to talk some back here."

The entire operation hadn't taken more than a half minute.

~

As THEY MOVED AWAY from the curb, Tyler, the young runner from the marshal's office who had driven the men back to their hotel—and told to keep an eye on the Westerner's movements—slapped the reins onto the back of his single wagon horse. He had been resting, half hunched down on the seat, as if he might be asleep, needing to avoid Rory's notice. But now, sensing his duty, he drove his wagon at a reckless speed, forcing a couple of other waggoneers to steer aside as they shouted their disgust at the young man's moves. He was able to get reasonably close to the hotel before he called the animal to whoa. He set the wheel brake and leaped to the ground.

The desk clerk came running out the front door of the hotel, hollering, "Saw it! Saw it all! I'm sure bett'n those two what done this 're on the side a' the angels. I don't want to be helping no other side."

The young runner said, "It's all right, sir. All under control."

The clerk heard the words as he skidded to a stop. In amazement, he looked at the four unconscious, or still gasping, men. A crowd was beginning to gather. The driver was crumpled into an unmoving heap, although he appeared to still be breathing.

"Are...Are...Are they dead?"

As if it were an everyday occurrence and nothing to get rattled about, the young marshal's trainee responded, kicking his toe lightly into the mid section of the man Rory had dropped with the carbine barrel, "This one might be, or perhaps will be soon. The others will wake up by and by."

As the startled clerk stood there in awe, Tyler said, "I'm going to need some help cleaning up this mess."

Glancing back quickly to see if he was needed at the hotel desk, the young man foolishly said, "What do you need?"

The answer to the question was, "Grab his feet." Tyler bent to pick up one fallen man by his shoulders.

Very reluctantly, but finally overcoming his squeamishness, the clerk did as Tyler asked. It took only a minute, or perhaps a bit more, for the four bodies to be swung into the back of the wagon. Shouting his thanks to the clerk—and hoping none of the men wakened to cause trouble before Tyler got the wagon turned around on the street and driven the several blocks to the marshal's office—he whipped the animal into action, standing in front of the seat, shouting, "Clear the road!" while urging the animal to put out more speed as he wove through traffic.

Tyler turned to the curb in front of the Marshal's Office, nearly lifting the fragile rig onto two wheels in the process. He called out to a couple of deputies that were just emerging from the big door.

"Hey, deputies. Could use some help here."

After their initial querying looks, the two men ran to the wagon. One took a quick look and ran back to the office. Within seconds, it seemed to Tyler, the street was taken over by deputies, and he was pushed out of the way. One man was going through pockets, removing weapons, letters, billfolds, and anything that might identify the men or their employers.

Marshal Jeramiah Kootenay soon emerged from the office. He gestured for Tyler to join him and then listened while the young man told the story.

"Good thinking, young man. I'm happy to finally have some of these thugs in our hands. I'm glad they didn't get away. But you saw nothing of the carriage after it left the hotel?"

"Nothing, sir. I was a bit busy right about that time."

"Right. Of course."

∼

MARSHAL KOOTENAY STEPPED over to the wagon. A couple of the men were waking up. They were all cuffed, hands and feet both. They weren't about to jump to the sidewalk and run away.

The marshal spoke to the two conscious men at once, "You men had no reason for that attack, personally. You're being paid by someone holding considerable power would be my guess. In fact, there's little doubt of that. There's also little doubt that you're an organized group of thugs. You're certainly more than a bunch of saloon rabble hired to do a single piece of dirty work. You're going to tell me all about it, but perhaps we should get you off the street and safely inside first."

With that statement understood to be an order, the deputies led the men, who were able to walk, toward the office. They carried the other two, one of which wasn't looking as if he was going to survive.

The senior deputy said to no one in particular, "Find a doctor for this man."

Two deputies pealed away and walked down the sidewalk, showing no real hurry. There was a doctor's office just a block away.

The wagon driver had awakened and was hollering his innocence and questioning where his carriage was taken.

Once inside the office, they laid the two unconscious men on the floor. The secretary, who seemed to handle everything from Marshal Kootenay's coffee needs to the controlling of funds, took a look and said, "Don't you dare let that man bleed on the carpet."

It was as if she saw dead or dying men every day. Regardless, a deputy jumped to attention and hurried off to find a bundle of rags.

41

As Cap directed the carriage down one street, then another, into a lovely park with a wide pathway through it, and then over to where the capitol building was still under construction—something he and Rory had decided the day before would go on for most of their lifetimes—Rory was digging answers out of the two men in the back.

"Let's start it this way, fellas. Just so you understand the situation. Personally, I don't much care if either of you live or die. I'm not eager to shoot another man, but on the other hand, it wouldn't put much of a damper on my appetite. So, here's what you're going to do. First, you're going to sit still and keep quiet until I ask you something. You move, you die. You holler out, same result. I've held to that position for several years. Seems to work well for me. And I'm not much interested in how you feel about it. This is not a democracy. You don't get a vote.

"The second thing is, you're going to answer my questions. Have no doubt about that.

"Now. Let's get started.

"First," Rory said as he jabbed the office man in the belly with the carbine, "Pass me your wallet or whatever it is you carry your identification and your money in."

The man hesitated but finally did as he was told.

Rory flipped the billfold open and studied the identification card. "Theodore Prescott." That's a name to remember. Of course, most men, with that handle tagged on them by overbearing parents, shorten it to Ted. But have it your way, Theodore. Now that we have that nailed down, why don't you just go ahead and tell me what your job is and who it is you serve?

If I was to guess, I have to say you're a flunky with no power or authority at all of your own, but you feel good about yourself because you serve either a high-ranking politician, or perhaps, a powerful bureaucrat. And this action this morning tells me plainly that you're prepared to do the dirtiest of dirty work. Or perhaps, it's more accurate to say that you hire scum like that one beside you, and you just come along to see the doing of the job from a nice safe distance. How about you just lay that out for me, Theodore?"

"I'll tell you nothing at all. You're a fool if you think you can get anything from me. You're a fool for even having touched me."

"Your boss is that powerful, is he Theodore? Well, we'll see."

Directing his attention to the thug, Rory asked, "And what would your name be?"

The thug glared hate across the width of the carriage and held his tongue.

Rory responded with a sharp jab of the carbine barrel, right where the butt had hit the man originally. The thug gasped, bent over, then threw up his breakfast onto the floor of the carriage. Rory managed to move his feet quickly enough, but Theodore barely reacted as the spillage soiled his pants from the knees down.

Giving the thug time to again catch his breath, Rory studied the two men. One of them was going to talk. He was pretty sure of that. But which one and when? What would he have to do, or at least promise to do, to make them release the information he wanted?

When the man was again able to sit up, he glared such hate as Rory had seldom seen.

"You do that again, or even threaten to, I'll come at you, gun or no gun."

"Tough man, are you? Well, perhaps you are. Tough enough anyway when you work with a gang at your back. But I'm tougher. You'd have just no chance at all. I could put my weapon down and take you any which way you choose. But we can avoid all that unpleasant expenditure of energy if you simply pass me your billfold and tell me what I want to know. I understand that this is not your venture. You were just hired as a hitman. Hired by scum like that one beside you. Men who live under the people's trust but, in reality, don't deserve anyone's trust. Men the world would be better off without."

Without waiting for an answer. A new thought entered Rory's mind. Feeling sure he was right, he said, "You're part of that bunch on the train, aren't you?"

The memory of how that attack had come down must have broken a dam in the man. Immediately, he said, "You killed friends of mine. I'll hate you to the day I die for that."

"Let's hope that day isn't today. But it could be. Could yet be. But to avoid that, answer the questions I already asked you. And one more question. Who is the leader of your gang? Who do you work for?"

In anger, the man blurted out, "I don't work for anyone. Never have. Never will. Others work for me."

"Ah. So, you're the boss. You're the one who sent men to kill a couple of prisoners on the train and the deputies guarding them. And all in the direction of this piece of waste flesh sitting beside you. And him acting for someone higher up, closer to the feed trough. The marshals will be happy to get that information, but much happier if you would tell them who hired you. I mean the man who really hired you."

The answer, accompanying the self-admission that his run of crimes had come to an end, said, "Best you ask old Theodore here. He's the chore boy. Carries the messages and the envelopes stuffed with cash. I know who he works for. It's no real secret on Capitol Hill. Calls himself executive secretary or something such as that. He's really nothing more than a flunky his boss would throw in the river and never think of again. The only thing that's secret is the dirty work they all do.

"Like a bunch of rangy dogs fighting over a carcass. Filth. The bunch of them. Call me a criminal, but they're ten times the criminals. Oh, there's good ones there too, thank the Lord. The good ones hold the country together, while these others feed off the people, hoarding money and power to themselves. Not caring who or what they hurt."

"Pass me your billfold, like I already asked you twice."

Rory opened the wallet after reaching across to take it from the man's hand. Frustrating the thug's intentions, Rory never moved his eyes away, giving him no chance to grab him or leap for the door handle. He had grinned as he held the wallet and leaned back. But he said, "Get that notion out of your mind, or I put the cuffs on you."

Silence reigned until Rory said, "Ezra Skittery, is it?

Or is that just a name you hold out to your criminal employers?"

No answer was forthcoming. Rory was tiring of the game, and the odor in the small space was enough to drive anyone into the fresh air. He leaned back and spoke through the small opening again.

"Cap. You lost? Or do you think you can find the Marshal's Office?"

There was no answer, but the carriage made a sharp turn, and the horses were urged into a smart trot.

42

THE DRIVE TO THE MARSHAL'S OFFICE TOOK NEARLY ONE-half-hour. Sitting in the rear of the carriage, Rory could only see what went by the windows. He had no idea where they were but hoped Cap was on top of the job. He was, and when they pulled to a stop, there were four deputies holding shotguns down along their legs—alert, but not making any threat, simply watching the road while they guarded the office doors.

As soon as the carriage pulled to a stop, Cap said, "Coupl'a men here you'll be want'n to escort into the office, fellas."

One of the deputies stepped forward and opened the carriage door. The waft of foul air caused him to cry out and take a quick step backward. He let a few seconds pass and then stepped forward again.

"You fellas like it in there, or do you plan to step out?"

Rory replied, "Take these two out first. I'll bring up the rear."

"Yes? And exactly who are you?"

"And I could ask the same of you. Now take these men into custody."

The marshal still hesitated, cautious and not understanding what was going on. Cap stepped down from the seat and reached into the carriage. Seeing that neither man had moved, he grasped the thug by the jacket lapels and yanked. It seemed to be a motion Cap particularly enjoyed administering. He had done similar things several times, to Rory's knowledge.

The thug fell to the sidewalk, barking both knees and tearing his pants. He had just started to rise when Theodore Prescott fell on top of him.

Rory emerged with a grin.

"Good work, Cap."

He looked at the deputies and said, "These men are under my arrest, but it would be best if you were to take charge of them. But either way, let's get them inside."

~

ONCE IN THE OFFICE, someone found an old pair of pants for Theodore to change into. He stepped out of his filthy and stinking shoes and left them outside along with his stockings. When a deputy reluctantly picked up the pants with two fingers and said, "I'll take these out to the burning barrel", Theodore cried out, "No. I'll get them cleaned. Just leave them where I can find them."

Marshal Kootenay laughed and said, "You're not going anywhere. And if there is any justice left in this country, you'll be wearing prison stripes for the rest of your life."

"I never did anything that hurt anyone. Just did as I was told."

"You cost the life of a fine young deputy and the

wounding of another. Who knows how much turmoil fills the steps you left behind. And probably the most cowardly thing I ever hear a criminal say is, 'I was just following orders.'"

The marshal hand-signaled for the two sheriffs to follow him into his office.

～

"GOOD WORK, men. I'm glad it didn't go the other way. Those men were loaded for bear with all the weapons hanging off them. Tyler, our latest trainee, showed quick decision-making when he disarmed them all and had the hotel clerk help load them into the wagon. They're all in the cells in the basement. They aren't going anywhere but to court, then to prison for a good long time.

"And these latest two you brought to me are a gift. Theodore Prescott, I know. Mostly by reputation and by the connections he has managed to assemble in the Capitol. I know who he clerks for. And I now know the outline that leads him to the stolen bank boxes and the dirty trail from there to here. We'll fill in the blanks alright, now that we have that outline.

"Sheriff, you maybe don't see the significance of your work, but you started this. With such a simple thing as a question about a tarnished gold coin, you put this all into action. And now your part is done. When I said yesterday that you were free to leave, I believe I thanked you on behalf of myself, the marshals, and the nation. I don't suppose either of you have forgotten that, but in case you have, thank you. Again. Go home. Put your lives back together. Greet that lovely young wife of yours, Rory. Look after that town and county you serve so well. And Cap. I don't know all of your story, but I've done some snooping. It's not much, but I've had one of my local people see to your ranch. He also cleaned up around the graves. There will be rewards paid out for some of these men. It will be for the two of you to share. It may take some time but look for it in the mail, by and by."

He stopped talking at that point, and then he grinned. "That was a smooth move with that herd of Texas cattle, Sheriff."

The three men shook hands and parted. Rory was wondering if there was anything this man didn't know or couldn't at least find out. Cap was thinking there was a tale to hear. A tale about a herd of Texas cattle. He would have a train ride over the width of half the nation to worm it out of the sheriff.

43

NEITHER RORY NOR CAP HAD ANY WAY OF KNOWING, BUT two days after they left Washington, while they were bored half to death on the train, Marshal Jeramiah Kootenay called in his best, most trusted men. He laid before them a list of names.

The almost non-stop interrogation of everyone involved in the gold coin theft, from Denver to Washington, from the mostly innocent—like Webster Cunningham with his Big C branded cattle—to the clearly guilty—ex-marshal Glover Harrison—to the men Rory and Cap had turned in during their stay in Washington, and a few Rory knew nothing about, had produced results. The names of the known actors were on Kootenay's list.

"Deputy Marshals, go arrest these men. Every one of them. Go in with enough force to get the job done. Go—without delay—to their places of work, their homes, the theater, if you must. I want none to be warned or to have a chance to escape.

"Here you will find the names of two members of

Congress. Men, the people laid great trust in. But, in reality, these are men without public purpose. Their every purpose is for themselves and their own betterment. It is not at all far-fetched to say they are involved in crimes without conscience.

"You will also find the names of top staff people. In short, these are politicians and their aides and fixers. Powerful men. Arrest them all. Do it publicly. I want them cuffed publicly and hauled out, not roughly, but publicly. Speak to no one. Leave me to talk to the reporters.

"Simply do your jobs. Search each man and lock him up. Treat them like any criminal. There are other investigators who will be looking through these men's desks. And perhaps their homes. But that is not your job today. Your job is to bring these men in. That's all, but that's enough. Now go."

44

Town Marshal Wiley Hamstead was sitting silently at his desk in the small office. The door between the office and the cells behind it was closed. The actions of the recent few days were troubling him. The shooting of Felix Tattersley was like a weight on his shoulders. On his mind. Was there some way he could have prevented it? Had he misjudged? As he was seeking evidence against Felix and Charity, did he go too far, tempting them to make a break for freedom?

There was no need for the man to take the risk of his escape attempt, and yet, together, he and Charity had done so. None of the charges against him called for a death penalty. Or, perhaps, not even a serious jail term. He, in all likelihood, could have been a free man in just a few years. With a good lawyer, he may have avoided prison entirely. But now he was in the grave, and his wife, Charity, was in a cell not more than ten feet away from where Wiley was sitting. What was his next move?

In reality, he knew what his next move was. His thinking on that was clear. It was the mechanics of the move that had him stumped. The mechanics and the question of who he would ask to assist if the federal boys didn't show up. Two or three deputy marshals arriving in town would be the final and perfect ending of the matter for him, but that seemed unlikely.

Still, clearly, Charity had to be taken to Denver. Sheriff Rory wasn't here to help, and Wiley had no idea when he would return.

He knew what Rory's response was going to be when he found they were involved with another federal case involving the marshals. But then, in truth, Rory wasn't involved. The crime was totally a town matter. Town, and eventually, federal—to be handled by the federal force headquartered in Denver.

Now, with those thoughts bringing some peace to his mind, how to get the woman to Denver? The train, of course. But he could hardly be expected to accompany her to Cheyenne by himself, spend one night in a hotel, just the two of them, and another day together on the train. No, that would never do. But Rory and Cap were away, and he had no other lawmen to either accompany him or to leave in charge at the Fort. He was clearly in over his head.

And then there was the wagon. The wagon and its contents. Someone was going to have to drive that to the big city. That was a full three days, perhaps closer to four.

Of course, he had already sent for the marshals. Turning the matter over to them was the obvious answer. Why try to pre-think the marshal's response? He could just wait and see. But did they even get the wire? And would the marshals come if they did get it? He knew they would come if the wire had been from Sheriff Rory. But none of them knew him. And they weren't known for running all over the country to investigate petty crimes.

He couldn't just let it all sit, with Charity Tattersley cooling her heels in that grim cell. He vaguely remembered something from his studies about justice having to be timely. The accused couldn't just be held until it suited the law. There had to be some expedience about the whole matter.

That got him thinking about his original purpose in suffering through the interminable days in stuffy classrooms. His goal had never been to become a small-town marshal. His goal was toward either teaching at the college level or hanging out his shingle as a lawyer. He had only taken on the deputy role in Cheyenne when he first came west to learn something about the culture and workings of the West. Now here he was, appointed to a one-man marshal's office, and his way forward was unclear.

Lacking any better idea, Wiley wandered over to the livery to check on the wagon and its contents again. Kegs sauntered over to see what the young man was up to. Wiley had folded the rear covers back and was standing with his arms crossed and resting on the top of the tailgate. When Kegs joined him, he held his silence for just a moment before saying, "Kegs. I'm stumped. This whole mess should be in Denver, but I don't know how to get it there. The wagon sits, taking up space in your barn. The woman is wasting away in that cell. And I don't hardly dare be more than a few feet from either. There's no telling what could happen if either the wagon or the woman was to be left alone."

Kegs had his own thoughts, but he seldom expressed them, feeling it was best to allow others to sort out their own matters. But privately, he was of the opinion that the marshal wasn't seeing the forest for the trees. The plain truth was that none of the stolen things in the wagon were ever going to be returned to their original owners. To think of traipsing back across the country, reversing Tattersley's travels just to return a ten-dollar desk, or a half-worn-out gun made no sense at all. The only real value rested in the team and the wagon itself. Still, the chances of someone traveling from eastern Texas just to retrieve the team and wagon wasn't likely either.

Wiley broke into the silence, pointing at the Yellowboy carbine.

"I'm thinking that could go back to Haraldson with no one likely to form up a complaint."

Kegs grinned a bit, slapped him on the back of his shoulder, and walked away, saying, "You just keep thinking that way. You'll sort 'er out."

～

THAT AFTERNOON A TRAVEL-WEARY deputy arrived from Denver. A well-put-together man, husky of shoulder, and tall. Strong hands, judging by looks. But young. Too young for what had to be done. Seeming to Wiley to be a bit overboard with self-confidence, the deputy burst into the small office. As if immediately taking charge, he said, "Deputy Marshal Maddison Pigeon. You have a situation you need help with."

Wiley actually laughed out loud. He studied the man, who was younger than Wiley himself, and finally asked, "And you figure you're the one to do the helping, do you?"

When no response filled the vacuum of sound in the small room, Wiley asked, "Where are the others?"

With a quizzical look, the deputy asked, "What others?"

"The others that are going to help you?"

"Sounded like a simple job to the senior deputy. Sounds simple enough to me too. There are no others."

Wiley stood and pushed his way past the deputy. He opened the connecting door and entered the cell room. With a gesture of his head toward Charity Tattersley, he said, "Deputy Pigeon, meet Mrs. Tattersley."

When neither deputy nor prisoner spoke, Wiley walked out and opened the outside door. He walked toward the livery, expecting the deputy to follow. At the livery door, he heard footsteps in the dust of the road. Assuming it was the deputy, he entered the big barn and moved toward the wagon. As he opened the rear canvas covers, Pigeon stopped beside him. Wiley waved his arm over the interior of the wagon.

"This junk is all stolen. Stolen over a thousand miles of travels. I'm sure some of these pieces looked good and valuable sitting in a shanty on the prairie. Kind of like grandma's old bedroom table. Valuable for memory, but sitting here hundreds of miles away, it's all just junk. Worthless for the most part, except for the few dollars it would fetch. Not enough money to pay for oats for the team. The wagon too. It's stolen."

Waving his hand over it all like a salesman trying for a buying offer, he continued, "You figure that's worth taking all the way to Denver? You have enough experience to make a judgment on that, Deputy Pigeon?"

Not waiting for a response, he dropped the canvas flaps back into place and led the deputy to the outside corral. There, among several other sale horses, stood the team. Four big-footed, harness animals were standing together, swishing flies off each other with their long tails.

Addressing the deputy, he simply asked, "Figure you can handle that team and wagon to Denver? And the two saddle horses that were also stolen. Three days, two nights on the trail, at least. Woman riding the seat beside you? Just you? And the woman, of course! Figure you're up to that, Deputy Pigeon?"

He didn't wait for an answer as he crossed the road to the dining room. It was early for dinner, but the meeting with Deputy Pigeon had set him off his routine. That was probably another sign that he didn't really belong in the law business. He tried to imagine what Rory would have done. He was left with the conviction that Rory would have told him to get back on the train and forget it.

Hoping his internal turmoil would settle down, he ordered and proceeded to enjoy his dinner, trying to put the other questions out of his mind. For the hundredth or more time, he wished for a telegraph closer than Cheyenne. And he wished he could somehow convince Denver to come up with a better plan than the one presently on the table.

Dinner had evolved into coffee time when Deputy Pigeon slunk his way toward Wiley's table. 'Slunk.' That's the word that passed through Wiley's mind as he watched the approach. Worry? Doubt? Fear? Silently pleading for help, or at least understanding? What did Wiley see on the deputy's face? He couldn't be sure.

"Mind if I sit?"

Deputy Marshal Maddison Pigeon eased into the chair when Wiley gestured at it with his coffee mug.

Pigeon was barely seated before he said, "You don't think much of me."

"I don't think much of those that sent you here on this fool's errand. What I think of you doesn't matter. What will matter are your decisions. When that is known, there will be time enough to sort out the rest."

"Marshall, let me start with an apology. I somehow assumed that it would be a simple matter of gathering up the prisoner, shackling her firmly, loading her on a horse, and riding back to Cheyenne in the morning. I was told nothing about a wagonload of stolen articles, a four-horse team, or the two saddle horses.

"So, I'd best back up to the start. In answer to your questions at the stable, yes, I can handle the team. I'm Eastern, but I'm farm raised. I was handling horses and mules by the time I could walk, seems like. Six horses, four of them needing harnessing of a morning, is a lot, but it can be done. I can do it. I'm confident of that.

"The wagon is not an issue. Once the animals are hitched, it just becomes a place to sit out the day. But the woman is another matter. Another matter altogether. And I believe you said she can't be trusted. Taken overall, it's a lot. I'd take it on anyway if it weren't for the nights. I'd have to sleep sometime. With six horses and a woman I couldn't trust, that would be a problem."

"So, what's your thinking now that you've got all that in your head?"

"My thinking is that we could do it together. I could handle the team and wagon easily enough. You could ride that handsome gelding, set up the camps, and find some firewood. Perhaps the woman would agree to cook up something edible. The woman could sit the seat beside me during the day, but shackled. I wouldn't turn her loose on a bet. What do you say? There's still time this afternoon to provision for the three days. We could start first light in the morning. And you could ride the rails home after."

Wiley leaned back in his chair and studied the young deputy with new eyes. If he wasn't alone, he'd be tempted. There was no telling when Rory and Cap might return. And he couldn't leave the town with no law at all. Think. What could be done? The thing had to be either dealt with at the Fort or transferred out. It couldn't just sit, waiting. Waiting for what?"

Tempted, Wiley started to think of solutions. Scheming, almost. Something he rarely indulged in. Stevensville. Ivan and Key. If Stevensville was quiet, in a crime-free way, perhaps he could convince Ivan to ride north until he returned himself. The Fort would only be without law for one day.

Deputy Pigeon sat quietly while the thoughts were churning in his table mate's mind. It didn't take long for the thoughts to become words.

"Here's what we'll do. Stevensville is just a comfortable day's travel south of here. There's two deputies there. We'll load up and go that far, at least. That will leave two longer days to get to Denver. If one of those deputies will ride here to sit in for me until I return, we'll go. If they refuse, I'll have to return here, and you'll still be without a solution, but at least you'll be one day closer to your goal. That's the best I can do."

"And it's good enough. You go do what you have to do to get the woman ready for morning. Perhaps the livery would have some grain for the team. The saddle animals won't be a problem. I'll see to the provisions."

45

THE NEW BUILDINGS IN STEVENSVILLE, THOSE THAT WERE replacing the burned-out ones, were nearing completion, but the cells weren't yet ready for occupancy. Charity Tattersley was housed in the hotel with the deputies taking turns sitting out the night at her door. Deputy Sheriff Ivan had agreed to put in a few days at the Fort. Wiley was freed to accompany Deputy Pigeon on what Wiley still felt was a foolish adventure. He would have suggested that Pigeon take Charity to Cheyenne, catch a train, and forget all about the wagon. But that option didn't seem to have any place in the federal deputy's mind, so he had held his peace.

BY MID-MORNING THE NEXT DAY, Ivan had arrived at the Fort and taken up his position in the small courthouse. Wiley and Deputy Maddison Pigeon were taking their nooning at a shaded spot along the south road. There was a small run of water tumbling down a bit of a hill nearby. Staying good on his word, Deputy Pigeon was caring for the animals. He didn't unharness the team, but after watering them, he walked all around, checking the harness fit and loosening the sweat-stained leather here and there. The gelding Wiley was riding was unsaddled and allowed to roll. Charity was putting some trail grub together over an open fire, with considerable skill.

As they were finishing up their meal, two riders approached. They entered the camp without the customary greeting or waiting for permission to come close. Neither man introduced himself nor asked anything about the campers. Appearing to be the roughest of men, unshaved and dirty, their good-looking horses loaded for travel, both Colts and rifles in plain sight, they said nothing, just rode close and began snooping around. When one rider came near the wagon and leaned over the seat to see what they carried, Wiley rose to his feet with his carbine at his side.

"Jest you set still there, sonny. Apt to live longer."

Unable to command the situation the way he knew either Rory or Cap would do, he stood silently but watchful. Deputy Pigeon stayed seated but held his hand on the butt of his Colt. Charity Tattersley looked terrified. They all gave a sigh of relief when the two swung their horses back onto the road and continued on south.

"That's trouble," were the only words Wiley could dig out of his mind. Neither of the others said anything at all.

They put the rig back together and moved out. Both of the men were extra vigilant, watching ahead and peering into every brushy copse. The uphill turnoff to a portion of the gold findings and to a series of ranches that had been settled in the high valleys was just ahead. Neither man had ever been there before, but the trail had been well laid out with scratches in the road dust by Ivan the evening before. From there south, there were more settlers, more farms and small ranches, and more road traffic. They were looking forward to being among people again. Still, they watched as carefully as they knew how. It wasn't enough.

The first shot, coming from behind a brush-covered rock, took Wiley out of the saddle and ended all his plans for hanging out his shingle for a law practice. He was dead before he hit the ground. Deputy Pigeon was driven back against the wagon seat by the force of a rifle bullet fired by the second man. He wasn't dead, but he was helpless. The bullet had taken him in the upper chest on the right side. With his right arm hanging uselessly, he twisted around, trying to reach his holstered Colt, but couldn't make it. His efforts ended when the gruff voice said, "Leave 'er alone, sonny. You'll be dead and gone soon enough."

With that, his Colt was lifted from his holster, and he was grabbed by his left shoulder and flung off the seat onto the road. The sudden shrieking pain was more than his mind could cope with. He sunk into unconsciousness and lay there, ignored by the outlaws.

Charity had been screaming since the first shot was fired.

A hard-knuckled backhand and the order, "Shet yerself up there, woman," was enough to quiet the shackled prisoner.

The man who had hit Charity, noticed the shackles. With a grin, he called his partner over, saying, "Well, looky here, Stubs. This 'ol gal has gone and had herself handcuffed to the seat. Must be a bad one. You a bad one, girly? Don't look so bad. Look mighty fetch'n if'n anyone was to ask me. Dig around in some pockets there, Stubs.

One a them fellas must have a key on him. Must be lawmen. They lawmen girly?"

Charity was too terrified to answer or hardly even think. She said nothing.

Within five minutes, one outlaw horse was tied to the back of the wagon, along with the two Felix Tattersley had stolen. One outlaw was handling the team. They moved south at a good trot until the uphill road pealed off. By that evening, the team was exhausted and trembling, but they had gone enough miles, first on the uphill and then across miles of a high ranch-strewn valley, to put them past cattle country and into the bush in the steeper foothills, not far from gold country.

46

DEPUTY MADDISON PIGEON WAS STILL ALIVE WHEN THE northbound stage came through, but in his unconscious state, he knew nothing as Tate, the driver, and a couple of passengers lifted him into the carriage. With some difficulty, the men managed to get Wiley's body laid out on top of the rig. After an hour of frantic, hard running, the team pulled to a stop in front of the hotel in Stevensville, with Tate hollering loud enough to call almost everyone from their stores, and Key Wardle from his unfinished combination of town marshal's and county sheriff's office. When Key heard that the federal deputy was still alive but hurting, he directed Tate to turn his rig around and continue to the doctor's office. Wiley was lowered from the roof and laid out in the doctor's shed.

~

KEY THEN SENT a rider north with the news. He stopped first at the Double J Ranch, just a short two miles north of Stevensville. He pulled George Jamison aside to tell him of the loss of Wiley. George's daughter, Hanna, had been stepping out from time to time with Wiley. Though no permanent commitment had been made or even talked about, the couple were clearly fond of each other. Hanna was teaching school in town. It would be unlikely the news would escape her ears. George immediately saddled up and rushed to town to comfort his firstborn child.

KEY TOOK his notebook and a pencil and walked to the doctor's office. The young deputy was still unconscious. The doctor explained that the way he had to dig around to find and remove the bullet, it was unlikely the fella would even survive, though he was still breathing as Key waited. He very much needed to talk to the man.

47

THE RIDER FROM STEVENSVILLE RODE INTO THE FORT AT just about the same time as Rory and Cap rode in from the north after their long train journey home from Washington. He found the two lawmen standing on the boardwalk, listening to Ivan explain why he was there, and Wiley was not.

Interrupting the talk, the rider pulled to a stop and said, "Got news, men. Not good news." He then told of the return of the deputies—one dead and one struggling to hang onto life—and the loss of the wagon and team.

The shock of the message could hardly have been harder. Ivan sank into a chair and held his head in his hands. Cap looked just like Cap always looked—wise, steady, and ready for what was to come. Rory looked stunned, as if he couldn't grasp what he had just heard.

Saying nothing to any of them, Rory walked to the saddle and gun shop where Julia was working. He tapped on the door to warn the dog to move away and then gave the animal a scratch on the ruff of its neck as the dog welcomed him with friendly whines and rubbed his shoulder against Rory's knees.

Julia rushed from behind the counter and snuggled into his arms. There was no need for words. The words would come later, when they were alone. With news literally bursting his chest, Rory pushed his young bride to arm's length and said, "I need you to listen to me."

At the news, Julia sank into his arms again and sobbed until it seemed as if she would never stop. Between sobs, she managed to say, "You have to go. I wish you didn't, but you must. So, go. Go and catch the murderers. When you catch them, shoot them until they're dead twice over. And then shoot them some more."

Rory ignored the suggestions. He pushed her to arm's length again, saying, I'll leave Cap here. Ivan will want to ride with me. I'll stop at the ranch to see Hanna and the others. We'll provision in Stevensville and hit the trail. There's not much to go on, but we'll do our best."

～

AT THE FIRST SUGGESTION, Cap started to object. Wiley had been his friend too. He hated the idea of sitting idle at the Fort while others were searching out Wiley's murderers. But, he finally relented after Ivan said, "Please, Cap. I have to do this."

～

THE SCHOOL DAY HAD ENDED, and Hanna had been brought home by her father by the time Rory and Ivan turned into the Double J. It was a saddened, weepy kitchen table everyone was sitting around. They didn't stay long. By the time they arrived at Stevensville, the federal deputy was dead. But Marshal Key Wardle had spoken a few words to the dying man first and had faithfully written down the deputy's hesitant, gasping answers.

The only information that was of any real significance was that Wiley had been very hesitant to undertake the venture, that the woman, Charity Tattersley, had been taken by the murderers, and that there were two of them.

Struggling through the pain and haze overtaking his mind, the federal deputy managed, with slurred words, to say, "Should have shot them as soon as they entered the noon camp uninvited."

He said no more. His eyes were glazing over. His face seemed to be turning from pale white to grey as he suffered from the loss of blood. After Key already thought the young man was gone, more struggling words came.

"Family. Love them. Tell."

But as the very last breath the young deputy would ever take was expelled, he gasped out 'Bonnie?' almost as an apology and a plea for forgiveness.

When Key began venturing into small talk about tragedies and sorrow, Rory cut him off with, "Later, Key. For now, we need the facts."

Tempest Wardle, Key's sister and Ivan's special friend, had come to the jailhouse to comfort both men. Ivan said, "Tempest, we need you to go to the mercantile and get us a goodly supply of trail food. Take that canvas pannier with you. Pack it in so it will ride well without throwing the horse off balance."

She left on her assignment but not without first

saying, "Mr. Ivanov, don't you be making the mistake of thinking I don't know how to prepare for the trail."

Ivan, preoccupied with other matters, ignored her.

With all else seemingly having been said and the trail supplies tied down, the two men swung into their saddles. Almost as an afterthought, Rory said, "Key, we have to get word down to the federals somehow."

"I already sent word with the afternoon stage. Best we can do."

Seeing no need for a response, the two hunters turned on the road and trotted to the edge of town before easing their mounts into a mile-eating lope.

48

THE WAGON TRACKS WERE UNMISTAKABLE. THERE WERE wagons enough on the trail; Stevensville was supplied by freight wagons from the supply houses in Denver. And then there were the two daily stages. But few had steel tires as wide as the stolen Tattersley wagon, and none of the other tracks were as fresh.

Without even slowing down, Ivan pointed out the lawmen's nooning spot to Rory. There was no purpose in stopping. There would be nothing helpful to see there, and the crime had taken place some miles further south.

When they came upon the murder site, it wasn't the wagon tracks that drew their attention. It was the conglomeration of hoof marks and boot tracks marring the road dust. Here they stopped. There might be something to learn from a thorough search. Ivan immediately spotted the brush-covered rocks two hundred yards to the south and walked that way. Rory thoroughly searched the murder site. He found traces of blood in two locations. He kicked dirt over both.

Looking for footsteps leading away—in the hopes that the woman may have found an opportunity to slip into the bush—left him disappointed and discouraged. He had not met Charity Tattersley, but that didn't matter. She was now a woman alone, at the mercy of two of the hardest type of men. She could expect no respect. No consideration. No mercy. Finding and rescuing her, even though she herself was a criminal, was as important to Rory and Ivan as was the capture of the murderers.

Ivan was soon back from his search of the bush. In his hand, he held two brass cartridge shells.

".44-40. Tracks. Boot and horse. No doubt. This is the place, and these are the shells. No need to follow saddle horse tracks. This wagon trail is all we need."

Rory had been almost beyond words since first getting the news. He used no words now either. He stepped into the saddle, swinging his leg high, to get over the protruding stock of the big .50 he had placed firmly into the left-hand saddle scabbard. He settled into the leather and led off at a trot. He knew this country from his previous travels. The original trail of the tarnished gold coins and the rustled cattle had led him to several uphill ranches in the area. His two cousins, Henry and Thomas, had been working at the local Triple T Ranch. Rory had received a welcome at the ranch several times.

The mountain valleys were populated with good folks. What depravations two men, such as the dying deputy had described, could do to welcoming people was not pleasant to think about. The ranchers could well take care of themselves if they were suspicious of their visitors. But to be caught unprepared could be a costly mistake.

All Rory and Ivan could now do was follow the

tracks. The team would soon enough tire and stop pulling. There would be no alternative to water, graze and rest. The murderers would have to hole up for the night. But that was the night before. They had a full day and a bit more lead on the searchers.

...the wagon going well enough. They had it rolling. They would be advantageous to water a few miles. The murderers would have to help up for the night, but that was the night before they had a full day and a half's lead on the murderers.

49

On the evening before, the evening Rory had been considering, the murderers spotted a mostly hidden track off the trail. They were well past the ranches and nearing the cross-trail leading both north and south to the gold fields. They weren't particularly familiar with the country, but they knew that much. And they knew that north would lead them to the newer findings.

South would eventually take them to Idaho Falls, an established and bustling gold town, and several smaller towns spread along the trail and into the gullies, offshoots of the main trail. It seemed there was gold almost everywhere up there, and where gold was found, men followed, breaking rock, digging holes, and moving on until they either quit in discouragement or struck color.

The fleeing murderers could find sales for the stuff in the wagon when they reached a populated area. They would clean themselves up, shave the wiry growth on their sunburned faces, and present themselves as traders, who have come to do business. The wagon itself was big and built heavy enough to serve as an ore wagon. The team would have any number of buyers waiting eagerly with cash in hand. They would sell the wagon load, the wagon, and the team, along with the two saddle mounts. They would then take to their own horses and ride out with money enough when it was added to what was already in their pockets.

The woman? Well, that was another matter altogether. She would have to be dealt with before they reached a town. Exactly what that meant, they weren't sure. Stubs was putting a fire together while Sandy, his partner, was caring for the team. Believing they were far enough from anywhere of safety for the woman that she would have no choice but to stay with the wagon if she hoped to eat, and sure enough, too, that if she ran off, they could easily catch her, Stubs unlocked the handcuffs.

"You go, girly. Do what you have to do. But don't you go far. Don't you be tak'n no notions. Don't get to thinking of runn'n off. I'll sure enough catch you if'n you try to run, and it won't go easy on you when I do. Me and Sandy, we got plans that kind of depend on you bee'n here. There's water enough in that runoff. Enough brush to get to your lonesome if'n that is your desire. You clean yourself up and do what you need to do. Then you get back here and put a meal together. You hear me now?"

Charity heard him alright. She heard what he said and what he didn't say right out loud. It was no more than what she expected. All afternoon the dread had been building in her. Death was beginning to look attractive. There were a few knives in the wagon, along with the stolen guns. But getting her hands on one seemed unlikely.

She held on to that unlikely possibility while she thought of everything, from throwing hot coals in their faces when she was cooking to jumping on a horse and riding for her life. She was a good rider, and bareback held no threat for her. If she could get a few fast strides out of the horse before one of them shot her or mounted a horse to give chase, she knew they would never catch her. She was half the weight of either man. A lightly burdened horse would leave the others in its dust. She could ride to a ranch and plead for help.

She finally put that daydream behind her, knowing it wasn't likely to be possible. Neither man would be that careless.

But she did get one opportunity that she might be able to put to her advantage. While she was shackled and the wagon was still moving, she reached into the space behind her with her free hand. When Sandy asked what she was doing, she answered, "My feet get sore. I usually trade these shoes off for moccasins. Feels much easier on the feet."

Sandy accepted that and could see no harm in it. Of course, it was all a lie. She had never worn moccasins, but she remembered the pair that had been in one of the trunks. Felix had thrown them aside as worthless. She remembered them landing right behind the seat, jammed between the trunk and the wagon box. She had trouble twisting her arm in that direction, with the unforgiving shackles holding her other arm firmly. But after a couple of minutes, she felt soft leather. Thankfully, the leather ties had been joined together, so the pair came out as one. Now, if only they would fit.

Again, working with one hand to remove her shoes and slip into the soft leather of the moccasin, was a challenge. They were a bit large for her, but they would be alright. She could make do. With the task completed and her feet secure behind the re-tied leather strips, she had freedom of movement and a covering for her feet. It wouldn't protect her well from sharp rocks or cacti. But for normal situations, it was fine. It was for sure a fact that she couldn't run in her normal walking shoes. Would she get the opportunity to run? If she did, she would be ready.

The opportunity came more quickly than she had ever imagined. The late afternoon high mountain air was arriving with a definite coolness to it. But the thought of the night was terrifying, even by comparison to what she had already been put through. The two murderers had no intention of being kind or pretending to be gentlemen. There was nothing left of that life in them, if there ever had been. When Stubs produced the key for the handcuffs and turned her loose, he said, "Now you'd best be remember'n what you've been told. You go clean yourself up and git back here. Don't you be tak'n no other notions."

Rubbing the feeling back into her chafed wrist, she draped her shawl over her shoulder. Picked a bar of homemade soap and a towel from the back of the wagon and stepped into the brush. Following the stream, until she was sure the men couldn't see her, taking a careful look around to identify a path she could follow, she kept walking. She made as little noise as she could as she kept moving away from the camp. She walked until she heard a man's voice holler, "Woman, git yerself back here. You hear me, woman?"

When she heard the crashing of brush behind her, she knew at least one, perhaps both, of the men were following her. She started to run. Being farm raised and strong, she had kept herself fit over the years. There had been no recent need for running, but she knew she could do it. And she was sure she could outrun the much heavier men who spent most of the time in the saddle, or judging by the gut each was carrying, sitting in a saloon or eating house. And so, she ran like she had never run before.

She tried to hold to a path that would keep her clear of the brush and undergrowth, but it was impossible. And with the increasing brush, there was the increasing noise of her running, and breaking twigs and small branches as she moved through them. The torn pieces of cloth from her dress, left hanging on the jagged ends of broken branches, would be enough to lay out her trail for the men to follow. The shouting now became almost frantic. The men were well aware that if she made an escape and found her way to safety, telling her story would doom the men to capture. If they mounted their saddle horses and ran, they might have a chance, but all their talk had shown they had dreams of the value of the wagon, team, and the loot from Felix's thefts.

A vertical wall of stone blocked her path. She had no choice but to leave the bush. The trail was only a short way off, but she had been trying to avoid that exposure. Now she was forced that way. As she burst through the last of the woods and onto the trail, she heard a clear shout. She paused just long enough to look back along the trail toward where the wagon still sat. There was Stubs, sitting bareback on his horse, holding to a walk while staring into the brush. She could see Sandy further back, standing half bent over with his hands on his knees as if he was gasping for breath. He must have been the one she had heard crashing through the bush.

Stubs, at first, didn't see her. He was more intent on his study of the bush. But he must have caught movement from the corner of his eye. Charity stood still, catching her own breath, until Stubs let out a holler and reached for his Colt. The two adversaries were far enough apart that they were reaching the outer range of Stub's .45. Before he could take careful aim, he squeezed off his first shot. There was no telling where it went or what it hit, but it didn't come close to Charity. She started running again, this time across the road and into the bush on the other side. Before he could take careful aim and get off a second shot, she darted back into hiding. Now she had no idea at all where she was or what lay before her. But she wasn't about to stop running.

From the bodily slump and the agony on his face, she judged she would have no problem outrunning Sandy. And Stubs wouldn't be able to force his horse into the heavy bush. *Run, just keep running.* She could sort out her location by and by.

50

A MAN CAN PUSH HIMSELF BEYOND LOGICAL LIMIT FROM time to time, but a horse needs rest. He might be forced into a few more hours, but eventually, the end will come.

Rory and Ivan knew better than to take their animals to the extent that they would collapse or be useless the next day. They had taken a late start from the Fort and an even later start from Stevensville. The miles of uphill grade, after they left the main trail, took the last reserves from both animals. It was with relief that Rory saw the distinct, high gate posts of the Triple T Ranch before them. He pointed with his chin and said, "End of the line for this one day, Ivan. Good folks up there. They'll make us welcome."

They turned in and walked the weary horses down the dirt ranch road. Rory wasn't surprised when it was Slim, the ranch foreman, who rose from the chair on the cookhouse porch and stepped into the yard to greet them. After careful scrutiny, the foreman laughed and said, "Howdy there, Sheriff. What brings you up the hill on this fine day? You hunt'n someone, or just in need of a decent feed'n, you and your gelding both? And who's your friend?"

"Evening, Slim. Place is looking good. Grass is good. Cattle fat. Spring rains have been kind to the Triple T. Must have made some money. I see fresh paint here and there. Now, Slim, say hello to my friend Ivan. County Deputy."

"Howdy, Ivan. You come to hold this fella's hand, or is he gett'n to where he can be trusted on his own?"

Ivan answered, "Does alright for the most part. Only he's not much with a cooking pot over an open fire. Kind of hoping we might be able to trade some firewood splitting or dishwashing or such for a meal."

"Firewood's all cut and stacked. But get yourselves down. Cook had a couple of steaks that were greening a bit around the edges. Didn't want to take a chance with the working crew, but I expect if he trimmed 'em up a bit and smothered 'em with onions, they could be 'et."

With a shout, the foreman turned toward the corral. "Yo. Carter."

Carter, apparently the yard man and probably the wrangler when they were working round-up, came on the trot.

"Come get these here geldings, Carter. Looks to me as if they've done some miles. See to their care and feeding. I expect these boys have miles to go tomorrow too, so see that they're ready for morning. Bring the bedrolls up and toss them on some unused bunks."

With the horses and the night's shelter settled, they wandered together into the cookhouse. Slim asked about the cousins, Henry and Thomas. They had been popular crew members during their stay on the Triple T. The conversation worked its way from one thing to another, finally landing on the fact that Rory was now married and settled in at the Fort. It took a bit of effort for Slim to work that through his thinking, but he finally extended his hand with a firm handshake and a sincere, "congratulations." Only after all of that, normal cookhouse talk on most ranches, did the foreman get around to what brought the law into the high country. Ivan glanced at Rory as if to say, 'it's his story to tell.'

"Murder, Slim. Two murders, in fact. And a kidnapping."

Without asking for details, Slim asked, "Anything the T can do to help?"

"You're doing it, my friend. That's enough. Unless you happened to take note of a covered wagon heading into the hills today."

"I didn't myself."

Slim lifted his voice just enough to be heard across the room. "Any of you boys see a covered wagon on the trail today?"

When there was no response, Slim said, "Ask around the crew and let me know."

Turning back to the lawmen, Slim said, "Kidnapping is rare enough up here so as to be non-existent. What's that all about?"

Rory held off on the back story, which he didn't really know the detail of anyway. The Tattersley fiasco had been overshadowed by the double murder and the kidnapping. Naming no names, he said, "Two deputies murdered. One federal. One town. Woman prisoner taken. We're sure it wasn't an inside job. It's very doubtful if the woman knew the murderers. Stole the loaded wagon and a four-horse team. Couple of saddle horses. Turned off the main trail leaving clear wagon wheel marks all along the way. We started out a whole day behind, but we can move a lot faster than that wagon. We hope to bring it to a close tomorrow."

51

THE WAGON TEAM WAS FINDING THE CONSTANT UPHILL trail to be a burden and a challenge. No matter what he wished for, Sandy knew that to push the team any harder was to end their day early, with a team that could go no further. He had never seen a problem with his cruelty when it came to men or women, but horses and dogs held a different place in his mind. He would care for the horses as if they were his own.

Stubs was off chasing the woman. He had walked into the bush minutes before the breaking of earliest dawn. The woman, he started feeling guilty that they had not even bothered to ask her name, had to be caught. As the wagon had creaked along, miles further uphill, Stubs had stepped from the bush.

"Seen where she lay to sleep. Pressed down grass all around. Trail going deeper into the forest. She ain't 'et, and she ain't slept proper. No way she can keep running. You follow the trail. I'll catch her soon enough."

Sandy thought Stubs just might be fooling himself,

but he never had gotten anywhere arguing with the man, so he let it go. When Stubs disappeared back into the bush, he urged the team into motion.

A grassy clearing with a trickle of water from off the nearby hill was attraction enough. Sandy stopped to water and rest the horses. The sun was about directly overhead. Noon, or close enough. There was a well-supplied grub box in the wagon. He would eat and set some out for Stubs in case he should put in an appearance.

The woman had said the men they shot were lawmen. One was a federal marshal. He had half believed her, but Stubs had scoffed at the idea. One thing Sandy knew for sure was that he didn't want the federals on his trail. But no matter who they were, they had laid on enough sliced meats and bread to satisfy without having to make a fire.

Sandy had nothing to do but keep moving. The pace was slow, and it seemed to him, the trail was long. One rider had passed him, riding downhill. He wasn't happy about being seen.

Stubs didn't stagger out of the brush covering until late afternoon. Sandy had gone into camp, watering and staking out the team while leaving the harness in place. He did the same for the saddle horses.

He was about to build a fire when a worn and much-scratched Stubs led his horse from the bush. He emerged about one-half-mile ahead of the camp Sandy was laying out and turned uphill. Sandy was pleased that he had been able to pull off the road far enough to avoid being seen. He stepped to the edge of the road and called Stubs back.

The way Stubs was walking, limping, and easing

himself along, he knew to not ask too many questions. Stubs could be awful sudden, sometimes regretting his actions later, but mostly not caring. And it was clear from past evidence that challenging the man with a Colt would have a shortening effect on a man's life.

"I was about to make a fire. Expect you could use a coffee."

"That's what you expect, is it? Well, in just this one instance, you might be right. What I really need is that woman."

"See any sign of her?"

"There's so much torn cloth hanging from the bushes I don't know as she's got much of a dress on anymore. Chased her over hills and through swampy bottoms. That there is the fastest runn'nst woman I ever did know. And I've known a few that tried to run. Shouldn't never have took the horse with me. Cost me time. Couldn't ride but once or twice when the woman left the bush."

Sandy hesitated to ask, but he needed to know.

"Any idea where she's at now?"

"All's I know is that she ain't here. Might be still runn'n fer all I can tell."

The camp was silent while Sandy built the fire and filled the coffee pot from the running stream. Building up his courage, Sandy said, "We daren't move into no big settlement without know'n where the woman is. She has to be caught again, or we'll have to leave all this and ride out. What are you figuring to do?"

"I figure we're safe enough for this night. We'll stake our own horses off a ways and sleep near them. If the woman leads the law here, we can mount up and ride off by ourselves."

"If she was to find any help at all, it's most likely the

woman would show up with a group of cowboys. Ain't much law in these hills."

"Well, a group of angry cowboys ain't no bargain neither. We'll eat now, put the fire out and move off like I just said."

52

Rory and Ivan had followed wagon tracks until they came to the previous night's camp. Again, they split up, with Rory searching for evidence around the camp and Ivan moving into the bush. Almost immediately, Ivan saw broken branches, tramped down grass, and here and there, a snag of cloth. With all that providing a trail, he was able to move right along.

The woman had been the one on the trail first. He could see that by the fact that the big boot marks were pressed into her trail, although he could see no smaller boot marks. He had no way of knowing about the moccasins. It wasn't difficult to follow the trail, but he was mystified when the boot tracks turned out of the brush and onto the dirt road. The woman's slight disturbance of the bush continued on.

When he came to the same rock wall that had forced Charity to turn, he was surprised to see that she had chosen to cross the road, exposing herself to any followers. It was impossible to sort out the timing, but he could see that the walker who had followed on foot had stopped on the road. One man on horseback had left clear hoof tracks. When the woman moved into the bush across the road, the horseman had followed. Ivan soon found where Charity had slept. The boot marks showed that the man had too, but much later, probably the next morning.

There was enough running water from any number of streams to meet her needs, but Charity would be without food. Nor was it likely she had a knife or any other way of killing anything to eat. There had been no indication of a fire.

Emerging from the bush, Ivan made his way back to where Rory had been sorting out the wagon camp.

"I never seen that woman but for a few minutes in Stevensville. No way to judge, but I can say she knows how to get through the bush. Easy trail to follow, though. Leaving pieces of torn cloth behind in her run. I'd say she was desperate. She was witness to two murders and would have no reason to hope for herself. She's running. I doubt she has any idea where she's going, but she's sure enough running. If the murderer can keep up her pace, he'll eventually catch her. Pretty sure that won't be in any way good for her."

Rory listened and thought. Ivan was a good tracker. From the description of the trail, he knew Ivan would eventually catch up. But when would that be? And would it be too late? And where was the wagon? Night was closing in, and they had seen nothing of the men or the wagon. The choices seemed to come down to a single matter.

"Ivan, we've got to find that wagon. There isn't enough light left for you to take to the bush again. The woman is surely without food, and she's been running for a night and a day, assuming we've sorted out the wagon camps correctly. Our only hope is to find that wagon."

Knowing Ivan was likely to see it the same way, Rory swung into the saddle. Ivan was right beside him, ready to move. The horses were worn from the long day, but they needed to find the wagon before dark. They would push for an hour or so. That was all the light they had anyway.

The slight curve in the trail allowed Rory and Ivan to spot the idle wagon pulled off into the fringe of the bush well before they themselves were exposed. With the little light left, they could make out the wagon alright, but the camp itself or the staked horses were unclear. They pulled to a stop, not wishing to ride into an armed camp with the murderers on alert and ready to shoot again. They just got very slowly underway again when a bullet ricocheted off a tree only inches from Ivan's head. Bark and debris stung his face and forced his eyes to close. His horse spooked in fright, stepping sideways, nearly unsetting him. A second shot missed only because of that sideways step.

Rory dropped to the ground, carrying his carbine with him. He used the gelding for shelter as he tried to figure out where the shots came from. He was far enough behind Ivan that he hoped the shooter hadn't seen him. Ivan got his animal under control before charging across the trail and into the bush. The entire mountainside sunk into silence. It felt as if the first person to move might be the loser in the game. Neither Ivan nor Rory moved.

When Rory realized that the shots hadn't come from the direction of the wagon, he was mystified. But he had never been one to question facts, so he took the evidence as it existed. The shooters were camped away from the wagon. Since no accompanying shots had come from the wagon, it was a good bet that both men were in the remote camp. That could indicate fear of exposure when travelers saw the white-topped wagon. Or it might show wise caution.

How smart were these shooters? Or, if not smart, perhaps cunning. And had they moved after taking those shots? And, more importantly, should he move? And, if so, move to where? Almost any move he made was likely to expose him.

When he made his decision, it was to leave the horse where it was, with the reins draped across its neck, an indication to the animal that he was free to wander and find some feed. Rory slipped quietly into the bush, moving toward where the shots had come from. Ivan would be doing what had to be done. There was a good chance that he was using the last of the light to watch what Rory was up to.

IVAN COULD SEE JUST ENOUGH to watch Rory slip into the bush. He decided he should go to the wagon. There could be another shooter there waiting for his opportunity. He also abandoned his gelding. It wasn't likely to go far. He eased along the trail just far enough into the covering brush to hide himself. In the darkness, small movements wouldn't be easily seen. It was noise that might be his worst enemy in the night.

Studying the situation as best he could, Ivan took note of the wagon camp. There was no fire. There were no smoky remnants of a cooking fire hanging in the air. The shuffling of horses was the only sound. Carefully, trying to see everywhere at once, Ivan crossed the road and ducked under the laid-down tailgate of the wagon. He heard a gasp of surprise and then nothing. He hadn't expected to meet company under the wagon. The gasp was small but clearly feminine. Had it been one of the men, he would have been in a position to shoot Ivan, but that didn't happen. Now, with two people only a couple of feet apart and with no knowledge of who else was in camp, Ivan was unsure of his next move. He finally took a chance, speaking barely above a whisper.

"Ma'am, I don't recall your name. I'm Deputy Sheriff Ivan Ivanov. I was in Stevensville when the two deputies came through. I'm the one that rode to the Fort to stand in for Wiley. You're safe with me. Can you tell me where the second man is?"

Charity raised her voice just a bit.

"They both camped in a hollow out there. I'm hungry enough that I took the chance to sneak in. Climbed under the wagon when I heard you in the brush across the road.

"I watched them slink off, leading their saddle horses. Going to run off, leaving everything behind if someone comes along. Cowards. Cowards and murdering bullies. Shot those two deputies from behind rocks. Shot them with no warning nor giving them a chance. Coldest thing I ever did see.

"They think they're safe out there in the darkness. If I can get my hands on one of these guns, they'll find out what safe means and doesn't mean."

Ivan almost laughed at the words. Not because he doubted her sincerity, or her determination, or even her ability. It was more because it all sounded so strange coming from the darkness after two days of running, hiding, sleeping without a blanket, and going without food.

"My friend, Sheriff Rory, is down there now. It's best if you leave it to him. In the dark, you could shoot him, or he could shoot you, not knowing the difference. I'm going down there right away too. You get yourself some food and stay hidden."

Then a thought came to him.

"Those two aren't getting away. I can pretty much guarantee that. The sheriff, with an anger on is a frightful sight. Those men shot and killed his working partner from up at the Fort. Rory's not going to forget that. Won't forget it or show mercy.

"I'm feeling some need here too. You leave it to us. But if you thought you could drive this rig, I'd hitch those horses for you, and you could head back downhill to safety."

He was about to say more, but Charity interrupted with, "You go kill a couple of murderers. I'll handle the team. I know those animals. You'd be putting them in all the wrong spots in the team, and they wouldn't pull right, wondering what was wrong with their master. I don't know what's to become of the matter of this stolen wagon and the junk in it, but right now, I just want to be safely away. If I end up in jail, well, that's how it will be."

"You push downhill and watch for the Triple T Ranch. They're friends of the sheriff. Good folks. We overnighted there. Tell them who you are and that you're waiting for us to ride down. We'll be along by and by. Might be a good idea to walk on the off side of the team until you're away. Just in case of a stray shot."

With that, Ivan slipped into the bush. There had been no more shooting, but very little time had gone by. Rory and the fugitives were probably all listening for movement through the grass or undergrowth, hoping to be the first to spot the other.

Ivan moved very carefully, walking first down the road to where Rory had slipped into the bush. He didn't feel that would be a good time to get shot, being so far from help and all, so he tapped the carbine barrel twice, just lightly, on the trunk of what he guessed was an aspen, although it was difficult to know for sure in the darkness. Tap. Tap.

There had been no planning for signals, so both men were taking some chance, but the single tap came in response. Tap.

If nothing else, the single tap let Ivan know where Rory was hunkered down. He would be very careful moving in that direction so as not to startle the men. There was a slight chance that the tap hadn't been from Rory, but the original shots had come from further into the forest, so he was fairly confident in his movements. He hadn't gone far when a voice said, very quietly, "I see shadows of brush moving. Identify yourself."

"Ivan here, partner. Where are those others?"

"Come closer so we can talk easier."

Ivan was lying flat on the ground, wiggling and squirming along, like a swimmer enjoying a warm dip in the summer sun, only they were now in total darkness, and the ground was sharp, with broken mountain rock, and the shrubbery was a collection of grasses, low growing agave and barrel cactus. It was not an ideal spot for crawling. But that shot that caromed off the tree back there was not fooling around. He could pull spines from his clothing and body later, but first, he had to live through the adventure.

Sliding up close to Rory, Ivan asked. "Got them spotted?"

"There's a shallow hollow just down there. Can't be more than three, four feet deep. Enough to hide a man but not a horse. The way the clouds are drifting, the spot is only slightly visible when the sky clears. Otherwise, I can see nothing. I'm guessing they were lying on the lip of that hollow when they took those shots. Cagy. Not taking any chances. Camped away from the wagon. Have their horses with them. Holding to their own skin even if they lose the wagon and all."

Ivan considered for a moment and then said, "I'm not so sure I feel like sitting here all night. Mountain air gets cold of an evening. I'm in favor of shuffling the cards a bit."

With no objection coming from Rory, Ivan fell to his stomach again and continued crawling. Rory watched until he was wrapped in total darkness.

53

Charity, working as quickly as she could after grabbing a bite or two from the grub box and loading a Colt she had stuffed into what was left of the oversized pocket in her split riding skirt, went to the team. Speaking right into the ear of the first horse chosen, she called him by the name she and Felix had given him and said, "Come along, you beautiful creature. You've work to do this night."

The horse, knowing his place in the grouping, stepped in without her guidance. She had the single tree connected in no time at all. The other three horses were no problem either, all responding to her kind voice and their long training. Pulling picket pin after picket pin, she tied the saddle animals to the back of the wagon.

Instead of climbing to the seat, or walking on the offside, as the deputy had suggested, she stepped between the wheel horses, lifted her foot to the tongue, and after wiggling this one foot until she felt secure, lifted the other foot. Now positioned safely between the two big animals, she wrapped the shortened reins into her right hand and gripped the leather of the harness closest to her left hand. Only then did she urge the team into a slow walk while she eased them out of the clearing and turned them until they were facing downhill on the road again.

Slowly they moved forward, and soon the noise of their passing was lost in the distance. When she felt enough distance behind her, she pulled the rig to a stop while she unwound the reins and climbed to the seat.

ALL FOUR MEN heard the wagon pass. To Rory and Ivan, the disappearing sound came with a sense of relief. Relief that the woman would be safe and could be dealt with later. Ivan came to the conclusion that the sounds of the wagon had shuffled the cards enough that he didn't have to take the chances he was prepared to take just minutes before.

To Sandy and Stubs, it was the sound of another failure. In their troubled and closed minds, they believed that luck simply wasn't with them lately. They weren't prone to self-analysis or the consideration of others.

The newest mistake the fugitives made was to think that with the wagon gone, and most likely the woman with it, escape would be as simple as climbing on their horses and riding away. Carelessly, they rose to full standing positions, intent on only getting to the horses. But it was right at that time that the clouds rolled away again, and the moon, together with the starlit sky, reflected enough of the far-off sun's rays to lighten the tableau that was unrolling in front of Rory and Ivan.

Still not exposing himself, Rory shouted, "Sheriff

Rory Jamison here, men. Me and my deputy. It's over. Stand down and surrender yourselves."

The answer from the men was a literal fusillade of shots that were fanned into the bush, tearing leaves and branches off trees and ricocheting off rocks. None of the shots came near the prone lawmen. When the shooting ceased, Rory decided the men were reloading. That was a good time to take a hand. For the first time in his life, he was satisfied that the murderers hadn't surrendered. He had known they wouldn't. With two recent brutal murders behind them and who knows what lying on their back trail, there was no chance of anything but death, either on the end of a rope, or with a bullet in the mountains.

Even with the starlight, it was too dark to run. Rory stood and stepped out as quickly as safety allowed, in a hunched-over walk, closed on the men and their horses. Ivan was doing the same, but he had a little different angle of approach.

Rory could suddenly see the first man clearly. They were separated by less than twenty feet of rocky rubble. He dared not run, but the ground was clear enough to step up his pace a bit. With a half-dozen rushed steps, he was on Sandy, although he had no way of knowing either man's name.

Rory grabbed the man's jacket collar and pulled him backward, allowing him to fall on his back. He had the muzzle of his carbine almost touching the man's head, but Sandy brushed it aside and turned into a whirling dervish. He was on his feet again so quickly that Rory was caught unprepared. They traded wild swings of their fists, although, in the darkness, neither landed an effective blow. When Sandy took a step away, there was just enough light for Rory to see the desperate man pull a wicked-looking knife from under his belt. The first wild swing came so quickly that Rory had no choice but to jump backward. Even then, he came close to being gutted. His heel caught on something, and he fell to the ground. The murderer was on him in a flash of time. With a frantic grab, Rory had a fierce grip on the wrist of the man's knife hand.

A chortling shout of, "Cut him, Sandy. Cut him bad." Stubs said the last words he would ever say. Ivan shot him dead center from ten feet away.

Ivan considered taking a hand with the knife fight, but the struggling pair were tossing and rolling so quickly that he feared being more hindrance than help. He stood close by though, waiting for his chance.

When Sandy tried to move the knife to his free hand, Rory managed to get his arm in the way. They were lying more or less side by side now. In an open and uninterrupted test of strength, Sandy would have had no chance against the sheriff, but rolling, standing, and falling, neither man found an advantage. Sandy was flailing around with his free arm, trying to grab something, anything, Rory's clothing, his gun, anything at all that would give him an advantage.

But Rory also had a free arm. He dropped that arm to his side and lifted his own camp knife. With a thrust upward, just below Sandy's rib cage, Rory sunk the blade to the hilt. Sandy expelled lungs full of fetid breath and sank to the ground. Rory, his knees trembling, took two steps to the side and managed to lower himself onto a rock. Breathing heavily, he watched Ivan go to Sandy, who was not yet dead.

Rory's blade was still sunk full length. Reaching for the blade, and doing something he knew Rory would not do, Ivan twisted the knife from side to side before pulling it out. Eight inches of blade will cut its way through a wide arc of innards. Its effect was almost immediate. Sandy, with a deep sigh, died.

Ivan took a seat on a rock just a couple of feet from Rory. The two lawmen sat there in silence. That silence was finally broken when Rory said, "I hate knives."

It was normally Rory who took the lead when the two of them were working together. Ivan reversed that when he bent to the first dead man, the one he had shot. He first unbuckled the man's gun belt and pulled until it slid roughly under his back. He set it aside and lifted the knife that was hung from the belt holding the fellow's pants up.

He next went from pocket to pocket, going by feel as much as sight, and lifted out everything—papers, tobacco sack, pocketknife, a small container of matches, and a mixed cache of items the man had accumulated, along with a small roll of bills. Feeling over the body, Ivan found one more hold-out gun. He added it to the small pile that represented the net worth of a fugitive from the law, a man who had probably reigned terror over the country for years, judging by how callously he had murdered a sheriff.

There was a bit more found on the second man but not much.

Ivan then brought in their horses. Guessing at which horse belonged to which man, he stuffed the pocket findings into the saddle bags. Searching the saddlebags themselves would wait until sunrise.

There was nothing more to do except dispose of the bodies. Here, Rory took a stand.

"Leave them. We can't see to carry rocks for their burying, and I'm not of a frame of mind to sit out the night. Bring the horses, and let's go.

Never before had Rory left a body uncared for. He probably never would again, but still, a bit later, he rode away without looking back or seeming to have a second thought.

Once on the road again, Ivan tied the dead men's horses while he and Rory went in search of their own. They hadn't wandered far, and soon their saddles were tightened, and they were ready to ride. But they hadn't talked about the wagon. Rory corrected that, asking, "What about the wagon? I'm assuming that was the woman who drove it away."

Ivan explained in a few short words, to which Rory responded, "Ride to the Triple T. Get some rest. Then take the woman and the wagon down to Stevensville. We'll move it to the Fort when I return. I'm tempted to say let the woman go. She's going to cause trouble no matter where she goes. But I guess you'd best hold her. We'll stand her before Judge Anders P. Yokam on the jailbreak charge. If the federals want her, they can send three or four men. I'm guessing it will take that many to get the job done."

Ivan tried to read his friend's face in the darkness.

"And what are you going to be doing during all that time?"

"I'm riding to Denver."

"Do I dare ask why you would do that? This case is settled. The murders were in the county, and it's in the county they should stay."

"I need to report on the lost deputy and return his few possessions. I have them in my saddlebag."

They turned their separate ways, but it wasn't but a few seconds when Rory called out to Ivan.

"Tell the Triple T that I'd be beholden to them if they

could send a couple of men up here to see to the covering of those two."

Ivan smiled to himself and waved his agreement as he put his gelding back into motion. There was no guarantee that Rory would have been able to see the wave, but he would know his words were heard and heeded. *My friend, Sheriff Rory Jamison. Tough as nails and gentle as a lamb. Can't leave a job undone even when he wants to.*

54

Rory, trusting to the strength of his big Jamison ranch-raised Blood Red Bay Gelding, had pushed through the night and into the afternoon of the following day. He was as weary as the horse, but they both perked up a bit when the skyline of Denver came in sight.

Just a bit more now, horse. You'll not get the rest you need, but a pail of oats should set you back up.

He dropped the gelding at the familiar livery and said to the hostler, "I'll be riding out again soon. Grain and water him. Check his shoes. We've been over some rough trails. Have him ready. And I'll want two more horses to take along. Tough animals I can depend on, switching my saddle from one to the other. I'll buy them or borrow them. Whatever works."

"Your money's no good here, Sheriff. You'll have to take the loan. I'll get them back soon enough. Anyway, your county still has a credit here from those last animals you left for sale. I've been going to bank it for you, but you know how it is. I don't have much use for a bank. Seldom go near one. But your credit's written in my book. You come back when you're ready. I'll have your rig on another animal and leads on the other two."

With a gesture of thanks, Rory took the saddlebags with the federal deputy marshal's small estate tucked inside and crossed to the Marshal's Office. He was struggling between anger at the thoughtlessness that had cost a young man his life, and the realization that no man or group of men was perfect. Things happen that can catch the best of men unprepared and looking foolish.

He turned the knob on the outer door and walked in. It was unlocked, something he had always believed was also foolish. Every head in the room turned to look at him. Block came from his small office and took one look at his friend before saying, "Rory, you look as if you've been through it. You need to get yourself a hotel room and some sleep."

"I need to go home, and that's what I'm going to do. First, I have to give this to Donavan Gaines."

"Do I dare ask what that is?"

"I'd have thought you would be expecting this. It's the gather from your dead deputy."

A total hush settled over the room and held for several seconds before Block said, "Dead deputy? What deputy? What's going on?"

"Am I to suppose the news hasn't come down this way yet?"

Branch Manager Donavan Gaines had come from his office.

"We've had no news from up your way."

"Well, I'm sorry to be the one to have to tell you. I wasn't there. Cap and I were on the train coming home from Washington when a situation arose. Your Deputy Maddison Pigeon was shot and killed trying to bring a wagon load of worthless trash and a prisoner to Denver. Deputy Pigeon and our Town Marshal Wiley Hamstead. Both shot and killed. The wagon and team stolen, and the woman prisoner kidnapped.

"Cap and I arrived just about that time. Ivan and me, we found the murderers and the woman. I expect they're back in Stevensville by now. Killers are dead."

Rory had held his tongue civil as long as he could. He looked directly at the office manager and said, "Donovan, your man is dead because a boy was sent to do a man's job. Actually, it was a job for two men. And our man is dead because he offered to help your deputy. I'm as upset by that as I've ever been upset. So, before I say something I'll regret, I'll ride for home."

Gesturing at the saddlebags he had dropped on a desk, he said, "There's what was gathered up from the deputy. I imagine he was buried in the town cemetery, but I've been away for a couple of days, so I can't say for sure."

There was no longer any pleasantness left in his voice.

With those hard words hanging in the room, he turned and walked out. Behind him, Donavon said, "Block. Take one other deputy and ride with that man till he's home. He's about ready to drop off his feet, but we know he won't stop until he's where he's set out to go. Hurry now."

55

THERE APPEARED TO BE A PARADE OF SOME SORT FORMING up when Rory and the two deputies, who hadn't been out of the saddle since they left Denver, rode down the street of Stevensville. There was a wagon at the front, pointing north, and everyone around the wagon was on horseback. But as they came closer, they could see it wasn't a parade to celebrate something—it was a parade of sorrow.

The first to spot Rory was his Uncle George. Rory was so tired, so worn, so weary of life and crime, that mostly what he saw was a blur before his eyes. It wasn't until George spoke that Rory turned his way.

"Rory, you've come home at a good time and at the worst time. We have all been worried about you. You and Ivan too. It's good to see you, even though you're as done in as I've ever seen you, and that's saying something."

"What's going on, George?"

"We're taking Wiley and the federal deputy up to the Fort for their burials. Coffins are in the wagon. That's Hanna with the reins. She insisted. Nancy's riding close by in case she's needed. Half the town is going. We sent a rider up yesterday to prepare the way. I expect there will be a lot of people in town when we get there. Are you able to ride another couple of hours?"

"Let's go. Wait, are you telling me that Ivan hasn't returned?"

"No, he's back. Him, that wagon, and the woman who started all this. She's the first prisoner Key Wardle has had in the new, mostly finished, cell block. Ivan's gone to the hotel to clean up, but he'll be along. We're all wondering what happened up in the hills, but Ivan said it could wait, and I guess it can."

Two and one-half hours later, the entourage entered the small town called the Fort. Julia sat her horse at the very edge of town, all alone, waiting for her sheriff husband. Praying he had returned safely. Rory rode at the very rear of the gathering, him and Ivan. Julia spotted him but sat quietly and reverently while the funeral procession completed its long, slow journey. As the wagon led the way to the cemetery, people rode or walked from every store, every corner of town. Dozens and dozens of people. Riders in from the ranches. Local farmers taking the afternoon off. All silent. All saddened. All tired of the crime that so often appeared in this wonderful, half-settled, half-tamed West. So often, it seemed, crimes without real purpose. Crimes without conscience.

Spotting Julia sitting her horse all alone, Ivan stepped his horse up just a bit to move ahead of Rory. The two federal marshals had ridden in the bigger group. As Rory rode close to Julia, she stepped her gelding alongside him. She reached out and took his hand. Holding to each other's eyes for just a moment, they turned their heads to the front again.

Later. Later would be time enough for a welcome home. At the moment, they had a friend to bury.

HIGH TRAIL TO UTAH

A SNEAK PEEK AT BOOK SIX

True to pioneer living, award-winning author Reg Quist delivers book six in a series following a young sheriff as he struggles to keep the people closest to him safe.

While Sheriff Rory Jamison is sent several towns over to dissolve a dispute between two warring ranchers, Deputy Ivan Ivanov is summoned to investigate a chilling double murder—a journey that takes him far outside the county he's been assigned to protect.

Swept up in the wilds of Northern Colorado, Ivan is forced to follow criminals through untamed lands and perilous situations. And as the investigation delves deeper in the untamed fringes of Utah, Ivan finds himself navigating uncharted territories in a relentless quest for justice to ensure restless fugitives face the law.

Meanwhile, Rory ponders his motivations and the path ahead as his beloved county's sheriff. With mounting incidents, his inner voice is questioning whether or not he's committed to protecting and serving the county he loves—at the expense of risking his life.

Full of intrigue and bullet-flying action, Rory and Ivan embark on separate quests to protect their county...and gain clarity on a future more uncertain than ever.

AVAILABLE NOVEMBER 2023

1

IN THE HIGH-UP MOUNTAINS, WINDING WHEREVER MAN
and horse could make way, there was a trail. In the
mountains that separated Colorado from Utah, collec-
tively known as the Rockies. But the Rockies, defying
the efforts of man, were too big, too grand, and too
varied to be enclosed in a single word. Or a single
description. The Rockies were much more than peeks
and valleys, snow caps, and wind-twisted trees. There
were many unnamed areas that made up the name Rockies. But no matter the name, it was a rugged land, fit only
for the brave or the foolish. Or perhaps, the desperate.

The follower knew only one name, that of the Red
Feather Lakes. He had left the lakes behind a week ago.
For the second time.

The trail was ancient. Few knew about it, and even
fewer had ventured onto it. No one knew of its origin.
Perhaps a man with a burrow or a mule, loaded with
beaver traps and great hopes, as he wandered the
streams connecting the many lakes, that had first blazed
the route. Perhaps. But it was more likely to have been

Indians. Feasibly, ancient Indians—the forerunners of the known people. For the Indians were always moving, exploring, and trading. But the blazes on the trees and the rocks cleared from the path spoke of white men.

Disappearing into the long grass in the valleys, skirting lakes and streams, and then appearing again as a weathered notch in a tree, or as rocks rolled away to clear the path, or the rotted stumps of downed trees— now overgrown by aspens that had sprouted where the pine had been felled—the trail led the wanderer on. But it was a difficult trail. Many who had begun had given up, the trail lost to them, beyond finding. Even their names and their stories were lost in time.

That some had succeeded in their western travels was shown by the fact that the pathway continued on, enticing the traveler to watch for the next notch in a tree and sometimes, again, where boulders had been rolled out of the way, lying uneasily in an unnatural row.

At one place, deep into the higher point of the trail, higher than any wise man would attempt to winter, was a small log cabin, no higher at the ridge pole than four feet, providing only room enough to crawl in for shelter. Rotting and turning back to the earth, its roof long ago giving up the struggle, the cabin, the work of a hopeful man, would soon be gone, leaving no trace in the harsh stillness of the mountain. It was said that bones had once been found in the cabin, bones of a man, gnawed and scattered, showing tooth marks of a predator.

Only a man intent on escape, or perhaps freedom unknown to him in past times, would push all the way to the end of the trail.

And such were the men Ivan was following.

Hunkered down on his belly, his rifle lying beside him, alone in the vastness and beauty of the rocks, lakes, and hills, he waited. The cover was good on the hillside where he lay. There was little chance of being seen. His horse was staked out far enough back into the lightly treed clearing that it was unlikely the other horses would sense it. And just below, well within rifle range, although he had no intention of shooting, lay the trail. He had seen the opening in the forest ahead the evening before, as the sun was laying its last light on the scene. He had been following fading tracks. For two weeks, he had followed, after being forced to return to a remote home-stead seeking help for Cap, who had broken his leg. But his query was again within sight, gone to camp for the night, unaware of their follower.

Immediately turning back, he skirted the trail by a half mile, paralleling the route the thieves had taken. Looking for a path to the higher country.

In his following, he'd had no need to study the country around or look for blazed trees. The movements of four men with their four horses, plus two heavily loaded pack mules, and the wagon team, were impos-sible to hide. He had only to stay far enough back to avoid detection and watch for any rearguard who had staked himself out in the bush that skirted the way.

When he was at a comfortable height and well ahead of them, he settled in for the night. Both he and the faithful gelding were beyond tired. But a cold bite from his camp supplies, and a belly full of the abundant grass, would put both man and horse in good condition for the day ahead.

ABOUT THE AUTHOR

Reg Quist's pioneer heritage includes sod shacks, prairie fires, home births, and children's graves under the prairie sod, all working together in the lives of people creating their own space in a new land.

Out of that early generation came farmers, ranchers, business men and women, builders, military graves in faraway lands, Sunday Schools that grew to become churches, plus story tellers, musicians, and much more.

Hard work and self-reliance were the hallmark of those previous great generations, attributes that were absorbed by the following generation.

Quist's career choice took him into the construction world. From heavy industrial work, to construction camps in the remote northern bush, the author emulated his grandfathers, who were both builders, as well as pioneer farmers and ranchers.

It is with deep thankfulness that Quist says, "I am a part of the first generation to truly enjoy the benefits of the labors of the pioneers. My parents and their parents worked incredibly hard, and it is well for us to remember".